HardBall
by
CD Reiss

This book is a work of fiction.
Any similarities to persons living or dead are purely because at the core of
each of us, we all want the same things and there's a universal difficulty
getting those things.

Thank you to Steven Weinberg for help with the Yiddish and to Rose He for
corrections to the Spanish. If it's messed up, it's because I misunderstood.

ISBN - 978-1942833215

Cover designed by the author.
Model is Ashley Gibson.
Photo copyright: Snooty Fox Images, 2015.

Hard Ball

Dash Wallace is a dirty talking, sexy professional baseball player who falls hard for the girl next door, but beware... your heart will take a beating as you watch him struggle with sticking to all he's ever known at the risk of losing the best thing that ever happened to him.

Hardball is one of those books that will suck you in and won't let you go until you devour every last, juicy bite.

~ *Sawyer Bennett, NY Times Bestselling Author of the Carolina Cold Fury Hockey Series*

Fiery hot and enticingly realistic, CD Reiss's captivating writing, complex characters and explosive love scenes make Hard Ball an irresistible modern day romance.

~ *Katy Evans, NY Times Bestselling Author of Real*

Delightful, sexy, emotional, exciting, exhilarating. I loved every single second of it! A sports romance with a DASH of kink....it doesn't get any better than that!

~ *Shayna Renee's Spicy Reads*

Unexpectedly emotional, beautifully written, and decadently naughty, CD Reiss once again owned me heart and soul. *Hardball* was an enthralling romance from start to finish!! And I never wanted it to end.

~ *Angie and Jessica's Dreamy Reads*

Hard Ball

CD REISS

Published by
Flip City Media Inc.

Also by CD Reiss

This one is for my fans.
There are no dark days
when you are in my corner.

one

Vivian

God save me from the Los Angeles Unified School District.

No.

God save the LAUSD from me because if I found an actual human being to choke for this ridiculous clusterfuck, I'd have to be peeled off them.

"It's right across the street," I said to Ursula, the school bus driver. "I can see the park from here. I can throw you and hit it."

"Girl," she said with a twang, looking me up and down, "you couldn't even pick me up."

I looked back at Jim, the phys ed teacher in charge of the field trip. He was wrangling back into the bus four third graders who had been hanging out of the windows. He was a bruiser, and patient as a saint, but we could only wait for the repair-and-tow for so long. I'd heard at least Iris complain that she had to pee, and we had at least three boys with unmedicated ADHD who were going to turn into clouds of hyperactivity if we tried to keep them seated much longer.

"It sounded like the battery," I said. "It's not dangerous."

Not any more dangerous than riding in the bus in the first place. The yellow clunker was a classic 1970s patch job that had escaped clean air laws and defied the principles of entropy. It had stopped dead a block from Lemon Grove Park, where the Los Angeles Dodgers were on the public field they maintained, signing balls for the underprivileged children of East Hollywood.

"Now you know the rules." Ursula waved at me. "If the

bus breaks down, the children stay on the bus until another one comes or the bus goes on fire."

"Do you have a match? I'm sure I can set a notebook on fire."

"I am not losing my job because you got your little yellow hairs in a twist."

"Try to start it again." I pointed at the ignition. "If it's the starter, it might catch."

Ursula rolled her eyes.

"Miss Foster!" Iris stood in the aisle, legs crossed, silver-capped teeth clenched. "*Tengo que ir al baño.*"

I spoke Spanish but encouraged the kids to use English by answering in it.

"You can go to the bathroom when—" I stopped mid-sentence as her light pink tights got dark on the insides of her legs.

Goddamnit.

I was just the librarian in a school that was lucky to have books. I wasn't qualified to manage a freaking urinary crisis.

Breaking every rule in a rulebook that made the Holy Bible look like a pamphlet, I reached for the ignition and twisted the key. The engine made the same grinding sound, but I kept the key turned—even when Ursula grabbed my wrist.

And the stupid thing started like an elephant poked awake.

"Go, go!" I shouted. "One block!"

Ursula was a bureaucrat and stubborn as hell, but she wasn't stupid. She put the bus in gear, looked both ways, and drove a block until she was behind the last bus—close enough to the park to let the kids out. She opened the front door with a *whoosh,* and the dry January cold blasted in. Seatbelts clicked open. Jim barked orders. Iris was crying. And amazingly, through it all, I was looking forward to the trip to Dodgers Dreamfield at Lemon Grove.

Iris was crying, half naked, bare feet on the damp concrete bathroom floor. Every tear cracked my heart. I wrung out her tights for the tenth time. Hairline veins of white bubbles spiraled and dripped.

Note to self—hand soap isn't meant for laundry. Iris was missing the event, and drying the tights under the hand dryer would be another wait.

I crouched in front of her until we were at eye level. I rubbed her tears away with my thumb. She hitched a breath. Touching her calmed her down. She didn't need new tights. She didn't need to be cleaned up. Not as much as she needed me to stop taking care of the practical things and look her in the eye.

Nice work, Vivian.

I slung the wet tights over my shoulder and took her hands. Iris had almond-shaped black eyes and a soft heart. She was easily hurt and took it on herself to right any wrong she saw. Such a small body. So much weight.

"It's okay, *chiquita. Podemos dejarlas secar en la biblioteca.*"

"Can you talk English to me? So I learn?"

"We can dry them in the library. It was an accident." I spoke slowly and deliberately. "Not your fault."

"Everyone saw." She looked as though she was about to burst into tears all over again.

I wanted to remove her memory of the incident. Physically remove it and burn it. "We can say you spilled soda."

"But that's a lie."

"It is." I took her shoes from under the sink and put them in front of her, opening the mouths and getting the tongues out of the way so they didn't smush in. "If you don't want to lie, you're going to have to own it."

"Own it? *En espanol?*"

I was about to give bad advice. I already wished I could take it back. Third-grade girls were relentless, and this lovely girl was already the butt of their attention because of her teeth, which were capped with stainless steel from a combination of bad diet and genetics. I didn't want her to own it. I wanted to keep her in the library all day and teach her to read.

"It's easier to say it was soda."

"My mother says not to lie."

Her mother was a rigid Catholic who often took Iris to clean offices at night because she couldn't find child care after six. I'd have let her stay with me, but that Bible-sized rule book wasn't a joke. Teachers didn't babysit. End of. So I let her come into the library at recess and sleep by my desk.

And she wanted to take ownership of her incontinence. She was going to be a wonderful woman, and I felt a swell of pride as if I'd had a small part in the creation of something beautiful.

"All right," I said. "Then if anyone asks, you say you peed and tough nuts if they don't like it."

"I give them the finger?"

"No!" I tried to be very serious, but I was laughing. "Just say, 'Too bad if you don't like it,' okay?"

"Okay."

"Give me a hug."

She wrapped her arms around me. I nearly fell over from the velocity of her affection, but I caught my balance and squeezed her.

I hustled the third graders onto the field where tables and lines waited. It was a zoo but a contained one. My kids lined up in front of Jack Youder, the veteran second-baseman. Of the twenty-five-man roster, seven players had shown up, including the mysterious Dash Wallace, who never showed up to anything. He was the one of the five I needed. The rest were easy-peasy.

I let the kids go first, staying at the back of the line while Jim guided the kids with autographs to the back of Charlie Finnegan's line. If the kids had nothing to sign, the player gave them a glossy stadium program. Three of my kids had brought hats. Iris had brought an old ball.

"And how old are you?" Youder asked when I got to him.

"Twenty-four." I didn't get the joke because I was pulling Diego from under the table.

"And what grade are you in?"

I smiled at Youder once Jim had control of the rambunctious child, and I handed Youder my dad's birthday ball. He rolled it around, looking for a space.

"Just finished grad school, sir. Hoping to be a grown-up someday."

He smiled at me. At forty, he was in his last years of play, and they'd been good to him.

"Me too." He found a space and signed with a Dodger-blue Sharpie. "I hear it's a drag though." He blew on the signature so it wouldn't smudge.

"You're a free agent after this year," I said. "Are you staying or going?"

"You're really up to the minute, aren't you?"

"Sorta."

"Well, we'll see. I don't think anyone's looking for maturity on the field right now."

Youder was always a charming presence at press conferences, with a warm smile and ready wit, but he took half a beat before the word maturity, and he looked suddenly rueful. I felt stupid for asking. It was like asking a woman how much weight she'd lost.

"We love you," I said. "You should stay."

He handed me the ball with dry ink. "I'll think about it."

"Thanks!"

I had Finnegan, Flores, and Jackson already. I got Trudeau and Bonneface while constantly counting kids in yellow Hobart Elementary hoodies. As I was about to get in Wallace's line, a whistle sounded.

A voice from a bullhorn followed. "Everybody to the tables for lunch!"

Suddenly the space in front of Dash Wallace's table was a ghost town, and I stood there with my ball in my hands and my heart in my throat.

Here's the thing about Dashiell Wallace: he was physically perfect. Six two and a half. Proportioned by DaVinci and sculpted by Michelangelo. In the middle of summer, he rolled up his sleeves, and the roped muscles of his tanned forearms twisted and tightened when he handled the ball. This perfection was apparent on the TV whether he was standing still or flying through the air. Nothing got past him. The space between second and third was his domain, and three Golden Gloves into his career, Dodger pitchers made it their business to make sure the batter pulled left, and the opposing batters tried to thread the first base line for all it was worth just to avoid him.

He was magical. And there he was. Right there. In uniform. Three feet from me, looking at me face to shoulders and breasts to hips with sky-blue eyes and black hair even more perfect than the TV could contain.

"*¡Señora Foster!*" a child cried from behind me. "*¡Necesitamos su firma para que nos puedan dar el lunch*"

Dammit. She wanted my signature. I was the sponsoring faculty, and I'd been the one to do the paperwork, so I was the one who had to release their hot lunches.

I held the ball out to Wallace. "Hi, this is for my dad, but I'm a huge fan."

"You're a teacher?" He looked me up and down again.

"School librarian. You're the second-to-last one I have to get."

He took the ball, turned it around, then locked his eyes on mine. "You have the whole roster on this thing?"

Another voice. "*¡La necesitamos!*"

"*¡Ya Voy!*" I snapped. They needed me, but I couldn't move. Dash Wallace had asked me something. What was it? I tried to remember as he rolled the ball in his perfect, strong hands. I tried not to think about how they'd feel on my body or anything at all except for making a sentence.

"It's for my dad. He's the most loyal living Dodger fan."

He found a spot and signed while he spoke. "You brought all these kids out here to get this signed for your dad?"

He handed the ball back without blowing on it. I'd wanted to see that. I'd wanted the little second of delay it would cause and the warmth of his breath on something I was going to touch.

But even in the time it took for him to hand me a ball with wet Sharpie ink, I absorbed what he'd said. Was he accusing me of arranging a field trip for my own ends? It wasn't that simple. Jim had the budget for a PE field trip, and I was a fan, so I'd agreed to chaperone, but who the hell was he to assume I'd dragged forty kids ten blocks in a broken-down school bus to get his damn signature?

I didn't say any of that. Somewhere, I had a really snappy joke about something, and he'd smile with those teeth—which were perfect except for the left front overlapping the right just a tiny bit—but the joke got swallowed before I could process it.

"Thank you. If it was too much trouble to sign without an insult, you shouldn't have bothered. My dad probably wouldn't notice it was missing." I turned my back on him before I could be more of an idiot.

I pocketed my ball and ran to get the kids their lunch. When I looked around, he was gone. Good thing. There was nothing more offensive than a man blessed with looks where he should have been given courtesy.

two

Vivian

My drive home from work was ridiculous. Friday traffic going west from East Hollywood was a running joke.

"Can you make it by six thirty?" Francine's voice came though my speakerphone as I stopped at a green to avoid blocking the box at Doheny.

"Not to Silver Lake, I can't."

"I want you to meet him. You have to meet him. That's it, I'm laying down the law, and he's going to enforce it."

I made it across before the light changed. It was the little victories that made life worth living. "If I date him, are you going to make cop jokes?"

"Hot cop jokes. Hot cop. Hot. With ink."

Francine had a listening problem. When I'd told her I wanted a nice guy, she confused that with good-looking, tattooed, and law-abiding.

"I'll be there as soon as I can."

"I'll try to hold him for you. But I can't speak for all the other girls there."

"If he's so desperate to get in someone's pants—"

"Vivian Foster. Don't even. Just get there and put a little mascara on, okay? And try not to start finding reasons to hate him before you even get there. Just go with an open mind. Have fun. You don't have to marry the guy."

"All right. I won't marry him."

I got stuck behind an SUV at a light. Couldn't see anything down the block, which I found the most frustrating thing in the world.

She blew me a loud kiss. "Love you, blondie."

"Love you too, brunettey."

We hung up. I wasn't the demonstrative type. I didn't say I love you all the time, and I wasn't girlish or giggly. I hated shopping in pairs and preferred staying home with a good romance novel to a girls' night out. But I figured sometimes you have to meet someone halfway. So if Francine needed me to escort her to the bathroom when we were out or say I loved her at the end of a phone call, I'd do it for her.

When Carl and I broke up six months earlier, she had been there for me. She took me out and let me cry on her new blouse. She got me drunk and made sure I didn't go home with anyone but her. But as the months wore on and I still wasn't interested in dating, she got more and more worried. Which meant she had to fix it.

I didn't want to be late for the setup with the hot cop, but when I pulled into my driveway, I was too tired to even think about wearing mascara.

My dumpy little Nissan with sun-damaged paint and a missing hubcap looked ridiculous on my block. I lived in Beverly Hills. It was almost embarrassing. Almost. Because having regular trash pickup and flat sidewalks wasn't a joke. Neither was feeling safe when I got home late. And the library was gorgeous. The school district was one of the best, which would matter when I had kids, and the restaurants were great when I could afford them. Which was never.

The front door was ajar. If I lived where I worked, I would have panicked. But this was Beverly Hills, and an open door meant I didn't have to worry about intruders as much as I had to worry about my stepfather.

"Dad?" I called from the porch. "Dad?" I said again, dropping my bag by the door.

Another reason to keep the doors and windows sealed in winter was the heat. We blasted it to keep Dad's joints comfortable. Warm and dry were the doctor's orders.

The house was built like the letter O, with a courtyard in the center, the public part of the house in the front and on the east side, the kitchen in the back, and four bedrooms and a den on the west side. The furniture had been top-of-the-line circa 1967, going out of style and back in again in the time I lived there.

I could cross to the other side of the house through the center. So I slid open one of the heavy, seven-foot-high glass doors that separated the living room from the courtyard.

"Close that!" a voice came from the kitchen. "I don't have stock in LADWP."

I slid it closed. "LADWP isn't publicly traded."

Dad stood in the dining room, leaning on his walker. It had tennis balls stuck onto the two back legs. We'd tried everything to get a controlled slide out of those back legs, and nothing worked like a couple of Wilsons. He was still young, but he had to have done something to piss off the gods because arthritis was crippling him before his time. "You keep saying that, but I was around when LILCO went public."

"In New York." I kissed his cheek. "We don't privatize utilities here in paradise."

"Such a know-it-all. A real *wisenheimer.*" He turned his hand into a flat plane and shook it at me. He'd brought his comedy *schtick* right from his family synagogue in Sheepshead Bay, Brooklyn.

Our kitchen was massive, and the appliances were from the same era as the furniture. Only Dad's handy repairs kept everything in beautiful working order.

I took the lid off the simmering pot. "Oh. Pot roast."

"You staying for dinner?"

He looked at me with his brown eyes. Mine were an icy non-color. Almost blue. Sometimes grey. His skin was olive, and mine was peachy. But he'd been a father to me since I was born.

As her divorce attorney, he'd fallen in love with my pregnant mother. He got her the house in the settlement and moved into it. I was six when my mom died. He hadn't blinked, adopting me without my biological father's interference. I didn't appreciate that properly until I was twelve, when he'd brought a woman home to meet me. I didn't remember her name, but she had red hair and was younger than he was. She ignored me so noticeably that Dad excused himself, picked up my plate, and he and I ate dinner in the kitchen while she finished alone.

She never came back. When I'd asked him about her later, he said he only needed one woman in the house. It was then that I felt chosen, and that feeling had never left me.

I put the lid back on the pot. I felt chosen, but I didn't want him to stay single the rest of his life.

"How did you peel the potatoes?" I glanced at his hands for signs that he'd aggravated his arthritis.

"They come peeled at the store now. It's like they read my mind. So I asked the deli to cut them. Then the lady back there, nice Spanish lady, she cut the carrots too. Even peeled the skins."

He shrugged as if to say, "I still got it."

"You didn't close the door again. We should get those lever handles so you don't have to grip a knob to lock it."

He waved again. "Such a *mensch*. Eat. Then go out."

"How did you know I was going out?" I got two plates and cups from the cabinet. They were my mother and bio dad's good wedding china.

"You're single and beautiful. It's Friday. You don't need to be a genius."

I couldn't stay home after that. He'd sulk if I did.

I set the table, and he made his way to his chair, tennis balls sliding across the linoleum. Some days he didn't need the walker and it was fine, and some days he broke my heart.

three

Vivian

"Well? What do you think?" Francine fidgeted with the fringe on her vintage crochet poncho. It looked like an afghan with a hole, and she looked like a cover model in it.

"He's a nice-looking guy."

He was Latino, built like a god, probably sang like Enrique Iglesias and fucked like James Deen. But I was barely fifteen minutes late because of an accident on the 10, and he was already making small talk with another girl at the bar.

"Those are real gang tats," Larry, Francine's boyfriend, said. He'd shaved his beard in favor of a Rollie Fingers curled moustache.

"He's reformed," she said with an excited smile.

My bones could feel how badly she wanted to jumpy-clap. I was her project. Sometimes I wondered if she put my face on Tinder and swiped right on my behalf.

I had a book burning a hole in my Kindle, and Officer Hotpants was coming at me with an LED smile and two glasses of something I was sure was alcoholic. My mother had been killed by a drunk driver, so if I had the car, I drank Sprite or took a cab home.

"Thank you," I said, taking my drink. How long could I nurse it? Maybe ten minutes. And I was thirsty. But I couldn't be rude and reject the glass, nor could I sound judgmental and tell him the real reason I wasn't drinking. So I figured I'd just hold it then go home sober enough to remove my mascara and read myself to sleep.

Francine took the glass from me. "Oh my God, I'm sorry."

She made an apology face at Officer Hotpants. "She's allergic to lemon. I'm sorry I didn't tell you."

"Cool, man, I hate lemon too." Officer Hotpants took the glass. "They look prettier than they taste, you know what I'm saying?"

He cocked his glowing handsome face at me. I had no idea what he was trying to say.

"Yeah," I said, smiling back.

"Larry, honey," Francine said, pushing Larry to the bar. "Can you get Vivian her usual?" She winked.

"Come on." Larry patted my setup on the shoulder, and they went to the bar.

"Thank you," I said.

"Baseball's on," she said, indicating the TV behind the bar. "He likes sports. You can talk about that."

Francine didn't know there was no baseball in January, because she thought of sports as played by other people and watched by men.

And she thought baseball was just another sport, which was incorrect.

I followed her gaze to the TV, where Youder stood on the Dodger Dreamfield in East Hollywood and said something, which was translated into the snaking black bars of closed captioning. I was going to explain to Francine that that wasn't baseball, it was an event I'd been at just hours before, when I saw what was behind him.

Me, taking a ball from Dash Wallace.

He was ten times more popular Youder was, but he didn't give interviews. He hadn't appeared in front of the cameras to accept any of his three Golden Gloves. He was never on television unless it was on the field during a game or in the background of some charity event giving a fan a ball, and when he made the gossip column with this girl or that, he wasn't facing the camera.

I watched myself tell him to fuck off and turn my back to him.

I watched him stare at me walking away.

I watched him put his fingers to his lips and blow me a kiss before shaking his hand as if I was too hot to handle.

Then it cut away to a beer commercial.

The whole incident was so small on the screen it wouldn't have been noticed by most people, but it was now taking up more space in my head than any other single event in my life.

Poor Officer Hotpants. He didn't stand a chance against the heat of my new fantasies. Oh sure, the kiss could have been a "fuck off, lady," and the shaking hand had shades of "bitch with a hot temper," but it didn't. Not on the HD screen. I could see it all because I was looking, and he thought I was cute. Even in my loose jeans and Hobart Elementary hoodie. Even with no mascara.

I sucked down my Sprite and claimed a headache, then I drove home on the empty freeway with Dash Wallace on the brain.

four
_____

Vivian

Despite my fantasies, it never occurred to me that I'd actually see Dash again. I was a public school librarian with a reading habit, and he was a mysterious and gorgeous athlete with the grace of the wind. Our paths had no reason to cross. So I just put my hands under the sheets and took care of my business, letting the whole thing fade over the weekend.

Except that one time I looked up Youder's interview on the Internet. Which I counted as one time even though I watched it about a hundred. I never closed the window and looked it up again. So, one time. Blow kiss. Blow kiss. Blow kiss.

He for sure thought I was hot, which was true in my little world, but from a guy who could have anyone he wanted, it was a Big Deal.

I bounced into work on Monday with springs in my shoes and a smile on my face.

Jim was getting coffee in the faculty room.

"Good morning!" I said, dropping a bag of apples on the counter.

"You look chipper."

"I am. It's just nice out. You know, the smog's all gone in winter, and the sky's blue. The air's crisp but not too cold."

"Probably a good time to ask you for a favor." He poured half and half from a tiny plastic pre-serve cup and ripped open another.

"Another Dreamfield trip?"

"Ah, no. I have this thing on Thursday night. The

17

Petersen's doing a fundraiser party, and I'm a donor."

The Petersen Automotive Museum stored classic and prototype cars in its comic-book behemoth building on Fairfax and Wilshire. He couldn't make enough to donate that kind of cash. We worked for Los Angeles Unified, after all.

I grabbed a cup from the stack by the coffee pot. "How much do you have to donate to get invited to stuff?"

"Small potatoes. But I won a raffle. It's formal. Want to go with me? Not a date or anything. Just I have two tickets and no sisters."

"Don't you have a girlfriend?"

"Not anymore."

"Ugh, sorry." After my breakup with Carl, simple sympathy was all I'd wanted to hear, so that was all I gave.

"Yeah, well…" He drifted off as if looking for words.

Seeing a big muscular guy broken-hearted hurt my insides. I blamed it on too many romance novels. "You all right?"

"She's going to be there with this guy…" He shook his head. Smiled to deflect. Shrugged to lighten the words. "Movie producer. She says they're friends, but I think it doesn't matter."

I took a sip of the cheap black coffee. Cream and sugar never helped it, so I just drank it black in all its bitter badness.

"You want me to make Michelle jealous? I'm all for it, but…" I didn't like seeing my friends hurt, but I'd met Michelle. She was a bodybuilder. I looked down at myself. There was nothing wrong with me, but a bodybuilder I wasn't. "I'm not the 'make the ex-girlfriend jealous' type."

"You're joking."

"My friend Francine? You've met her. She might do the trick, and she loves cars."

"Okay." He put down his coffee so he could talk with his hands. His mother was Sicilian, and he'd gotten his gestures from her side. "I want you to know it's not like that between us. You're my friend. I enjoy the hell out of you in a totally platonic way. But you're gorgeous. Even with the glasses and baggy shirts. You're bomb sexy. Not for nothing."

I looked at my coffee and cleared my throat. He wasn't lying, but that didn't make him right. "If I argue, you're going to think I'm fishing for compliments."

"I won't think that. But don't argue. Come on. If you're sexy enough for me, you're sexy enough. It'll be fun. They have games and exhibits. It's crazy. I'll drive so you can have a drink."

Why not? I had contact lenses and a closet full of designer dresses. If I didn't make Michelle jealous, so what? I could keep Jim company and have a good time with him.

I was totally putting on mascara for this.

"Let's go have fun then," I said. "I'll take a cab over to your house, and we can go sit in the Batman car. I have a dress that will knock you over. I hope she sees it."

"You're a good sport, Viv."

The bell rang.

"This is going to be the height of my week," I said.

I grabbed my bag of apples, turned on my springy little heel, and walked out.

Carl hadn't been a bad sort. There was nothing technically wrong with him. He wasn't scary or arrogant. Wasn't too confident. Just an approachable, low-key guy who didn't shine too bright or demand too much. I'd felt comfortable about him right away, and we slipped into three years together without thinking. He took my virginity without hurting me or being intentionally gentle. He freaked out a little after at what he'd done and who he'd be for me for the rest of his life. I told him to take it easy. It wasn't that big a deal.

We never fought either, which had seemed great. Who wanted to fight? I didn't. I wanted to come home and relax, watch some tube, have sex (or not), and go to sleep. So that was what I got. Everything was copasetic.

Then there was a day like any other. I came home from a

rough day at Hobart. It was a Friday, and I was looking forward to going out for a drink with Francine and a few of Carl's friends. He was on the couch after his own rough day of cranking out coffee and saying "yes" a hundred times, binge-watching a show about people who actually did things.

I asked him if he wanted to come with me to meet Francine and the guys.

He kept his eyes on the TV. "Nah. You go."

"It's okay. I'll stay here with you."

I texted Francine to bail on Friday and plan for Saturday and plopped onto the couch.

I don't know if it was ten minutes into the show, after a few jokes and bonding comments, or an hour later. I just don't remember. His feet were entwined with mine and half-buried in the space between couch cushions.

"I'm bored," he said.

"Wanna go out? It's not too late."

"No," he said, poking at his popcorn as if he was unsure what he wanted out of the conversation. "I'm bored overall."

"I get it," I said, not getting it at all. "Maybe take some art classes? You can do nights at the coffee shop."

"Listen to me!" he hissed. "I'm dead inside. I'm dead in this apartment. I feel like I'm a rat in a glue trap."

For months, I couldn't get over how he'd seemed angry at my suggestion. How he'd tightened his jaw as if I was a complete imbecile. He'd never spoken to me like that. We'd never raised our voices at each other. I thought that was the mark of something good and strong, but it left me unprepared for his venom that night.

"This is going absolutely nowhere in the biggest hurry." He tossed the popcorn aside as if he'd just had it with everything.

My eyes must have been the size of saucers. I'd never been so surprised by anything he'd done.

"Okay?" I tiptoed around his emotions, which seemed more toxic and messy than usual. "So what do you want to do?"

He leapt off the couch. "Be done! Just done! I can't be here anymore!"

"With me? You're breaking up with me?"

"Yes!"

In retrospect I understood that he really wasn't angry with me but had to whip up his emotions to initiate the breakup. He was a complete pussy, but I didn't really believe that until months later. At the time, I was convinced I'd done something to piss him off.

"What did I do? I don't understand."

He leaned on one foot. He had a flake of popcorn on his T-shirt. I always remembered that. Focused on it. The way he didn't notice it. I thought it was because he was so mad at being stuck with me that he was a mess, but no. He always had crap on his shirt. He always looked as though he'd just rolled out of bed. He didn't give a shit and blamed it on me.

Pulled between the sure knowledge that this horrible turn of events was my fault and the fact that it had nothing at all to do with me, I stood, upending the popcorn onto the carpet. "I'm moving out."

The words came out of my mouth before I'd thought them out, but I knew they were right. I felt the relief in my guts, the lightening of my shoulders, the way every corner of my mind was suddenly illuminated.

"You're a loser, Carl. You're the biggest loser I've ever met. I'm not responsible for making your life exciting. No woman is. And I swear to God, you're going to regret this until the day you die alone in some cheap studio in East LA."

He left while I packed, probably to meet Francine, Victor, and Larry, which was what I'd wanted to do in the first place. I was mad and hurt and victimized by my own hard words to myself.

I moved back in with Dad and then… nothing. I was the same. I went out more, read a ton of books, made some friends, got deeply involved in my job, and ran away from romance. Even when Carl tried to bring back the friendship, I pushed him away. His idea of friendship involved kissing me, and as heartbroken as I was, I wasn't interested in going backward.

Carl got his life together because he had to. He'd taken the risk of breaking up with me, and he had to prove he'd been right to do that. At least that was how it looked from where I sat. He got a job at Disney as a receptionist, then he got promoted to development. I saw him at Trader Joe's buying wine. I didn't even recognize him, he was so cleaned up and put-together. I was stopping for apples on the way back from work, and I looked as if someone had wrung me out.

Maybe it hadn't been Carl. Maybe it was me. Maybe I really had been a dead weight on him. Maybe I was my own dead weight—living with my dad, working a government job that paid in the smallest satisfactions.

I made conversation with him at the checkout, deflecting from talking about myself so I could hear all about his blossoming adulthood. Every one of my victories and good days seemed clouded by the fact that I'd kept my boyfriend from reaching his potential. He'd been a loser because of my presence in his life.

Naturally, I went home and cried. Then I got over it. Then months went by, and I stayed numb. I had ups and downs, but they blurred into one another.

The Monday after Dash Wallace had blown a kiss behind my back was no more up than any other up. I was amped and happy walking to the library, swinging my bag of apples. I had a fun event to go to with a nice guy. Dad's ball was almost finished in time. I had a job I loved. The sun was shining, and all the world was...

I turned the corner. The world was... weird.

The library was locked, and outside it stood a man in charcoal pants and a jacket. Pale blue shirt undone at the neck. I almost didn't recognize him in dress shoes. I thought he was some overdressed LAUSD administrator coming with a surprise talk about a reduction in funding for libraries, how there was a public library three blocks away, how they were going to just have some shelves in the hallway, how they needed the space for a classroom. I was already listing the phone calls I would have to make to stop whatever it was he'd come to do.

Not until he was two steps away did I swallow a ton of professional antagonism.

"Are you Miss Foster?"

"Vivian," I said, neck bent to look up into those damned blue eyes. "What brings you here, Mr. Wallace? If you want to make a big donation to the library, the children could use it."

"You can call me Dash."

Because he never gave interviews on camera, I'd had no inkling of how resonant his voice was. Out in the park, with the ambient noise of the wind and children, I hadn't noticed it. But in the stark hallway of a brick-and-stone building, it vibrated against the center of my body.

"Dash then." I unlocked the door. "You got past security."

"I autographed a banner, and they patted me down." He smiled, and I kept my cool. "Things have changed since I was in school."

I opened the door and let him into my modest domain. I felt suddenly ridiculous that I had a full-time job managing this tiny room with two tables and kid-sized chairs. A couch. Two Ikea padded chairs. The windows had bars, and the top shelves were empty.

He didn't know how hard I'd fought for a water cooler and that I paid for the cups. That I went to sales on weekends to find new books. How I fought to use the Dewey Decimal System so the kids would know how subjects were organized even though computer searches were now the norm.

"This is really nice," he said.

I spun on him, this anomaly in a custom suit. Was he making fun of me? He was a god, expanding all over the simplicity of this simple room. Nothing had ever been so incongruous as his presence in my library.

The way he looked at me, those lips tightening just a little, his hands crossed in front of him—he meant it. Or he meant to be polite. I couldn't tell past the glow of perfection. My every intuition misfired. His looks and stardom were short-circuiting my senses.

"Thank you." I indicated the metal folding chair across my desk. "I have only one other grown-up-sized chair."

He nodded and sat in it. I didn't think the little library had ever contained a man like Dash Wallace. He was tall, of course, but he also cut the space he moved in like a scalpel, and when he crossed his legs, the angle of his legs against each other was the opposite of awkward.

"So…" Opening my apple bag gave my hands something to do. "If you're not here to fund my palatial library, what brings you?"

"Well…" He cleared his throat. "First, I wasn't trying to insult you on Friday."

"What were you trying to do?"

"Make conversation."

I dumped the apples into a big yellow bowl on my desk. "I'm sure I was oversensitive." I shook out the last apple. It tumbled to the top of the pile, bounced, and went to the floor.

With a speed that defied the laws of physics, Dash shot his arm out and caught it. The rest of his body barely moved. His fingers tensed around the fruit just enough to hold it, as if he was about to throw it to second base. Those fingers. The way they curved. The flesh on bone. How would they feel against the curve of my hip? The inside of my thigh?

"You catch it, you keep it," I said, looking away.

He put it on top of the pile. "Leave it for the kids."

"Breakfast doesn't always happen for the kids who get here at seven thirty." I sat behind my desk, comforted by the furniture between us. "And they don't all get a good lunch. The ones who fall between the free hot lunch program and lunchmeat on bread. There aren't enough fruits and vegetables. And everyone loves an apple."

He nodded, looking at my face as if reading a book. Was I babbling? Was he reading my attraction to him like a story he only needed to skim? He was sucking the breath out of me.

"You're right," he said, taking his apple back. "Everyone does."

"I have a class coming in five minutes." I didn't mean for my voice to be husky and low. I cleared my throat. I'd done enough talking. I just met his gaze. Let him read my story. He was a beautiful man, and he knew it.

"I have a problem," he said.

"Oh, looking for a place to make an endowment?"

"Let's not start on my endowments."

My throat did something that made a sound, and my jaw clamped shut to prevent me from responding. He was smiling. I was dying thinking about his endowments.

"Sorry," he said, and I remembered that blown kiss on the TV.

He thought I was sexy, and he didn't know that I knew. Why was I letting a little joke between adults make me feel small? I should have felt terrific. He may or may not have wanted me, but he certainly found me physically appealing. I could choose to feel good about that.

I cleared my throat and decided on a new start. "Don't be. I brought it up. This problem. It's something I can help you with, I assume?"

He fingered the apple as if it were a baseball, thumb looking for stitches, turning, feeling, turning. A body in motion tends to stay in motion, and Dash Wallace was a man in motion. "I had something before your students came to my table on Friday. When they left, it was gone."

My body went from warm and aroused to cold and tense. I had to work to not get defensive right away. "Really?"

"A glove. It was in my things under the table. I need it back."

My kids. He was accusing my kids of stealing his glove. That was a problem. No matter how poor they were, they weren't supposed to steal things. I felt personally responsible. I wanted to apologize profusely, beg forgiveness, sell something to pay for it.

But couldn't he buy another glove? For Chrissakes, he had only one glove in the world? He'd signed a seventeen-million dollar two-year contract. Who did that then came to East

25

Hollywood looking for a missing piece of equipment? How much was the most expensive baseball glove? Five hundred dollars? A thousand?

As if reading my mind, he said, "It's not just any glove. It's important to me."

"I understand." I didn't. Not at all. I sat in my creaky chair.

He leaned forward, elbows on the desk. My desk. I couldn't move. If I leaned forward, I could have kissed him.

"I came to you because I remembered you. If I went through my agent, he'd make a stink. I don't want to make a big deal about it. But I need it back."

His body held so much power, so much forward motion. His stare was a swing in my direction, and instinctively I curved. I held my hands folded in front of me, and all my tension flowed down from my shoulders. I squeezed my hands together as if I was cracking a walnut between them.

"I'll ask the kids. If it doesn't turn up, we'll find a way to pay for it." I wished I could swallow that last sentence back. There was no way I could cough up enough for whatever that thing cost, and the LAUSD would laugh me out of a job if I asked them for it.

"I don't want money." Ever so lightly, he tapped my desk with the tip of his middle finger. It was the only movement of his body, as if he was conserving his energy to spring. "I have the money. It's the glove. *That* glove."

"It's the glove you love." I smiled at my joke and felt like a dumbass at the same time.

"You're a poet."

"I know it."

He laughed, really laughed at my silly rhyming game. Oldest joke in the book, and he laughed.

The bell rang.

"I'm so sorry this happened," I finally said. "I'll make it my business to get it back."

He regarded me, my face, my eyes, my posture. The look was so deep I felt not physically naked but morally, as if he were stripping me bare to see if I was not only capable of finding his glove but if my desire to do it was real.

I scribbled my number on a scrap of paper. "Here. I'm personally responsible for this. You can call me and harass me any time."

I slid the paper across the desk. He'd probably throw it in the trash and call the school's superintendent, who would fire me outright for not watching the kids.

He took the paper and folded it in half against his thumb. "You buy the apples with your own money?"

"Yeah. Oranges sometimes, but the peels get messy."

"You seem like a good person." He slid the paper into his breast pocket.

My response burst out of the base of my throat without taking the usual route through my brain. "And you're very handsome."

I turned red—I knew from the hot tingle in my neck and shoulders—but oddly, his cheeks went a little red as well. He always seemed so cocky, in part because I only saw him on the field, but maybe he wasn't.

You're a school librarian. Did you even brush your hair this morning?

That little voice brought me back to reality. Dash may have turned a little red, and he may have been a little awkward, but that made him charming and sweet to more accomplished, more beautiful women. It did not put him in my league. I was triple A, and he was the majors.

The bell rang. He stood.

"Thank you." He buttoned his jacket.

I didn't look at him as I walked to the door and opened it. "I'll ask around. Do you have a deadline? It could take time."

"Opening day's my deadline." He handed me a card. "Call me if you find it. Or just have it sent to the address on the back."

"I will."

A line of second graders made their way down the hall, and they parted for him as if he was an unseen wall with a space all his own. He turned back as he walked, giving me a wave. I wished I hadn't told him he was handsome, and I wished I didn't have to interrogate the entire third grade on his behalf.

five

Vivian

I hated going into Mom's closet, because she wasn't around anymore. It still smelled like her. As soon as I slid the door open, I was assaulted by rosewater and memories. I sighed and stepped inside.

She hadn't been born to money, but my bio dad had gotten the house cheap when his four-minute-long career had turned a corner. My stepdad was a hard-working divorce attorney in a city that didn't take marriage seriously, and he was generous and kind, but his career had skidded when his arthritis took over his life.

In the years he'd been married to my mother, he treated her like a queen. She never wanted for a dress, and what became apparent as the years went on and I plumbed the depths of her closet, she often didn't want for a choice of dresses for any occasion. Some still had tags. Some were too expensive for price tags but had obviously never been worn.

I was an inch shorter than she'd been but the same shoe and dress size. As the years wore on, the contents of the closet had gone from dated to cutting edge, and in the hours before the Petersen event, I ran my hands along the sleeve of a matte gold gown that looked as if it had been smelted by a goldsmith.

"She never wore that one," Dad said from behind me. He was having a good day, and the walker was in its little hallway, waiting for the rain.

I pulled the hanger off the rod and draped the fabric over myself. "It's too much."

He waved. "Please wear it. It's a waste not to."

Dad hated waste. I didn't know if that was a new thing or if the excess he'd poured on my mother was the result of a surplus of love.

"All right," I said, turning to the side and back again. "But if I can't find the shoes that go with it, I'm changing to the blue one."

Dad stood against the doorjamb with his arms crossed. His eyes stared in the middle distance. It was his Missing Mom Face.

"Dad?"

He snapped out of it. "I think the shoes are in the bottom rack."

I crouched to hunt for them. Couldn't miss them. Matching matte gold stilettos. Insane.

"You look just like her, you know."

"Like mom?" I huffed.

That was a load of crap. My mother had been ethereal. She'd stopped modeling when she got pregnant and never got back to it because it was more boring than being a wife and mother.

He snapped open a drawer and rummaged around before pulling out a little velvet box. He handed it to me open. Two gold hoop earrings each strung with a single pearl.

"Wow. They're gorgeous."

"She was wearing them when we met. She said they were lucky."

I couldn't deny him, so I put them in my ears.

"Have you thought about dating?" I asked.

"You get married first."

"Oh, please."

"Who is this guy tonight?"

"A friend. I'm not his type, and he's not mine."

"What's wrong with him?"

Of course he'd never address the fact that a man wasn't interested in me. He thought any sane, straight man would want Vivian Foster.

"Nothing. He's just, I don't know. Nice, but I work with

him, and—"

"He's not a star in a romance novel?" I snapped the light off, but he kept on. "Those men don't exist, peanut. We have flaws. We're a little nuts but not in the ways you like."

"I'm aware."

He'd never understood why I didn't go back to Carl when he called. Maybe I hadn't articulated it well enough. Whatever forward motion Carl had without me had happened because I was gone. If I went back to him, I'd blame myself for every stumble in his life. I couldn't shoulder his life as well as my own.

I put in my contacts, which I hated doing. I didn't like touching my eye, and the whole thing made me nervous. But I blinked twice and looked at myself in the mirror. The mascara would look great without the glasses. I snapped my fingers. Blink. Blink. Boom. In.

As I got dressed, I reminded myself that my father was only looking out for me. He never spoke a word that wasn't out of love. That train of thought took me to his sixty-fifth birthday in April. I had another signature to get from last summer's twenty-five-man roster. Duchovney had gotten himself on the sixty-day DL mid-season for a meniscus tear, and that was it. He hadn't been around to sign anything.

Not that dad would count to twenty-four and be disappointed, but I liked all my players in position.

Hello. I'm checking on the glove. Any word?

Lord help me. Was it him?

I rushed to my work purse and fished out the card Dash had given me. The numbers matched. It was him.

Not yet. We'll find it. I have a thing with the gym teacher tonight. I'll ask him if he saw anything.

A thing?

I froze. A thing. He was asking. Why? And why had I said *a thing* in the first place?

> An event at the Petersen

I hit Send just as his message came in.

Sorry. Wasn't prying. I typed before I thought about it.

How could texting be so awkward? I felt unbalanced. Should I wait to answer? Not answer at all? Soothe him immediately? What was the difference? I wedged my foot into the gold shoe with the six-inch heel, nearly falling over.

> I get it. Sometimes I'd like to put a cock in my mouth

Wait. What?

That can be arranged

> No! I meant to hit the backdoor butt

Crap! Was my subconscious doing the typing?

> backdoor

> Goddamnit! Back-space not knees

> What? And button not nuts

> Butt

> Not butt

For the love of…

> Are you still there?

Still stuck on the cock in the mouth

> Kill me now

Autocorrect has a new fan today

I laughed. I had no choice. It was that or die of shame, and since I hadn't meant it, and he knew I hadn't meant it, I was going to live.

See you at the Petersen

See you at the Petersen?

Oh. My. Fucking. God. Jim had better not have a problem with me talking to Dashiell-motherfucking-Golden-Glove-move-like-the-wind-hit-like-Tyson-with-a-body-like-a-Renaissance-god Wallace because I was going to see him and stand next to him s-o-c-i-a-l-l-y. My face tightened into an excited grimace I hoped to the good green gods I didn't make in front of him.

I looked in the mirror again. Hair. Check. Makeup. Check. Dress. Body. Heels. Check, check, check.

How would I stand?

One heel out? Lean on a hip? How would I laugh? Big smile? Titter? Belly laugh?

No. Not that.

The mirror didn't like that.

"Peanut," Dad called from the doorway, two rooms closer than I expected.

I tipped a little as I buckled the second shoe and righted myself, dropping the phone to my side as if I were a preteen hiding what was on the screen. "What?"

"The guy's here. The *schlamiel* you're not interested in."

six

Dash

A librarian in slacks and a bright yellow hoodie wearing sensible black flats on the winter grass of a park field. No makeup. Glasses. Baseball clutched in un-manicured fingers.

Not my usual, to say the least. But I could see her body under the clothes, and the way she went off-balance when she pulled a kid away from a collision with another one had a certain sexy grace. Her voice didn't screech. Her laugh was like a purr. The first thing I imagined was pinning her under me, holding her hands over her head, immobilizing her while she came. My fingers had tingled when I handed her back the ball. Weird.

Then the glove was gone, and I immediately knew I had to contact her myself. Just to check. To see if I'd lost my mind. I didn't like glasses or T-shirts. I preferred women who were finished. Polished. I hadn't gone for that type since I was eleven.

But there was something to the surprise of what was under those slacks. What she'd look like in heels and a dress. And what the heels and dress would look like on the floor.

I was mad about the glove. First at myself because I thought I'd misplaced it, then at whomever took it, then at God and the universe because it was just another sign that shit was going belly-up.

I had my assistant get me the number for Hobart Elementary, then I stared at my phone.

What was I supposed to do? Call the principal's office and accuse an entire class of underprivileged kids of theft? I made four point three million a year to catch and hit balls. My father would have been ashamed if he was alive to see it.

But I needed that glove back. *That* glove. Daria's pin was on it. Losing it meant losing her.

I could go to the librarian. The one in the yellow sweatshirt. With the slim neck and the little gold chain around it, curling on her skin where her trapezius rose and fell. That cleft of space between the bulky hood and her body was somehow more sexual than a hundred miles of cleavage.

I had a meeting that afternoon, so I put on a suit. That was what I told myself, but when I pulled my cuffs and matched my socks, I wasn't thinking about my agent, who didn't care what I wore. I was thinking about hitting the Hobart Elementary library first.

I was one of LA's most eligible bachelors. I didn't let that run my life, but the papers mentioned it frequently enough that it had become a fact. I could have a ton of women, and I did. But when she'd blurted out that I was handsome, it didn't feel like part of her strategy. It felt like approval I hadn't known I needed.

So I tried to wait, then I couldn't.

> Hello. I'm checking on the glove. Any word?

Not yet. We'll find it. I have a thing with the gym teacher tonight. I'll ask him if he saw anything.

Of course. Why wouldn't she have a boyfriend? Just because she was wearing a yellow sweatshirt and flats didn't mean I was the only one who saw a sexy woman. And it was rude to ask. Completely out of line.

> A thing?

An event at the Petersen

What kind of answer was that?
An answer to a question you have no business asking.

36

> Sorry. Wasn't prying. I typed before I
> thought about it.

**I get it. Sometimes I'd like to put a cock
in my mouth**

Wait. What?

That had to be autocorrect.

But I'd done enough dirty texting in my day to not discount her intentions entirely. Putting my cock in her mouth was on a long list of things I wanted to do to her, and my dick stiffened as I thought about it.

If she wanted to play dirty, I was ready, willing and able to play dirty.

> That can be arranged

No! I meant to hit the backdoor butt

I snorted a laugh.

It was autocorrect. She must have meant sock or shoe or foot. Who even knew? But before I could stop laughing and reply, a rapid fire stream of filthy mistakes buzzed my phone.

backdoor

Goddamnit! Back-space not knees

What? And button not nuts

Butt

Not butt

I hadn't laughed that hard in a long time.

Are you still there?

> Still stuck on the cock in the mouth

Kill me now

> Autocorrect has a new fan today

I had to see her. I had a few weeks to kill before spring training, and she was a lot of fun. If she was having a thing with the gym teacher, I'd just back off. Or not. Whatever.

See you at the Petersen

I didn't wait for a reply. I made a call.

"Jack?"

"That's my name, Wallace. What do you need?"

"You're a member at that car museum? The one on Fairfax that looks like a comic strip?"

"Yeah."

"There's a thing tonight?" I asked.

"Yeah."

"Are you dragging your wife again?"

"She's trying to get out of it."

I heard her in the background. "I hate cars, Dash. I hate them!"

"I love them," I said. "Take me. I'll buy you dinner and bring you flowers."

"You gonna try to suck my dick too?"

There was a scuffle as the phone was snatched from Youder's hand.

"Are you offering to go? Please go. I can put on yoga pants and watch *Scandal*."

"Deal. Go get your yoga pants on."

She hung up before her husband could refuse her. Gotta love that woman.

It had all started with the avocado tree.

The first thing it did wrong was make fruit in June instead of September. I hadn't known about off-bloom years, when a tree just went apeshit a few months early. I'd come back from a losing series in New York to find my front yard had turned into a minefield of squirrel-chewed fruit. That gave me the first inkling that the thirty-foot tree would be a major encroachment on my routine.

I called the same guys I always called to come harvest the fruit. They thanked me and hauled away ten bags, leaving me one I tossed around on the plane the next time we traveled.

That could have been nothing. Really. But I knew it wasn't. I carried around a kind of discomfort I didn't have the will to release. Like a tiny rock in a lace-up boot. You figure it's not so bad, not bad enough to warrant the unlacing and relacing of the entire boot.

Not until a pipe under the house broke and I found out it was the avocado tree roots pushing on the foundation did I know why the off-bloom had bugged me. The tree was going to be a major pain in my ass. So I had it cut down. Had the stump ground out. Roots dug out as far as they could be without sending my house down the hill.

Then my patio was too sunny. The front of the house wasn't on the street. It faced south, right into the giant eyeball rising and setting over the east and west sides of the horizon. I was home half the summer, and I spent it trying to manage the shade in my front yard.

I was in a tucked-away enclave in the Oaks section of the Hollywood Hills. I'd bought it for the view and kept it for the quiet. I was easily distracted by anything sensory. Everything found a way into my eyes and ears. Even a strange taste could distract me. A shirt seam half undone and rubbing my skin could drive me nuts. So the ambient noise of the city was great until a truck was a little too loud or the neighbors two blocks away let their smoke detector battery go dead and I was assaulted by chirping every thirty seconds.

In my house, I controlled my distractions. I could have as much sensory input as I needed to work out or run my business. No one watched me up in the hills. One side of my house faced the cliff and Los Angeles. One faced the narrow street. The back faced the neighbor, a movie director and his wife who were home half the year, and the other side faced an acre of nothing.

But the avocado tree had been a sort of good luck charm, and that off-bloom, and the crushing roots on the foundation, had fucked everything else.

The girl I fucked in New York found a boyfriend. The one I fucked in St. Louis tried to get me to commit to I-don't-know-what. Mary in Oakland was fine, but we only played the A's once a year unless they got in the playoffs, which was unlikely. So I went without pussy for too much of the summer, and the bad luck built up.

I made an error in game three of the playoffs.

I didn't think of things as going to hell. None of those individual craptastications spun together to make a shitstorm.

At Christmas, my mother had announced she was selling the house and moving into an apartment with her boyfriend. I was happy for her but felt unmoored.

Still, I could juggle all the little things. I'd work it out.

Not until I looked under the table and saw my glove was gone did I put it all together. Things were going wrong. General things. Every piece on the board had shifted, from my personal to my professional life and everything that linked them.

I needed to put it all back.

I backtracked. The tree. Well, there wasn't much I could do there that wouldn't take eighty years to fix. But I planted a fig tree and hoped for the best. I'd find new women where I needed them, and I bought the house I grew up in. My mother still left it to live in town, but the house? I had that.

Then Daria's pin.

Losing the stupid insult of a pin reminded me that I hadn't fixed a thing. All I'd done was plaster over the leak. I needed Daria's pin. I couldn't play without it. Not successfully. I didn't know where the leak in my charmed life was, but I knew the luck was seeping through it.

Going to the Petersen and seducing a school librarian was exactly what I needed to keep my mind off everything. An easily achievable goal that would fill the well of shitty circumstances.

Vivian the librarian.
Vivian with a bowl of apples on her desk for the kids.
Vivian with a neck like a lotus stem.
She'd do nicely.

seven

Vivian

Jim opened the door of his green Saturn to let me in. He was a gentleman's gentleman, looking into my eyes when he spoke despite the low-cut liquid silk of the dress, complimenting me chastely, and keeping the conversation light.

"Security told me Dash Wallace from the Dodgers was in the building Monday," he said. "I wonder what he wanted."

I told him about the glove and the conversation after, leaving out the double entendre about endowments and the part where I blurted out how handsome he was. "So it's this big deal because you can't go around accusing kids of stealing, but we have to solve the issue if there is one. We've searched backpacks and lockers—"

"Third graders don't have lockers."

"But they have brothers and sisters and cousins, yada yada. It's such a disaster. If one of our kids took it, it's not in the building. So we're contacting parents, and it's going to be an ugly mess, I'm sure."

"Did he say what was so special about it?"

"No. Just that it was important. I don't have high hopes."

The museum rose at the intersection of Fairfax and Wilshire. Gigantic wind-shaped comic-book swirls made of brushed metal covered the building, lit from behind in deep red. In one sense, the building was ridiculous and fake, out of proportion, overly ambitious, poorly yet grandly designed to look like a birthday cake or to represent the absurd cartoonishness of Los Angeles itself, a city so driven by cars that they had their own museum. In another sense, if the designers had wanted to go big or go home, their mission had been accomplished.

Jim pulled into the lot, the only entrance to the building (it was a car museum after all), where we were stopped by a valet. Flashes went off for everyone getting out of their limos and foreign sports cars, but he and I were able to walk up to the doors without a glance from anyone.

I caught a glimpse of Michael Greydon and Laine Cartwright with two of their children. Brad Sinclair was there. Monica Faulkner, the singer. I scanned for Dash. Every face. Every body. Would I see him first, or would he see me?

One guy. From the back. Brown hair and a perfect body next to a woman in a copper up-do. I gulped. Of course he wouldn't be here alone. The man turned to kiss the woman.

Wasn't him. But it was a reminder. Dash was a beautiful man. He was rich, talented, and sought after. He wasn't coming alone.

"Wow, this is some raffle you won," I said as I clung to Jim's arm. I was glad I'd worn the gold dress. It was appropriate. Whoever Dash's date was, I was about to give her a run for her money.

We got on the white-lit polymer steps to the second floor. Below us, the first floor was designed like a freeway clover, and inside each leaf was a car on a turntable. One from each of the major auto-producing nations: Japan, the US, Italy, India.

I scanned for him below. Nothing.

"Who are you looking for?" Jim asked.

"Dash Wallace said he was going to be here."

"The roof is the VIPs," he said as we crested the second floor. "He's probably up there."

I deflated and felt relief at the same time. I could stop looking for him because I wouldn't see him unless he came looking for me, which was unlikely.

As soon as we stepped off the escalator, we were assaulted by a cacophony of bells, whistles, whirring, and tapping. The floor was crowded with people and games, machines, tables, and an announcer.

"Looks like all the fun stuff is here," I said.

"Your specialty."

"I'm *fun*? I'm not fun."

He laughed. "Yes, you are."

"What do you want to do first?" I straightened his satin blue tie and patted his lapel.

"Batman." He pointed at the Batmobile. "Gotta do Batman."

We headed to the exhibit that had inspired the party. The museum had acquired each incarnation of the Batmobile from the 1970s TV show to the most recent reboot. We grabbed drinks and got in line to sit where Michael Keaton had sat while the car shimmied in front of a screen depicting the chase scene with Superman.

Michelle appeared when we were at the front of the line. Her smooth ebony skin seemed to stretch for miles from her neck to her sternum. Her breasts were covered with two strips of shiny white fabric belted at the waist so precisely placed that not an inch of inappropriate nudity could be seen at any angle.

I saw her just as Jim and I were giggling about bat signal-worthy crises at school. Out of apples. Bat signal. Inappropriate language. Bat signal.

"Ex-girlfriend at two o'clock," I said.

"Bat signal," he murmured, looking behind me.

"Not your two o'clock, you dolt. My two o'clock."

She tapped his shoulder so hard it must have hurt then triangulated between us. I guessed I didn't have to worry about him stalking her. She had no problem being in the same room with him.

"Hi, Michelle." His face lit up like the city at sunset. He loved her, the poor sod.

Her lips pressed together, and her eyes burned two dime-sized holes right in him.

I held out my hand. "I'm Vivian."

She glanced at me as if deciding it was safe to shake my hand, then she did. I looked at her and tried to think non-threatening thoughts, averting my gaze after a point and looking over her shoulder. At which point I swallowed my own face.

"Bat signal," I squeaked.

The guy running the Batmobile attraction undid the velvet rope. "You two next?"

"Yes," Michelle said, slipping between Jim and me.

He looked at me, silently asking if it was all right, but I was still speechless that a man I hadn't seen anywhere but on a TV screen was five feet from me for the third time in a week.

"Mr. Wallace," I said.

He smirked. "Almost didn't recognize you without the glasses, Apples."

"Did you forget my name?"

"No, but I think he did." Dash pointed toward Jim and Michelle having it out in the front seat of the Batmobile, so deep in discussion that they weren't paying attention to the attraction.

I turned to face Dash. He'd shaved for the event, and though I liked the scruff he'd had before, the angles of his jaw looked extra sharp without hair to soften them. His tux brought out the width of his shoulders, and the open jacket let me see the flat perfection of his waist. I didn't want to think about the rest. Not while I had to form words.

"I hope they stay together this time," I said.

"You look..." His eyes scanned my body, and I felt prickly heat all over. "What are the words?"

"Nice? I look nice?"

"You could conduct electricity in that dress."

I laughed. Part nerves. Part space filler. Part delight over an obscure fifth-grade science reference.

I flattened the gold fabric against me. "I was going for more insoluble."

"You've just out-scienced me."

"I help the kids with their homework after school."

He pointed his chin at the Batmobile. Jim and Michelle were talking quietly among the blasts and screeches of the screen. "I think you lost your date."

"Yeah. Well, I don't want to keep you from yours."

She was a five-foot-eleven triathlete with a PhD, no doubt.

"I came with my sackmate."

My brain skipped as if tripping on a crack in the pavement. Sackmate.

A friend with benefits. That was my first thought. Up on deck, the consideration that a casual fuck buddy made him kind of available. In the hole, the actual definition of the word sackmate.

A shortstop's second baseman. Double-play partner. Jack Youder.

Not a fuck buddy unless you'd just hit a grounder to short with a man on first. Then you were fucked.

It had taken me forever to unravel that, and he watched the process, probably wondering if I knew what he meant. I couldn't stand in public with a baseball god and look like a deer in headlights.

"What are you going to do when he goes free agent?" I asked.

He stiffened, unamused and seemingly unimpressed. Fuck. Foul ball.

"He's not going anywhere," Dash said.

"You'd have a hard time finding a mate as good to sack."

I was trying to lighten him up, and it worked. He smirked and looked at me the way he had when we'd met at the park. He looked at me as though he was trying not to. As if I was a magnet's north and his gaze was stuck on me like magnetic south.

"You have a way with double entendre, don't you?"

"Don't let it fool you. I'm a librarian. You don't get more boring than that."

Jim and Michelle got out of the Batmobile. I didn't know what to do with my hands. They wanted to touch Dash

47

Wallace, but my brain wouldn't let them, and the energy it took for mind to command matter drained me of any conversational material. I'd never felt so stupid in my life.

"Is there someone in your life, Apples? A guy type?"

I shook my head.

"Is that a 'no'?"

I nodded. God almighty, what was wrong with me?

He bent toward me, and I could smell his cologne. Pure heat and crackling ozone. Spice and musk and something that could only be described as lust in a bottle.

"Was that a forward question?" he whispered in my ear. His breath was warm, and with every syllable, I knew how his tongue and lips moved to make the sound.

"No. I don't think so. I mean, I guess that depends on what your intentions are. If you're just curious, then it's forward and inappropriate." *You're babbling.* "But if you're trying to come on to me, it's probably one of the first questions you should ask because a gentleman would establish consent."

You implied he wanted to come on to you.

I wasn't the feisty heroine I imagined I was. The whole conversation had no place in a romance novel, or even life. I was supposed to feel his heat and still parry/thrust with clever comebacks. I was supposed to push him away while I beckoned him closer, all leading him to chase me until I could no longer run. For every hundred times I had been told by my father and my friends that romance novels were fake, life proved it true two hundred times.

"I found the word for that dress," he said.

God, I hoped it wasn't *vintage* or something. "Tell me."

"Molten."

My insides went as molten as my dress, and I saw him and what he was saying in a narrow tunnel. He liked the dress—and my body in it.

This was the best night of my life. Ever.

I was losing my crackers. I needed a distraction.

"Look," I cried, pointing at a guy in a top hat and white face paint approaching us with a stack of iPads.

"Play the trivia game!" Top Hat handed me one. "We're giving away a trip to Cancun."

"Oh," I said. "I'll play!"

"Keep your eyes on the screen!" He pointed at a flat screen behind the Mercedes exhibit, then he handed Dash a tablet and took off for the next willing victims.

"Wait!" Dash held up his tablet and put it back on Top Hat's stack. "I'll play with her."

"Play with me?"

Top Hat took off, and I was left with a shrinking space between me and my double meanings.

"Yeah. Like sackmates."

Dash seemed to like sexy entendres, and everything I wanted in the world right then was for Dashiell Wallace to like me. I didn't have to promise him anything, and he didn't have to deliver after we left the event. All he had to do was stand near me. Let me be in his orbit.

"What if we win?" I said.

"Let's cross that bridge when we come to it. Now..." He leaned over me to look at the screen. "We need a nickname. Apples?"

"Apple Dash."

"Sounds like a delicious dessert." The glow of the screen washed the surfaces of his face in blue light as he tapped in the name.

I didn't even know what the nickname was supposed to mean except we'd become a team while I wasn't looking.

I was going to die with happiness. It was temporary of course. But I couldn't stop smiling. I knew then why women threw themselves at the feet of men like Dash. Actors, musicians, athletes, the kings and gods of the world. The social alphas. The gifted ones.

It felt good. Really, really good.

The screen flashed. Ready-Set-Go.

"The suspense is killing me," he said, glancing sidelong at me.

"You better watch it," I said. "Trivia's my thing."

The screen flashed.

First category. Three questions.

"Really?" he asked.

Literature.

"Yes. Really."

In what play was the phrase *beast with two backs* **coined?**

The word was almost out of my mouth, but I didn't get past the initial vowel before Dash had typed the answer.

Othello.

I tapped Send, and a big gold star filled the screen.
"Talk about double entendre," I said.
"He's the king."

Who created Lenny and George?

"That's so vague," I grumbled.
"Do you know it?" His fingers hovered over the screen as if a batter was switching his stance to send it his way.
I scrunched up my face and let it go when I realized how unattractive that was. I did know, but I didn't. "Skinny book. Tree on the front."
"Right. Uh..." He shook his head as if loosening the information. "Unemployment. The Great Depression."
"Steinbeck."
"Has to be." He tapped out *John Steinbeck*.
Gold star.
We high-fived, and for a second, his fingers curled into mine. I pulled my hand away. I would have burst if he'd held

my hand. Just exploded into hot, sexy bits-of-Vivian all over the automotive museum.

What 2012 American novel ended with an unfinished sentence?

It was a hard question because the book wasn't on any bestseller list, nor was it part of popular culture. It was thirteen-hundred pages long, and the only way to know that was to finish the book, which no one had. Except me. That was where I earned the prize. The other questions were bullshit.

"I got this," he said.

"Don't send!"

He couldn't know. He was going to type in the wrong book entirely. I would correct it before he hit Send, saving the win for us and impressing the hell out of him with how much time I spent alone on my couch with a Kindle.

But his fingers tapped the glass confidently, and the letters that appeared were exactly right.

Eternal Joke.

He knew.

"Right?" he said.

"Right." I hit Send. "Did you read it?" It was a stupid question. I was supposed to assume he had, but where had he found time to read that monstrous doorstop of a book?

The screen flashed beneath us. I knew why. Gold star.

"I like long books." He shrugged.

"I've never met anyone who finished the whole thing. Did you like it?"

"Loved it. Right up to that last comma."

Winners will be chosen randomly from players who answered all three questions correctly!

Next Category – Pets!

"It was beautiful," I said. "Do you read a lot?"

"Yeah. It helps me."

"Helps you what?"

He didn't answer but handed me the iPad. "I travel too much for pets. Do you want to do this one?"

Without him? Did I want to answer questions about pets without him? No, I didn't. I just wanted to ask him what else he'd read, his favorites of all time, everything. I pushed away the iPad.

"Paper or Kindle?" I said.

"Paper."

"You're missing out! Look, I have my Kindle in this tiny bag." I opened my gold clutch, revealing my slim grey device. "I can catch a couple of pages anywhere, any time. It's the best thing!"

He dropped the iPad on Top Hat's pile and guided me around the room. "I'm not a couple-of-pages-at-a-time kinda guy. Once I'm in, I'm all in."

"What are you reading now?"

I practically jumped out of my fancy shoes. I was sure he wasn't reading about Jax the sexy banker and Harriet the waitress as they explored a hundred ways to have sex, but that was okay. I was sure he was reading something that had come across my path, and the thought... oh, the thought that we could talk about *books* of all things was so exciting I couldn't contain myself.

"*Reaper's Weekend,*" he said.

"Oh! That's..." I caught myself before I said *hard.* "Postmodern."

"The denser and more opaque, the better for me. Slows me down, or I go too fast."

We ran into Jim. Michelle was on his arm.

"Hey," Jim said, pointing at me then Dash. "Shortstop. Dodgers. Three Golden Gloves."

The men shook hands.

"He was with me the whole time you were in the Batmobile," I said. "You notice *now*?"

He jerked his thumb toward Michelle. "I was distracted by her beauty."

She elbowed him playfully. I didn't know what they'd fought about, but it obviously wasn't anything a little jealousy couldn't fix.

Jim turned to Dash. "What's up with Youder? What are you gonna do when he goes free agent?"

It was a normal question, yet I didn't know what to expect from Dash since he'd tensed up on me when I asked. He and Youder were great partners. Almost psychically connected. They'd led the league in double plays for three of the last five years, and I just figured if he could do that with Youder, he could do it with anyone.

But no. Dash's expression was clear. The impending free-agency of his fielding partner bothered him. "I'll figure it out."

Youder was a sore spot. Jim hadn't done anything wrong, but I wanted to pop him.

Michelle nudged Jim, and he said to me, "Meet downstairs when it's over?"

"Yeah."

"I can take her home," Dash said.

My mouth opened. Words came out.

No. Nothing came out. They got caught in a mental bottleneck.

I probably looked like a choking victim.

Sort it out. Fast.

What Dash had intuited was that Jim wanted to go home with Michelle. He was right. Jim didn't need me dragging him to the west side.

But Gentleman Jim wouldn't allow me to get in a strange car with a strange man no matter how famous he was.

And what did *I* want?

"No," Jim said in the split second it took me to separate the mental wheat from chaff. "I brought her. I'll get her back."

Michelle interjected her two cents right after. "Girl, he

brought you. He delivers you home. Don't worry about me."

"Of course." Dash nodded.

"I'll take a Ryde." I waved away their objections. "I'm fine. Thank you, guys. But I got it."

"It's decided." Dash held his arm out for me.

I slipped my hand in the crook of his elbow. The wool of his jacket was warm to the touch, the arm under it hard with muscle. The moment lasted forever. I was at Dashiell Wallace's side. Thank God I was wearing Mom's dress. Even if I wasn't the most glamorous woman in the world, in that dress, I could pretend I was.

Dash pulled me away from the crowd to a less-populated room housing concept cars from the eighties. A solar car. A one-person car. A three-wheeled car.

"I feel like I haven't earned this nice treatment," I said. "I haven't found your glove yet."

"You will."

"I can't guarantee it. There's not much time until spring break." I stopped the stroll around and faced him. "I just want to tell you the odds aren't great. I can't search everyone's house. In the end, it's just us hoping one of the kids is honest."

He walked a few steps along the guardrail to the card for the wind-powered car, but his eyes didn't move with the lines. They locked onto the middle distance. I shouldn't have broken the moment with stupid pessimism. Now I felt like an interloper in this moment.

It was just a glove.

Right?

"I don't like losing things," he said before his gaze flicked to me. "It bothers me."

"Yeah, I understand. It's disruptive."

He tilted his head, blinked, looked through me as if my skin were made of glass. "Yes. That's exactly right."

I had about four minutes' worth of babble in me. The cost of attachment to objects. The time spent looking for the old glove versus the time spent getting used to a new one. I discarded all of it in favor of letting him look at me like that.

"How long did you have that glove?" I finally asked.

He took my hand.

He was touching me. Skin to skin. This whole scenario was impossible.

"Not long." He led me around the perimeter. "I got a new sponsorship at the beginning of the year, so I switched."

I would have broken in with a question, but he was still holding my hand. I could barely think, much less gently and subtly question why a new glove would mean a damn thing to him.

"It wasn't the glove," he continued.

"No?"

"No."

He led me to the elevator banks. A few other people in eveningwear waited.

"Where are we going?"

"The VIP event's upstairs."

The doors slid open. People got out in their black ties and sparkly gowns, tittering and slurring, holding up purple tickets.

A man in a burgundy jacket stood by the elevator control panel. "Do you have a ticket?" he asked me.

"I do." Dash took out his ticket. "The lady's with me."

Burgundy Jacket turned around, took a look at Dash, and nodded. The doors slid closed. "Yes, sir."

The elevator whooshed, and I felt the enormous pressure under the soles of my stilettos. We stood side by side, facing the door, arms pressed together. He was an immovable wall against me, all muscle under his tux.

"Rule-breaker," I mumbled.

He leaned down to my ear, and I breathed in his cologne, memorizing it, shifting the angle of my chin just enough to feel the skin of his cheek on my jaw.

"You make me reckless."

My knees went weak, and I lost the capacity for words just as the elevator stopped. I lost my balance, and Dash put his arm around my waist before I fell, drawing me close.

"You all right?"

"I'm fine, thank you." I moved an imaginary piece of hair behind my ear.

"You're blushing."

I thought I'd been aroused before, but his words and his physical presence activated every nerve between my legs. I sucked in a breath to keep from moaning at the feeling.

Was he turning a little red again? Because I was for sure. The heat in my cheeks didn't lie, nor did the deepening color of his.

What a strange man. What a bundle of contradictions. Like that slightly overlapping tooth in front. It was awkward but somehow a necessary part of the whole incredible package.

I wasn't tall enough. Fit enough. Rich enough. Smart enough. Accomplished enough. Exciting enough. I was a dead weight to a man. Didn't he know that? Couldn't he tell I'd drag him down?

I wasn't supposed to set my sights too high. My mother had told me so. My father—not my real dad but the man who had given me my DNA—had been "beautiful as a Michelangelo and smart as Einstein." That was what my mother had always said. Even when I was only a first grader, she'd leaned over me as I ate my blueberry oatmeal and was very, very clear about how I was to react to that kind of guy.

"Don't be fooled by the handsome ones or, God forbid, the rich ones," she'd say. "Look for a beautiful heart."

I was six. I remembered it because of her intensity. If she'd lived, she probably would have had to repeat it a hundred times before it stuck. But she didn't live, so her advice went into the vault, only to be trotted out when a rich, handsome man like Dash Wallace held my hand and I didn't know why.

But, Mom, I want to. Can I just do this one thing?

The elevator doors slid open, and I knew my mother would tell me it was all right.

Just this once.

eight

Vivian

The rooftop party was less carnival and more soirée. The winter night was cold for LA and clear by the same standard. When I looked up, I could see all of Orion, not just the belt.

Dash knew people. He waved, said a few words, but he kept his hand on either my arm or my back, subtly guiding me to the edge of the roof. He'd said he didn't have a plan, but he knew where he was going and never deviated.

I pretended I belonged there, standing straight and holding my purse in front of me. I looked at all of the other women's expressions and imitated them, faking it all the way. I didn't fit in, but it didn't have to be so incredibly obvious.

I may have been uncomfortable and self-conscious, but I was elated to be next to him. He took me to the edge of the roof that overlooked the city and held his hand out for me.

"You're cold," he said.

Understatement of the year. I hadn't been prepared to go outside, and it had to be sixty degrees. "People from Minnesota would laugh."

He shrugged out of his jacket and, in one fluid move, draped it over my shoulders.

"But you'll be cold," I said.

"This isn't cold."

Of course it wasn't. Between rewatches of the Youder interview, I'd spent some time on Wikipedia, getting the facts on Mr. Wallace. He was from upstate New York. Albany or something. A small city so buried in snow it looked flat white in satellite pictures for a third of the year. His brothers threw snowballs, and he caught them.

"This doesn't feel fair," I said.

"How is that?"

"I know all kinds of things about you, and you don't know anything about me."

"Tell me what you think you know." He put his elbow on the slate ledge and cupped his perfect chin in his perfect hand. His body was half-stretched out, half-curled in on itself, as if he was ready to spring for a grounder.

"You're not cold because you're from Buffalo."

"Ithaca."

"Upstate New York. You were drafted out of high school but made a deal so you could play minor league ball when school wasn't in session, and you played for Cornell the rest of the year."

"All they wanted was for me to stay sharp until they could call me up. My parents didn't think I was really going to play major league ball, so I went to school to make them happy. None of this is relevant."

"Really?"

What was relevant to him? I had the feeling it wasn't numbers or stats. Maybe it was the way he caught a ball off-balance and spun on his left toe while he threw to second behind his back, cutting three milliseconds off his time, to make the out? Or the way he wore down a pitcher with foul balls, risking the at bat in favor of a longer ball later?

"Why don't you give TV interviews?" I asked.

From his expression, my question was relevant but not what he'd expected. "It's a distraction. Anything I have to say, I say on the field."

A closed-door answer. Dad the lawyer had named all of my teen argument techniques, and this was a non-sequitur meant to cut off further discussion on the topic.

"My turn." He leaned on the wall. "Where does a librarian get a dress like that?"

"That's a long story."

He shrugged. "I don't need to be anywhere. Do you want

to sit?"

"Yeah, actually."

He pulled a chair out for me, and he sat on the opposite side of the round cocktail table, elbows on the marble, waiting for me.

"It's my mother's dress. She was a very glamorous woman."

"Was?"

"She was hit by a drunk driver on Wilshire and Rodeo. I was eight. My stepdad raised me. He kept her house, her clothes, all the things she loved."

"Her daughter too."

I pulled the lapels of his jacket close around me. It smelled like him even in the cold outdoor air. Dusty and masculine. Grass and sky and everything in between.

"The glove," he said, picking at the leaves that had dropped off the centerpiece and gathering them into a neat little pile. "I know it's trouble to find it, so I want to explain. It's not the glove. I can buy another glove. I even have time to wear it in. I have ten spares. But I had a sister. Her name was Daria, and she died, God, seven years ago now."

"I'm so sorry."

"Thank you. It was undiagnosed leukemia. Which is crazy. But there it is. That's not even the point. The point is when I went to college, we traded pins. The kind with the snap in the back. I gave her one of my Eagle Scout *fleur-de-lis*. To annoy me, because she thought I should have just skipped college and gotten drafted, she gave me a princess pin she got at Disney. I wore it inside my glove."

"It was inside the glove that was taken?"

"Yes."

The missing glove had gone from inconvenience to serious business. Just about every step of the way, I'd failed. I'd been unable to prevent the theft and assumed the worst of the victim when it came to light. I was guilty on both counts.

"I feel terrible," I said. Three words to describe a much more complex web of self-reproach.

"I wasn't trying to ruin your evening. But not telling you why I wanted it back didn't seem right either."

"I want to run back to work and start making phone calls."

He took my hand again, and again, I was swathed in shock.

"Thank you for taking it seriously," he said.

"I'm all about serious. I'm wearing my dead mother's shoes."

"The shoes too?"

"I have enough to get me through middle age as long as I don't gain a hundred pounds."

He laughed. He was going to say something. It was going to be terribly witty, then I was going to stutter nervously and his seduction would be complete. He would win in thirty minutes or less.

But he never said anything because a man in an Armani suit approached with a boob job on his arm. I shot up, nearly toppling the chair.

"Vivian?" Carl said. "Hi! Wow! I can't believe it. You look va-va-voom!"

He reached for me with his hands splayed and his arms bent, the Angeleno sign for "I'm hugging you now," except low, as if he was going to grab my tits.

Dashiell Wallace of the lightning reflexes and recently discovered jealous streak stood, grabbed Carl's shoulder, and yanked him back, sending my ex-boyfriend off-balance and forcing Boobjob's mouth into a lipstick-and-collagen grimace.

"It's okay!" I said. "He's a friend."

Dash was being an ape, but he wasn't a stupid ape. He let Carl go with a push, letting me know with the tilt of his head that he felt justified.

Carl straightened himself. "Sorry." He glanced at me then Dash.

"You caught me by surprise," Dash said, slapping him hard on the back with a big smile.

"Cool, cool, it's cool. Hey, yeah, Viv and I know each other from a long time ago." He turned to me. "This is Cherry." He indicated his date.

"Nice to meet you. Dash, this is Carl. Old friend."

Did I feel smug? Sure, I did. I was standing at a VIP event in a designer dress, on the arm of a professional athlete who could have any woman he wanted. If that wasn't the antithesis of boring, I didn't know what was.

Handshakes were exchanged, and it was very clear Carl had no idea he was shaking hands with a two-time World Series champion. Dash didn't wear his ring, not that Carl would have recognized it. We had a gender switch with regard to sports. To him, sports were for illiterate clods, and baseball hearkened back to a dead agricultural past. I'd agreed with him and followed the game despite his disdain. Wives dealt with sports obsessions they didn't understand all the time, and husbands went about their business, loving what they loved without apology. I'd done the same. To Carl, that had proven I was boring and provincial.

"You hurt me," Carl said, hand over his heart. "When was I demoted to old friend?"

Jesus Christ. Was I really supposed to answer that?

Cherry put her hand on Carl's shoulder and looked me up and down. "This the Viv who dumped you, baby?" She held her hand out for mine. "Thank you for setting him free."

My jaw came unhinged from the rest of my head. I couldn't imagine how unattractive that was because I was too busy imagining what kind of situation would lead Carl to lie about how we'd ended.

I put my finger up to accuse him of something. Not just lying but manipulating this woman's heart. She was obviously defending him and pumping up his ego. It was nice. Too nice for him.

I pointed at her. "Don't believe a thing he says."

"It's complicated," Carl mumbled.

A weight snaked across my shoulders. Dash Wallace's arm pulled me away. I heard him say, "Nice to meet you," but I didn't feel fully present. I walked steadily on those tricky shoes but didn't feel balanced.

What. A. Dick.

I must have had a black squiggle over my head because Dash didn't say a word. He kept his arm around me, pulling me close as he guided me to the elevator, down to the parking lot, and to the valet. He opened the passenger door of his black Mercedes.

I wasn't supposed to let him drive me home, but I didn't care anymore. I got in, and he shut the door.

I got my phone out quickly to text Jim.

Don't need a lift home. Everything good

I shut off the phone. I didn't even want to let him tell me good-night-see-you-tomorrow. I just wanted to go home and say the most terrible things to myself.

But Dash was driving, and he didn't know where to go.

"West," I said. "Left on Spaulding. Right on Hilgreen. You'll wonder if that's in the Beverly Hills city limit. It is. It's a gorgeous house. You'll wonder how I can afford it. I can't. You'll see it's behind on upkeep. You can deduce why."

"He really pissed you off."

"You're the one who nearly belted him." My words were tight and accusatory. I didn't know how to lighten up.

"I saw how you reacted to him. I'm sorry, I—"

"Because fuck him."

I was forgetting to be happy. I was in a car with a dream guy, and I was still hung up on the douche who had crushed me two years earlier. I couldn't control my thoughts or emotions. Couldn't choose the fun thing over the sad thing.

"He dumped me. He just one day up and decided I was the reason he was a loser. Well, I never called him that. I never treated him like the piece of shit he was. And one day, he gets himself all pissed off over nothing and leaves. And guess who's devastated? Me. And who's the one who moves? Me. Who only goes out with *our* friends when he's doing something else so she won't be uncomfortable? Who watched him get his life together only after he dumped me? Who was boring? Who's lower than shit? Me, me, me. And now he goes around playing victim with all his new girlfriends? What the fuck? He stole everything from me, and now he steals my victimhood? Well, no. He can't have it. I was the wronged party. Fuck him. That's mine."

Was I crying?

No, I was not crying. Given another minute, maybe. But I crossed my arms and, clamping down on the tears, looked out the window as Dash drove past the closed storefronts of Olympic Boulevard.

"You could give it to him," Dash said.

"He gets nothing." I waited a minute as the storefronts turned to apartment buildings. "Give him what?"

"Your victimhood. You don't really need it."

"Fuck you too," I said softly.

And wrongly. He didn't deserve to be cursed. I was still wearing the jacket he'd surrendered so I wouldn't be cold. He'd known me a total of two hours and had been more attentive to me than Carl had been in five years.

He stopped at a light, and I faced him for the first time since I'd started cursing.

He looked back at me. I hadn't hurt him—I knew that much from the smile he was trying to hide—but that was no excuse.

"I'm sorry," I said.

"You're something when you're mad."

I laughed nervously and looked at my lap. "Yeah. I've heard that."

"Have you ever considered boxing?"

The light went green.

"I used to ice skate, and when I was mad, I'd go to the rink and just pound the shit out of a double lutz. Hours and hours. I was mad at everything, so I got real good."

"You don't skate any more?"

"Nah. No time. No money. Not enough talent. Turn here and bear right."

He took the direction, and when he came to my house, I wanted him to keep going. Pass it by. Stop someplace that was fully mine. A house that didn't bear the scars of someone else's difficulties. Something new and fresh. I didn't want to leave my house, but I didn't want him to see it either.

"Stop right there." I pointed at the spot in front of my house. "The white with blue trim."

I'd forgotten to think about my living situation and how unattractive it was. Sure, I lived in a big house in Beverly Hills, but it had been won by my mother in a divorce settlement, and my stepfather lived there. I couldn't ask him in.

Not that I should have.

Maybe my living situation was saving me from myself. Because I didn't want this thing with Dash to end. Not now. Not yet. I wanted to extend it for as long as I could. He might never call again if he didn't get laid tonight, but if I did take him inside and I never heard from him again, I'd feel worse.

"Thank you," was all I had. I popped the door open.

He reached across me and closed it. "Wait."

He got out and walked around the front of the car then to my side. He opened my door and held out his hand for me. I took it and let him pull me up.

We walked side by side toward my steps. Mrs. Scotson's yappy dog barked. A bus rumbled down Olympic. The little brown crickets chirped, and above me, our sycamore tree rustled in the wind, dumping a rain of fluttering leaves.

We stopped at the front door.

"Thank you," he said. "The whole night would have been boring without you."

"Really?"

"Why do you look so surprised?"

"I don't know," I lied. "Anyway. I liked seeing you. I'm going to do my best to find your glove."

He leaned down, mouth near mine, breath on me, and whispered, "Good night, sweetapples."

He brushed his lips on mine, and when I responded, he held my jaw while he kissed me. I parted my lips enough to let his tongue slide against mine, warm and wet, demanding attention. The rustling of the dry leaves slid away. The traffic on Olympic was silent. The universe existed only where our bodies met. My hands on his wrists. His hands on my neck. Our mouths locked in a dance whose steps coursed down my spine to the neglected space between my legs.

He pulled away, and I gulped for air.

"Yes," I gasped.

"Yes to what?"

"I forgot the question. But it's yes."

"The question was, 'How many times do you want to come tonight?'"

"I..."

How many times?

Was there a number above one? Or sometimes?

He put his finger on my collarbone, at the center of my neck, and moved it outward. My brain shut down to feel the sensation of his finger pushing my neckline aside.

"You're a beautiful woman. I've been looking at your body all night. I want to see it wrapped around me. I want to feel you come."

Yes. Yes yes yes yes. Yes and yes. God, yes.

I reached for the doorknob. The door was ajar.

"Oh, Dad."

I couldn't bring Dash Wallace inside. My father was probably up. What would I do? Introduce this man to my father then slip him into my room, telling Dad we were going to listen to records?

"Dash..." I slipped off his jacket and handed it to him. "I'm sorry. It's a bad time."

He took the jacket languidly, draping it over one arm while reaching for me with the other. He drew me close and put his lips against my neck, holding me up while setting my body on fire. "When's a good time?"

I couldn't answer before he kissed me with an urgency I hadn't felt before. He kissed me as if now was the only time in the world because this heat was all there was. I wrapped my arms around his neck, and his hand went down my back to my ass. He pulled me into him, hitching my leg over his waist.

I gasped into his mouth when I felt his erection. My body

was about to go from matter and mass to pure energy as I pushed against it. I didn't care about what he wanted outside sex. Didn't care if Dad was up. Didn't care about anything but that dick grinding against me, those hands, that mouth. He pushed me against the doorjamb and moved against me, with me, nose to nose, watching my face as my body pulsed toward him, soft to hard—Goddamnit, what was I doing?

I pushed him away before I had an orgasm on my front steps.

He smiled like a cat who'd just eaten a pet shop full of canaries, taking my hands off his chest and holding them. "Not tonight. That's fine." He kissed my right palm. "I want to see you again. This week. Next week. From now until I leave for spring training."

He pressed his lips to the inside of my wrist. "You have no idea how many times I can make you come in the next few weeks. You're going to beg me to stop, and guess what? I'm not going to. Not until you forget how to speak."

I swallowed. "The next few weeks?"

"I'm offline when I'm in Arizona. And after that, I'm hard to get. By November, we will have both moved on."

His hands out in apology, streetlights brash on his face, and all the warmth of the past minutes gone, I felt the same as when my teenage cousin had shown my eight-year-old self how to play 52 Pickup. I'd begged him for a game of gin rummy, and he'd thrown the cards all over the living room.

Pick them up and put them in order in less than ten minutes.

Make sense of this in three seconds, or you'll look like an ass.

We both worked nine months out of the year.

But completely different months.

Was he saying he only wanted to have this relationship until spring training?

That wasn't what I wanted.

He'd be traveling half-to-two-thirds of the time between April and November.

How did people usually do it?

What did I want from him?

"What do you want?" I asked.

He held his coat open by the neck. "Right now, I want to get you warm."

"I don't want your jacket. I think this might be a short conversation. What do you want here? With me?"

"I like you."

"You like me but?" I asked.

"There's no but. I like you, and I want to spend the next few weeks with you until I have to go to spring training."

I realized how well I'd gotten over Carl when I felt the air go out of my lungs. After he left me, I'd spent months with a collapsed chest, and the transition back to normal had been so slow I hadn't noticed it.

Now there I was, freezing my ass off in the street while Dash tried to put a jacket on me, feeling as though someone had squeezed my lungs flat.

I hated feeling like that. I pushed the jacket down. "I'm sorry. I don't like expiration dates. I'm not saying I want more from you or anything like that, but it's too risky for me. The whole thing."

"Promising anything past March—"

"I don't need a promise."

"Promise is the wrong word. Attempting. Trying. That's risky." He wasn't committed to putting his jacket back on, and I wasn't accepting it, so he stood there holding it between us.

"We have opposite ideas of risk," I said. "Things last until they don't. I can't do this your way. Thanks for the lift home."

I pushed the door open before I could change my mind. The warmth of the house blasted my face, and I stepped away from him. Into the foyer. Turned. He stood there with his jacket over his arm, his posture telling me I could still change my mind.

"Nice running into you too," I said. "I'm still looking for the glove. I'll have it sent if we find it."

"Okay," he said.

"Okay. Bye." I gently closed the door. *Click.*

I didn't lock it. I didn't want him to hear the clack of the deadbolt. It seemed rude.

I watched out the window as he got back into his car, revved the engine, and sped away. I ran into my room, threw off the shoes, and got under the covers. It seemed as though it took forever to get warm.

I regretted that he couldn't see it my way. I regretted that I'd given him so much of myself while getting pushed against the door, but I didn't regret saying no to his proposal. I knew the limitations of my heart, and having a relationship with an expiration date would have hurt me more than cutting him off on my front steps.

I didn't want an expiration date. I wanted to go in with both feet. I wanted to be blind and dumb when my heart was ripped out of me. To go in faithfully, with everything, so when I stood alone again, tears welling up, I could tell myself that he was the asshole. He'd fucked up. He was awful, and my mother was right. Too good-looking, too talented, too rich. How was I supposed to soothe myself if I went in knowing when it would end?

Cynical. The whole idea of it was cynical.

Eventually I fell asleep in my mother's gold dress, feeling as though I'd dodged a mess of heartache.

nine

Dash

Youder came by to work out. The weeks before spring training were spent making sure we didn't get our asses kicked in Arizona. We were out of shape, lazy, sloppy. Youder and I had worked out together three times a week from January to March the same way for the past five years.

We took the old stone steps down the hill to the southernmost point of my property and turned right around. The hill looked like a sheer face with bushes and rocks latching onto the dirt to defy gravity. We scrambled back up the hill on well-worn trails, hitching and heaving, working out arms and legs against our own body weight.

Twenty-five laps per session in January.

By the first week in April, we could do a hundred even if it took all afternoon.

He had his foot on the top of the fence separating the patio from the baby fig tree, stretching, and he spoke as if what he was saying wasn't supposed to mean anything to me. "Trent's pushing me to move." He took his leg down and put up the other one.

"That's how he makes his money." I twisted at the waist, stretching the sleeping back and shoulder muscles.

"Yeah. He says Baltimore's got a young team. They're looking for maturity, and they have a third-base coach moving into retirement."

Jack would make a great coach. He was a natural leader and a clear-and-unemotional thinker. He knew the mental game. He'd mentored me when I was at Cornell, and he'd been on the team that wanted me the most. He was the reason I was playing for Los Angeles and not Pittsburgh.

"Barnett's never retiring," I said.

"Trent says otherwise."

"He doesn't know shit. He's an agent."

"He knows plenty. He's an agent."

I stopped stretching. "You're not going to Baltimore."

He regarded me seriously, putting both feet on the ground. "I might."

I took a deep breath and looked toward the horizon, over the stretch of the Los Angeles Basin, to the stadium, like a bird's nest on the east side of Elysian Park. At night, it looked like a spaceship landing, but in the day, it was just a grey cleft in the city.

"You'll be all right," he said. "We have three winning seasons behind us. They can pay the best—"

"I'll be fine," I said. "But Baltimore's a loser. For you."

I didn't wait for an answer but trotted down the old, cracked steps that led to the southernmost, wildest, and lowest edge of my property. My meds hadn't kicked in, and I was going to say something impulsive.

It was his career. He could do whatever the fuck he wanted.

He caught up to me at the bottom, and without a word, we started up. My anger at Jack abated as my body expended energy, dealt with pain, opened my thoughts.

I don't like expiration dates.

I pulled myself up on the trunk of a bush, needles catching my arm and going for my face. I was impervious to accidents and pain. More stimuli to get me through and distract me enough to let me pay attention.

Expiration dates.

The treadmill was impossibly boring without a book. Free weights were no better unless I had an audiobook in the headset. Counting reps literally caused me psychic pain, the urge to run was so strong.

This I could do. Climbing up a hill I could fall down was

good. I could give it attention, and the stakes were high because falling could lead to a career-killing broken bone.

Things last until they don't.

I threw myself up the hill and back down again. One step at a time. I'd built the charms in my life one at a time, and one at a time, they'd collapsed.

So one at a time, I'd have to build them again.

I didn't have women in Los Angeles, yet the hopefulness of that thought brought Vivian to mind. I tried to shake her as I climbed. I had reasons for the rules.

So no.

But I tasted her in my dry mouth. Heard her in my gasps. Once her voice came to my mind with its talk of expiration dates, I couldn't shake it. She was in my invigorated muscles and the ache in my arms, and the harder I pushed, the harder she did.

Maybe I could break the Los Angeles rule.

It seemed reasonable. If things were going to fall out of the bottom, I couldn't just fill from the top. I had to rethink and remake the setup of my life then hold fast again.

One step at a time with her. No rushing. I could have her by the time I went to the Cactus League. I would have her. Own her. Make her body mine. Satisfy my unreasonable, disproportionate craving for her. I gasped for it with every wrench up the hill, every burning muscle, every drop of sweat down my face.

As I climbed the hill, lifting myself by a tree branch, leveraging enough weight to get my leg up to a ledge in the slope, I passed Youder for the third time.

"Last lap," I said, breath heaving.

He gave me the thumbs-up and scrambled behind me.

When I got to the top, I grabbed his bottle and sat on the edge. I'd never gotten this far ahead of him.

He threw himself on the flagstones at the top of the hill, where my patio started. "Jesus." He barely had enough breath for the two syllables.

I leaned back and handed him the bottle. "You have two

months to get it back."

He sprayed his face with water even though it was freezing out, then he downed half the bottle. "I won't." He sat up. "This is it. This is where the shit starts filling up the bag."

"Whatever."

"The age thing. It's real, son."

"You're just lazy. Julio Franco played until he was forty-nine."

"I'm not Julio."

He wasn't Julio. I wasn't saying he was. I couldn't tell if he was being intentionally thick or if I was bent out of shape for no good reason. Let's face it, I didn't make the effort to figure out the difference.

"People look up to you. They look at you, and they see a guy who could play ball to the end. You start getting soft, you work through it. Get a little older, work harder. If you leave, you just prove this game's like all the other ones, okay, but it's not. And it's not because guys like you play."

"Old guys?"

"You know what?" I stood and put my hand out for him. "You're not a free agent until October. I'll see you tomorrow."

He grabbed my hand, and I pulled him up. He clapped me on the back.

I drank a quart of water when he left. It took so long to drink that much water, and I had to stay still for it. Jack getting too old to play hurt me in places I didn't poke too often. The place where I couldn't play. The place where an injury took me off the lineup. The place where my life was turned upside down and death fell out.

I had a book to read. I'd stop thinking about Jack leaving and playing without Daria's pin and the missing ports-of-call women if I buried myself in it.

Fifteen minutes in, when I laughed at a line so clever it seemed to twist on itself, I wondered if Vivian had read it.

I was sorry she hadn't been able to let me finish the job at the same time as I was grateful she'd refused me before she went full psycho. I respected that. Admired it. She had a lot going for her. It was too bad about the circumstances.

Another line cracked me up, and I realized the book I was reading was by Dwayne F. Wright. The same guy who'd written *Eternal Joke*.

It didn't all have to be about sex, did it?

We could be friends. That could be part of the New Rules.

I grabbed my phone.

Have you read The Underling?

ten

Vivian

I don't want you to think less of me. I don't always read the opaque stuff. I read a lot of romance

I read the Story of O

What did you think?

(...)

(...)

Are you there?

Yes

(...)

I liked it. Eye-opening

How?

You're curious, aren't you?

About you? Yes.

(...)

(...)

I didn't like that her first master shared and abandoned her

**She was better off. Once you make a
woman yours there's no sharing**

Make her yours how?

How?

Let me tell you, exactly

**When you take a woman who has never
been tied up before, and you loop her
wrists over the headboard and her legs
to the footboard. And you blindfold her
so she can't see where your hands are.
When you touch her body everywhere,
suck her nipples hard, play with her
until she's so close to orgasm she's
begging for release. When you say,
you're mine you beautiful thing, no one
else will have you. Then there's no
turning back.**

(...)

Have you ever done that before?

Everything through "release"

**And I shouldn't ask this. We're just
friends**

But I have to

I haven't

Done anything like that, I mean

I was going to ask if it turned you on

(...)

(...)

(...)

Vivian?

Was that inappropriate?

It was inappropriate

And I am very turned on

eleven

Vivian

"You look tired." Francine poked our slice of apple pie.

Pie was the new thing, replacing macaroons, which had replaced cupcakes as the most stylish way to end up with a closet full of clothes that didn't fit.

"I was up all night texting with Dash."

"Mr. Winter? Really?" She'd dubbed him Mr. Winter because he'd slated the relationship to end in spring. "Were you texting about how many times he was going to fuck you before he split?"

"*Shh!*" I glanced around the coffee shop.

Everyone must have heard her. They were just being polite. Thank God. She pushed the pie to me, and I speared an apple.

She fiddled with the white pom-pom on her pink hat. We were both dressed in jeans, but hers were original Sergio Valenti's, and mine were Gap. She was one of seven stylists in Los Angeles making money. I thought I should try to let her dress me one day. If she saw my mother's closet, she'd explode.

"What were you texting about then?"

"Books. Until three in the morning. He is—I mean, I can't believe I'm texting *Dash Wallace*. I feel like I won the lottery."

"You should fuck him," she said, dropping her voice on the word *fuck* as if that kept anyone from hearing. "And quit this lottery talk. He's just a guy."

I flashed on feeling the rock hardness of Dash's dick between my legs. His hands gripping my arms to keep me up. His knees pressing my legs open. I'd brought myself to orgasm twice thinking of him and the things he'd texted. After the discussion of *The Story of O* and whether or not it turned me on, we moved to safer subjects, but I'd throbbed for him all through it.

I flushed hot pink. "We're friends. We agreed."

"It's been years, Vivian. Years."

"I can't sleep with him until spring training and just stop."

"Do it."

"I can't."

"You're practically a virgin. Come on! He's so cute. And I bet he moves like a champ. Please. You've slept with one guy your whole life. Just a few weeks. For fun!"

I rolled my latte between my hands, letting the warmth spread over my skin. "I'm not that way. I'm not judging. Everyone has to do what makes them happy. But I'm not in the market for a fling. I like serious relationships."

"Like the one you had with Carl, you mean?"

"Shut up. I just... it's not like I want to marry the guy. I don't even know him. But I don't want to make it cheap."

"Who said anything about cheap? Make him take you out," she said.

"See what I mean?"

"What I'm saying is, how do you know you won't like a fling? You've never tried it. And if you start having 'feelings,' you just end it before they're too much."

I put my cup down and blew on the surface of the latte until the foam was a white crescent against the edge. Francine sounded logical and right. What could it hurt?

"I saw Carl the other night," I said.

"I know," she replied, sitting back.

Carl and Larry were still friends. We hadn't split our friends in the breakup. We just kept all the hurt feelings away from friends we shared. Except Francine. She was a vault.

"How did you feel about it?" she asked.

She was a vault for Carl as well. If Carl told Larry anything and Larry shared it with Francine, I'd never know.

"I looked awesome," I said, meaning every word. I'd even

felt beautiful. "He did too. He was with this girl. Woman. Big tits and lips."

I didn't have big tits. Mine were great, perfect for me, but not Ds. And my lips were also fine, but not Angelina Jolie pillow pets. Was that what Carl had been looking for?

I realized I didn't care. That was new. I used to use all of my shortcomings as a reason to beat myself up about Carl, and now, in the coffee shop with Francine, I just didn't care what kind of woman he wanted that I wasn't.

"What did Jim think?" Francine asked. "Did he paw you to make Carl jealous?"

"He was with Michelle. I was talking to Dash at that point. I have to say, I've seen Carl a few times since we split up, and every time it gets easier. He looks more together, and it gets easier anyway."

She reached across the table and held my wrist. Her hand was warm from her cup of chocolate. "You're ready." She tilted her head to make eye contact. "I know you think I've always thought you were ready. But I knew you were hurting, and I was looking for a Band-Aid. This is different. I know you don't believe it. I know it's hard. But I mean it this time. You're ready."

I let her hand stay there. Maybe I was ready to look for a man again. But I wasn't ready to throw my body around until April. I hadn't changed that much. "I'm scared."

"I know," Francine whispered back. "I know, and that never goes away."

twelve

Vivian

I couldn't keep my mind on my work. I had a stack of books to get back on the shelves and a bunch of late notices to slip into backpacks. Iris had eaten two apples during recess and four after lunch. Which was fine, but now I had to get more. I had to write requisitions for new books. I had a proposal with the public library pending that would have them send a book for every child off the semester's reading list. I could do all of it. I wasn't overwhelmed, necessarily.

You're ready.

By Wednesday morning, the physical memory of him had faded and been replaced by the plain intellectual excitement of seeing his texts. We were reading *Goalpost* together. I couldn't keep up with him, but trying was so fun that I'd been up late again on Tuesday night, talking about the characters and making predictions. It wasn't my usual romance fare, but I didn't miss the alpha guy getting the girl, losing the girl, getting the girl. A break was nice once in a while.

I got the go-ahead to send an email to all the third-grade parents about the missing glove. By lunch, I was catching up on all the things I'd let slide in my Dash-induced haze when Iris came in with a plastic grocery bag.

"*Lo siento, señorita Foster.*" She apologized, placing the bag on my desk, head hanging like a puppy.

I knew what was in the bag. I asked her why without even opening it. "*¿Por qué?*"

"*El pin era rosa. El color rosa es de niñas.*"

I tried not to laugh. This was serious. She shouldn't have

stolen, even if the glove had a pink pin and pink was for girls. There would be a punishment for sure, but I hoped to keep it gentle. Consequences were important, but Iris could get derailed easily. Her parents were very strict already.

"In English, Iris."

She screwed up her eyes and made her brain work. Good sport. She never fought hard work. "I was just looking at it."

"Under the table?"

"*Sí.* Yes. I put it on my hand. There was a pink pin. Pink is for girls."

"So you took it?"

She hung her head, nodding.

I opened the bag and was flooded by a smell I'd forgotten. Dash Wallace. I tried not to groan in front of Iris. Opening the glove, I saw a little hole in the leather but no pin anywhere. I took it out of the bag completely and inspected it.

"Where's the pin?"

She didn't say anything. I assumed that was what she'd been talking about when she mentioned the color. She understood English well enough to look at the carpet in shame.

"Iris? There was a princess pin."

"My brother flushed it down the toilet."

Uh-oh.

Baseball players were notoriously, crazily, famously superstitious, and a third-grade girl with a seventh-grade brother may have just ruined an entire season by flushing a good luck charm.

I escorted little Iris down to the principal's office, telling her she didn't have to cry.

I was sure I didn't want a short-term fling with Dash Wallace or anyone, but the news was too bad to deliver by phone.

And, yeah, I wanted to see him again.

thirteen

Dash

I took my run down the hills of the Oaks and up again. I took two a day in the winter, when heatstroke and dehydration weren't a concern. Everyone in the neighborhood knew me, and the streets I ran were so far off the beaten path I was unlikely to see anyone who wasn't used to me trotting by all the time.

My knees ached more than usual. I'd had a hard time getting out of bed. She'd kept me up late again.

I'd only fucked women who didn't keep me up that late. This was exactly why I set limits. During the season, I had lights-out early no matter the time zone. No errors from fatigue. No strikeouts from a lack of sleep. Early dinner. Back to their place. They came three times, I came once at the end, we had a few laughs, and I went back to the hotel. Everyone happy.

The cold burned my lungs, and I tried to focus on my steps, my breath, the rhythm of my body.

Limits and lids. I imposed limits and kept the lid on emotional highs and lows. Five years of it, and I had it down to a science. No media attention on my personal life because it effectively didn't exist. No distractions from the game because that was all I had to pay attention to. Beautiful women were easy to find, and I could spot one with a dirty mouth who liked getting a pink bottom. We kept it short and sweet. A series in Baltimore where Eva liked to be bound so tight she couldn't move. A two-week stay at home in Los Angeles, then to Pittsburgh, where Joanna preferred my belt to my palm. All good. Just to relax. Just to maintain the feeling of control I had on the field. When things went off the rails in my personal life, it affected my performance, and I'd worked too hard, given up too much to let another human being fuck with me.

I was sure I was right.

But I liked talking to her.

I felt as if I was bending the rules anyway.

I was at war with myself.

My front door led to the stairs to the house. Opening it, I stepped into an outdoor area that seemed infinite. When I'd been looking for a house, I didn't like seeing the stadium from the front steps, but eventually I got to like it. I wasn't seen. I was only seeing.

I turned on the lights. Music. Opened the windows to the cold. I was still coated in sweat and breathing like a runner. My thoughts were disorganized. Unusual after a run.

She had felt safe.

I'd let my guard down with her. She may or may not have intuited that, but I knew it, and it was disruptive. I grabbed a ball and fingered the stitches. I had them all over the house. None had seen a game. I just wore them down with my thumb and fingertips. I juggled them, three, four, five. I had a way of letting things fall through the cracks in favor of new sensory pleasures. I could focus while juggling baseballs, and I had to focus right now on one problem I'd avoided solving.

The glove.

One, two, three balls in the air, and my hands hit a rhythm my thoughts had to follow. I let them flow instead of trying to organize it all. There was a relief in letting go of the pretense that I had to remember any of it.

I had to stop texting Vivian. Cop to wanting to fuck her. Okay, I want to fuck her she's not going to work out with Youder because he needs to re-up with Los Angeles is not the place for a girl who's serious and has told you so when she said you shouldn't finish Cornell, and you should just do what you love because how old are you now? How many years before you break a bone or cartilage or a heart like your own, which is made of tight knots, and spanking an experienced girl who *oohed* and *aahed* was nice, but a buttoned-up librarian begging for my cock in the filthiest terms possible, mouth open, lipstick on my cock, mascara running up and down the hill twenty-five times hold on to everything. No more slipping no more slipping no more slipping she's not a plaything.

I dropped a ball and caught the other two. Turned one in my right hand. I'd done my signature real big on her ball because I thought she was hot and it was my stupid way of letting her know. So it was my fault from day one.

I couldn't stop thinking about her. She was a fucking infection.

The look on her face when I'd told her how many times I was going to make her come. Shocked. Scandalized. Aroused. All of it. Saying it and watching her expression had been like plowing new snow or knifing the satin-smooth top of a new jar of peanut butter.

I could fuck her maybe. A few times. Just to crack the label.

Before I'd been diagnosed with ADD, I did crazy shit for the sake of doing it. I broke crayons to hear the snap of the wax. Punched a kid two years older than me because the buildup of energy needed a place to go. Yelled too loudly when I lost and slapped my own face when I struck out. I was a balloon that constantly filled to bursting. I had to release the energy. I had no choice.

The meds started when I was twelve, and the feeling of control was such a relief I almost cried on that first day.

To get her naked in front of me and tie her hands behind her back. To watch her adjust to my control. To accept it as she'd never accepted it from anyone else.

The space between second and third was mine, and nothing got past it. Nothing. My domain. The first season I got control of my fielding, after Daria's death, that was the year I stopped feeling the eyes on me from the stands because they didn't matter. Nothing had felt so good as seeing them as a wall instead of people.

Getting a girl like Vivian to kneel when I told her to would be that difficult, and feel that good. But I didn't have space in my life to be master of two domains. And I wasn't giving up the field. I'd worked too hard for it.

So she'd have to move on her way. No more texting. I couldn't give a woman more than a minute's attention during the playing season because I didn't have enough attention to give, and she'd need more. She might not be clingy or crazy, but I couldn't fuck with her. Couldn't break her in then break up with her. She wasn't a plaything—that was obvious.

If I could stick with one decision, that would be great.

I was going to start this damn day over.

fourteen

Vivian

I sat in my car and turned the glove over in my hands. I pressed the opening to my face. The place where his hand went. Pure man. Adrenaline and endorphins. Sex.

Going to his house with the glove but not the pin was dangerous. I didn't know how he'd react. But I parked halfway down the street, where the curb wasn't red. Engine running, glove in my lap, sun setting over the city at the end of the block, I wondered one thing.

What did I want out of the guy?

I asked myself that question the entire half-a-block walk up to his door. I didn't even know if he was home. Looking up at the house, I saw all the lights were out. I knocked, confident no one would answer, then emboldened by the silence, I rang the bell.

Nothing.

Relieved and sad at the same time, I waited another second. I couldn't leave the glove there. The mail slot was too small. I could have it sent. That was the wise thing, of course.

I walked back to the car, staring at the glove. What had the pin looked like in there? How had no one noticed it? Maybe he wore the pin backward?

The impact as I crashed into him yanked the last breath from my lungs. I jumped. He jumped.

"I'm sorry, I—"

"You found it!" Dash held out his hand.

He had on a Dodgers cap, grey sweatpants, and a grey T-shirt even in the cold. His arms were slicked with a sheen of sweat, and his breath came faster than it should have. He'd been taking a run. I'd almost missed him.

Great and not great.

I didn't give him the glove. "I have something to tell you about it."

"Okay?"

"The girl who took it, she's sorry. Her parents are really strict, and they want to offer their apologies. They're disciplining her."

"They don't have to."

"I'll tell them you said so." It didn't matter what he said. They had their own way, and they didn't make their poverty an excuse for bad behavior.

"They're not beating her or anything?"

"No, no. Just no TV. That sort of thing. She's their only girl. They have big expectations. Dash, I—"

"There's no pin," he said when I stalled. "I can see from here."

I handed the glove over. I couldn't look at him. "Her brother found a princess pin offensive and flushed it. I'm so sorry."

He turned the glove around in his hands as if the pin would appear. I wanted to die of shame.

"You know in *The Grapes of Wrath*, the way the Joads lose everything?" He looked up from the glove at me. "And it's not all at once, it's just piece by piece?"

Was I supposed to tell him he wasn't close to that level of poverty or apologize again?

"Yeah," was all I could say. I was getting cold, and I couldn't stop thinking about the warmth of his body against mine.

"This isn't anything like that," he said. "But it feels like it, you know?"

"I do. I don't know how to make it right." I made some gesture toward my ratty car as if I had to go, which I didn't. I didn't have a thing to do after this silly sidewalk conversation, but he probably did, and I didn't want to keep him in the middle of the street.

"You're probably busy," he said.

"Not really."

"Do you want to come in? I won't bite unless you ask me to."

A little twitch of his eyes, a stiffening of his lips, a swallow after he said it made me want to ask for his mouth on my body. A bite. A kiss.

It took me too long to answer. He was reading me like a book, looking into my eyes and seeing the filthy images behind them.

"I won't ask then," I said.

He held out his hand, indicating the house on the corner, behind the gate. We walked back up the hill. Again I asked myself what I was doing, and I didn't have an answer. Then he opened the gate, and I was committed to being in the same room with him.

The house didn't face the street but the city, and the front yard was a steep slope down into the basin. To the right, the steps up led to the house, and to the left, a little plateau with a set of chairs around a fire pit seemed like a pedestal over the city. It was only five at night, but the sky was already just a few shades lighter than navy, and the air was frigid.

"This is nice," I said.

He was halfway up the steps, looking down at me. "Yeah. It's quiet. Do you drink coffee? I have a pot on a timer, but it's caffeinated. I have decaf instant."

"Caffeine doesn't keep me up."

"Me either."

We went up the stairs and into the house. It was Mission style with thick walls, a tile roof, and arched windows. The inside was floored in tiles and dark wood.

He dropped his keys on a thick-legged side table and faced me with his glove tucked under his arm. "You look nice."

His words were flat and noncommittal, but his voice and gaze were laced with sex.

I looked down at myself. Button-down floral shirt. Slacks.

Sensible flats. Work clothes. I'd tucked my hair into a clip before I arrived and made sure none of my lunch was still stuck in my teeth, but my appearance wasn't worth mentioning.

Last night, I touched myself thinking of you.

"What's a girl got to do to look like crap around here?"

He trotted over to the kitchen, which was open to the living room with a stone bar counter and stools. I sat on a stool. He dropped the glove on the bar and got two mugs from a cabinet. Sitting still, without the wafting winter air from the open door, I smelled the coffee as it gurgled in the machine.

"Be somebody else, I guess."

His hand on the cup, the other on the pot. Would I ever compare another man's hands favorably to his, with his powerful wrists and long fingers? Every digit was articulated and active. Not an ounce of fat on them. No roundedness. No tapering at the tips. No softness at all.

"I'll take that as a compliment," I said, looking at the bottles of vitamins behind the glass cabinet doors. The juicer. The calendar on the fridge. Anything but the way his jaw squared when he smiled.

He held up a cup. "How do you take this?"

"Black is fine."

He took his black as well and came around the counter to drop the cups in front of us and sit next to me. I wrapped my hands around my mug and sipped. The coffee was thick and strong. He had his glove. Pin or no pin, that was our connection right there on the kitchen counter. There was no reason for us to talk anymore.

"How will it be without the pin?" I asked.

"Who do you want to answer? Mr. Reasonable or Mr. Real?"

"I know what Mr. Reasonable would say."

"Mr. Real is panicking."

"Why?"

"This whole game is built on luck. If you have a run of bad

luck and you can't get out of it, you're fucked. Well, I'm having a run of really shitty luck, and all the things I do to give me good luck are falling apart. Pin included. My fucking avocado tree. Jack Youder going up for free agency. I'm sunk."

"Will you not do that thing anymore? Where you twist around and throw to Youder behind your back like this…" I twisted my arm around, my shoulders followed, and I looked over my shoulder in a cheap imitation of a move he made mid-air.

He laughed as if I'd embarrassed him. "Yeah. That's the thing. Doing stuff like that, I'm an injury waiting to happen." He waved his finger at me. "One injury. That's all it takes. One."

He put his foot on the low rung of my stool. It didn't put his body any closer, but I was aware of his encroachment into my space. The inches between us shrank, and what I saw was nothing compared to the scent of him fresh after a run. Not gross or sweaty, he smelled like cool air outdoors.

"I've realized something about you," I said.

"What's that?" He put the glove down next to me. He was closer with each move. Now the coffee cup, putting it where he had to reach in my direction.

"You're very risk-averse."

"Off the field, maybe."

"This deadline for us?"

"Yes?" He leaned toward me.

How did he get so close I could see every hair on his jaw? Every lash? The brown fleck in his left eye?

"It's risk management." My voice barely worked.

"And? What about you?"

What about me? With the safe job. Living with my father. Driving a Nissan. "I'm not a big risk-taker."

"And that's why you don't like the deadline."

"Yes. And you can get in my space as much as you want. I'm not changing my mind. I was hurt once. I like you, but I'm not walking into it again."

He bit his upper lip then relaxed his mouth. He took a long

time to answer, as if deciding not just a response but a course of action.

"That guy?" His voice was husky and low, suggestive without even suggesting anything. "He's an asshole. He fucked you like a middle schooler."

I gripped my cup with one hand and held onto the stool with the other. I was so close to going liquid. So close. "You don't know what you're talking about."

I said it even though I knew it wasn't true. He seemed to know exactly what he was talking about.

"I do know what I'm talking about. I can't stop thinking about you. Imagining you with this little blouse off, these no-nonsense trousers dropping. I can see the shape of you under these clothes."

"No deadlines." My voice was no more than a breath.

"Reconsider. Take it back. When I fuck you, I'm going to take it slow. You'll come twice before I'm even inside you." He put his hand on my knee and slowly moved it up, pressing harder with his thumb. "First with my fingers, then I'm going to lick your pussy until—"

"Stop!"

My back had straightened as much as it could while still keeping me on the seat, and my underwear... well, I wanted to weep for them because they'd taken a deluge before the word "fingers" left his lips.

"It's working. All right?" I put my hands on his shoulders, intending to push him away, but the pushing part didn't happen. "It's working. I haven't even done half the stuff you're telling me you're going to do and—"

"I haven't even said anything yet." His voice was full of promise, as if he hadn't gotten to the good part.

I closed my eyes so I didn't have to look at his perfect face and held up my hands as if warding him off. "I've been with one person my whole life."

"Wait." He leaned back. "What did I say that you haven't done?"

"The licking thing."

He stopped. Crossed his arms. Tilted his head as if trying to solve a math problem above his grade level. "The licking thing?"

"Yes. That. TMI?"

"He never ate your pussy?"

I got hot everywhere. The bottoms of my feet and the top of my head. I must have been a sunburned shade of red. I looked away and crossed my own arms, but there was no hiding.

"It's not TMI," he said. "Just tell me."

I huffed. Why should I tell him? I didn't owe him an explanation. I'd never even told Francine, and I'd known her since sixth grade. But there was something about Dash Wallace that felt safe. Maybe it was the way he'd shut down all the fuck talk to hear what I had to say, or maybe it was the way he never made me feel as though he was doing me a favor by wanting me. So I blurted it out.

"He thought it was gross."

I wanted to cry. I was ashamed that I'd let Carl say that and that I'd repeated it. I felt gross. I felt awful inside and out. God, I shouldn't have said anything. Because Dash's eyes had gone wide and his lips parted a little, then a lot, and his tongue was fidgeting with his teeth.

"Stop looking at me like that."

"I'm stuck," he said.

"Stuck? What does that mean?"

"Between wanting to punch him and wanting to eat you out until you scream. I don't think I can do both at the same time."

"Well, he has a point, I mean—"

Dash reached for me so fast I couldn't finish and put his hand over my mouth. "Don't you dare. Don't you say it. You taste like heaven, and I'm going to prove it to you. You have no choice now. You're going to see me. You're going to let me take you out. I'm going to put my face between your legs and experience how delicious you are."

I'd die of course. And I was going to tell him that if he did,

I'd explode into a hundred twenty pounds of pleasure pieces, but he moved his fingers and kissed me. His lips were on mine, but the space between my legs blossomed with the promise of what he'd just described.

"No expiration date," I said, low and firm. Amazing since I'd gone soft and molten inside.

I felt the war inside him. Mr. Reasonable was battling with Mr. Real, but I had no idea which was fighting for me. One millisecond he looked hard enough to send me out the door. The next his face changed subtly, like the ripples of the ocean, and he looked as if he'd agree to anything I asked.

"No expiration date," he said. "But no promises either. I've never had a home field girl."

I opened my mouth to ask a question, and he ignored me, laying a kiss on me that pushed out every objection.

Never had a home field girl?

Wait. You should ask—

He pulled up my shirt, bra and all, releasing my hardened nipples. I didn't have a second to protest before his hands were on my breasts, cresting at the nipples, stroking, twisting. I groaned, and he sucked in a breath, pulling away so I could see his face.

"You want this," he hissed.

"I do."

"Unbutton your pants."

The way he said it, as if there was no question of obedience, as if it was my job because his hands were busy with my tits, sent my fingers to my waistband. I undid my pants.

"Slide them down, sweetapples."

I was already halfway off the stool when he asked that.

No. He didn't ask.

He'd stated a fact. I slid off the stool and pushed the waistband down as far as my arms would reach. He leaned back, his gaze taking me in, face to tits to my panties.

"You're so fucking sexy, and you don't even know it." He slipped his hands between my legs, inside my thighs, to my soaked white underwear. His finger hooked the crotch and made room to get to my center.

"Oh, God."

"I'm not going to eat your pussy tonight. I'm going to make you wait. But you're going to see me. You're going to let me take you out. And after that, I'm going to lay you in my bed, and this here?" He brushed his finger along my clit.

I exploded. He owned me. He could do whatever he wanted. When he brushed the finger back, I was so close to orgasm in two strokes.

"I'm going to suck on it, and then I'm putting my tongue right here." He slid two fingers inside me. "You're so wet. Wait. Wait until I take this with my mouth."

He drew his fingers over my clit again. I was so close and not there yet. As if he knew, he slowed down.

My fingers dug into his shoulders. "Dash, I... God, I—"

"Do you want to come?"

"Yes."

"How bad?"

"So bad. Please. I'll see you. I want to."

He put two fingers on my clit and shifted them just enough to take my breath away. "There's going to be a lot of fucking and sucking."

"Okay. Yes."

"You want that."

"Let me come. I want it," I begged.

"I call the shots. You understand?"

"Yes."

"You're so fucking hot." With that reminder, he flicked my clit, stroked me back to front, and brought his fingers back to my swollen nub and pinched it.

I buckled as if my skin had been pulled taut, mind broken, body transcending all pain, all pleasure. I cried a long call to the kitchen counter, the stove, the tiles under my toes. I didn't even realize he was holding me up with his free hand or that he was sucking on a nipple. The tornado of release had whipped away my consciousness and littered the landscape with its shredded pieces.

Dash Wallace, who could leap ten feet for a line drive and hit anything thrown at him, who was a mysterious and graceful figure in a billion-dollar sport, had given me the orgasm of my life.

He took his mouth off me, removed his hand from my pants, and showed me his wet fingers.

"You are not gross." He put his middle finger in his mouth and pulled it out with a pop. "Your body is nectar to me. Taste it."

He laid his index finger on my lower lip, and I opened my mouth. He slid it along my tongue. The taste of me was pungent but clear. Bright. Tart. Not terrible. Not gross. Kind of nice.

"That's what I'm going to taste when I eat your pussy."

I puckered my lips around his fingers as he drew them out.

I didn't do things like that. I wasn't repressed exactly. I just wasn't sensual or confident. I wasn't kinky or experimental. I liked being on the bottom, and I didn't talk much during sex or ask for what I wanted. If you had told me a month ago that I was going to let a man put his fingers on my pussy then in my mouth, I would have made a lemon-face. But I wanted those fingers. It felt good to suck them and see the way he clamped his jaw tight and breathed through his teeth.

"I like you, Dash," I said when his fingers were out. "But I have to be honest. You scare me."

He straightened, making sure I didn't fall. He put his arms around my waist and pulled up my pants. "You don't scare me."

I buttoned myself up. Reality pushed against the walls of my fading orgasm. He'd opened me as if I had a latch and hinges. If I'd known he could do that, I would have run down that hill so fast the sidewalk would have broken under my feet. If I'd known he'd expose me so definitively and, with his warmth and gentleness, make me all right with it, I would have stood stock still at the front door and not known what to do. None of this was what I had expected. He was supposed to be a cavalier jerk. He wasn't.

"All right," I said, having thought it through at the worst time and in the worst way possible. "But I want to warn you I'm not cynical or casual. If I start to…" I searched for the words, and they were all too loaded or too cold. None accurately described the breadth of my fear. "If I start to have feelings or if you're careless with me, I'm cutting it short. Just for self-preservation."

"You're risk-averse." He gently pulled down my shirt.

"Yeah. Also, I know what we just did, but no guarantees on the first date."

"I have to do something tomorrow. Let's do Friday night. Let's not waste time." He smirked as if he knew damned well he was getting my clothes off on the first date.

I was pretty sure I wouldn't be able to resist him, but I didn't want to rush. Even looking back on him having his hand down my pants scared the living hell out of me. The thought of going so far, so fast made me shake.

I would just ride the break the next time I saw him.

fifteen

Dash

I had no idea what the fuck I was trying to do. I was a man who had control of his impulses, who knew what he wanted. A man who had made fucking decisions about his fucking life, not a fourteen-year-old with an amateur pituitary gland.

But I'd kissed her the whole way down to her car, and now, an hour later, I still stood watching the spot where it had been. A Lexus was parked there now, but all I saw was that deathtrap of a Nissan. I'd never cared about teachers' salaries until I saw that car.

I could still smell her pussy on my fingers. I didn't want to jerk off. I wanted her. I wanted to want her as much as I wanted her to just disappear so I could live my life.

I wasn't supposed to have a girl in LA, but I'd figured it wouldn't be a big deal if it ended in the spring. Then I'd agreed to continue past that. Well, I'd agreed to not dismiss the idea. I'd keep up my end of the deal with her. I wouldn't end it definitively or give it an expiration date. I couldn't imagine I'd have any interest from Arizona though.

But man, she was something. I got in the shower to get the sweat off me and took one last whiff of her before handling the soap.

I didn't chase after women generally. They chased me, which was convenient, or I did without. I didn't do without very often.

I wasn't an asshole. Or maybe I was. I didn't want to get attached when all I did was practice and travel, and nothing was going to come before the game. Nothing. Being clear with myself about what I wanted from a woman was a virtue, not a sin. And I was honest with every one of them every time. It was easier that way. I was a shitty liar.

Getting involved with Vivian was a rule-bender, but she had something.

I jerked off anyway.

By the time I was dressed, I was late. I had an assistant to help me manage my time with the team, but when I was alone, time management was a struggle. I lost track of how long things took and wildly over- or underestimated any amount of time that could be measured with a clock. I was only good with split seconds.

I rinsed out her coffee cup before leaving, rubbing along the place where her lip had touched.

Get it together, weirdo.

She wasn't completely broken or completely whole. She was guileless without being naïve. Vulnerable and strong at the same time. A locked box with a tiny window that let me see something shiny inside.

When I was a kid, I had been obsessed with two things: locked doors and baseball. Baseball remained endlessly interesting, but the locked doors didn't fare as well. Eventually I found out that they usually didn't have anything exciting behind them. The size of the locks, the hiddenness of the door, the warning signs to stay away and be careful added to a curiosity that ended in disappointment. The places they hid held garbage bins, dull offices, shelves full of nothing I cared about.

But I had to find out what was in there. It would be nothing at all. She wasn't half as special as she seemed. No woman could be. But I had to find out—just in case.

I was only human.

"Why you looking at the floor, Wallace? You going left on me?"

We were at the Joe Westlake's annual general manager's dinner, and there was a penny on the carpet.

I picked it up and brandished it for Youder. "Heads up for

good luck."

The GM's house was a palace north of Sunset in Bel Air. Wives, girlfriends, players, and kids mingled with the game's heavy hitters. An invitation to the dinner came with the most expensive skyboxes, and I was supposed to mingle. I usually did all right. I wasn't anxious with people, just cameras.

"Joe made a casual offer," Youder said, checking to make sure the room was empty. "It's pretty good."

"For you to stay?" I tried not to look as if Santa had just come in June, but that was what I felt like.

"No, to leave, asshole. Of course to stay."

"Because you're not going to lead the league in double plays without me, and you know it." I swirled my vodka around the glass. What had Vivian said about drinking? And her mother? The details eluded me, but I put the glass down.

"My wife wants to stay. She's got no need to freeze her ass off again. And she has friends."

Youder didn't have friends outside the team. None of us did.

"You should stay, dude. It's not even about baseball anymore. It's about your life."

"Coming from you, that means exactly nothing."

"Fuck you. Is Duchovney here?"

"Nah. He's…" Youder shook his head. "His knee's not getting better fast enough. He's low."

"Low" was a nice way of saying he was too depressed to get out of bed. We were all used to working our bodies to the point of exhaustion, and between the lack of physical activity and the prospect of never playing again, a bad injury crashed us emotionally. No one talked about it, but it was a fact.

Randy swaggered over. He was in his second year with us. He was young and cocky with a terrible (or great, depending on how you looked at it) reputation with the female population of Los Angeles. "Hey, you seen Shawn? He's been training with Edwards."

I didn't care. Not about Shawn or Edwards or what any one of my teammates was doing to get in shape for spring. I was in the mood for neither camaraderie nor pissing contests. "You know what? I'm going to slip out of here."

"That time of the month?" Randy asked.

"Cramps are killing me." I gave Youder and Randy hugs with loud claps on the back, and I left while things were looking up.

Sunset Boulevard was a constant traffic jam from Silver Lake to Beverly Hills, but west of that, it was a winding road with few traffic lights and nothing to see on either side. It was easy to lose yourself thinking about what you wanted to do to a certain librarian's body, the prospects of a winning season, making an effort to forget what had happened to your sister's pin, whether or not you should call your parents tomorrow or the next day, the clusterfuck the avocado tree had started, the librarian, the season, the pin, your parents, avocado, Vivian, baseball, pin, parents, tree-sex-life-Daria-momdadtreefuck—

The car moved sideways, and I turned the wheel, thinking that would fix the way the car slid across the road as if it were on a sheet of ice. I knew what to do on ice. I'd grown up in Ithaca. But turning the wheel didn't do anything, and my brain registered the crunch of metal and the force of impact a split second later.

Professional athletes were freaks. The average height of a pro basketball player was six foot seven. Football players were built like bungalows. Baseball players had hand-eye-mind coordination that was hard to measure but just as freakish.

Which was how I'd felt the car moving before the sound of the crash registered. I'd been T-boned from the side street and was moving sideways into oncoming traffic.

Not really much I could do but skid.

And hit the brakes.

And turn off the car.

Took as much time to do as to step left once, calculate the trajectory of the ball, catch it, move my right hand to the glove, take it, calculate the speed of the runners, line up the throw, execute.

Thup.

It was done.

Blink. Blink.

Silence.

Fingers. Toes. All wiggle. All move.

My head turns.

My name is Dashiell Wallace.

It's Thursday.

Someone is screaming.

It's not me.

The passenger side door is an inch from my elbow.

I get out.

I can stand.

Walk.

Make words.

I can carry her out of the way of traffic.

Call 9-1-1.

Assess her injuries like an Eagle Scout.

Relay the information calmly.

Convince her she's going to be all right.

Walk away.

When the paramedics tell me I'm the luckiest guy in the world, I believe them.

sixteen

Vivian

Vivian, are you there?

I'm here

Where?

Trying to sleep. It's midnight

About what happened today

(...)

Yes?

I washed you off my hands. I want it back. Having you on my fingers feels like good luck. I bet I hit .400 with your pussy on my lips

You can wait. You don't have to hit anything yet

I'm going to open your legs and have a field day on your clit. Just a little with the tip of my tongue. Then I'm going to suck on it. Pull it between my teeth. Do it all over, flicking just a little. I can make you last a long time

(...)

(...)

(...)

Are you touching yourself

No

Now I am

Are you wet?

Yes

I want you to come

Okay

Just imagine what I'm going to do to you and how much I'm going to love doing it.

(...)

Graze on my lips, and if those hills be dry, stray lower where the pleasant fountains lie

(...)

(...)

(...)

(...)

Are you coming?

You quoted Shakespeare. I didn't have much of a choice

I'll make a note

I'm so sleepy now

Good night, sweetapple

Good night, Dashiell

seventeen

Dash

The Dodger batting cages were tucked in a warehouse downtown, on the east side of the river. The building was the best kept on the block—unmarked, guarded, with a small parking lot. No one from the street could see the helipad or the world-class training facility inside.

The machine clicked and whooshed. My bat made contact with a *thwock*. Line drive to left. Too low to get over the shortstop. I set up again. *Thwock*. Good for triple A. I had a long way to go here. No worse than I'd been any other winter.

Randy waited by the gate in a Nickelback T-shirt and old Nikes. "What happened to you?" He pointed at a bruise on my forearm.

"Accident on the way back from Joe's."

"Fuck." He shook his head. "No one knows how to drive in the rain here, man."

Everyone said that, and it meant they thought people drove too slow or too fast, but no one knew what it meant to drive in Ithaca winters.

"I got T-boned," I said. "It was bad. Car was totaled."

"And you got a bruise?" He raised his eyebrows in shock. "*That* bruise?"

"Yeah."

"What did you eat before? Did you have the fucking fish?"

I shook my head but didn't answer. What was he talking about?

"Eat that every day. I'm telling you, whatever you did to get that luck going, do it every day." He pulled a bat out of the bin. "The universe just gave you a big heads-up."

He closed the gate and got ready to bat.

Trust Randy to tell me what I already knew.

eighteen

Vivian

Mom's closet had been a disappointment. I didn't know what I'd expected, but nothing worked. Too formal, too farty, too much my mother's taste.

Francine put a long pleated skirt up against my waist. It was too *her*.

"No," I said, getting jostled by a woman with a big tote. The sale section in the back of the store was a wreck at the end of the day, and we'd found nothing. "Too long."

"You have three hours," she said, clicking through hangers. "Let's do this. Tell me your vision when you imagine yourself going on this date."

"Sexy. Not slutty. But I want to look..." I waved my hands in circles and lowered my voice to call up the only adjective I could muster. "Delicious."

She raised a perfectly-manicured eyebrow. My cheeks tingled.

"What are you going to do tonight?" she asked.

"I have no idea. He didn't say."

"But what do you say?"

"I say we're going to do fun things. Alone together kinds of fun things."

She looked at her watch. "We're in the wrong store."

She took my hand and pulled me out of the sale section, through the expensive stuff, past the designer cosmetics and shoes, and out to the fake courtyard of the Grotto. The tree was still up next to Santa's village, but the sparkle had left both in favor of CAUTION tape as they were dismantled. SALE signs were plastered over every store window.

"Where are we going?"

"Do you trust me?" she called back.

"I do. Mostly."

She didn't answer as she wove through the crowd, over the stone pavement, past the fountain, the movie theater, the high-end storefronts, and down a small pathway between the mall and the street. A candy store. A custom shoe store. And...

"No way..." I said.

"Yes way."

"I can't," I said when we were outside her destination. "He'll expect it. I don't want him to expect it. I can't wear this."

"Oh, you can, and you will. Not for him and not for what he thinks. But for you." She poked me in the chest. "Because there's nothing wrong with feeling sexy, and this stuff does it."

She took me by the elbow and pulled me into La Perla. The bustle and rush of the mall was shut out the moment we entered, and we were engulfed in undulating music, dark corners, spotlights, and perfectly formed mannequins in garters and stockings.

I clutched my bag. "I can't."

"Can I help you find something?" the salesgirl asked. She wore a man's shirt opened to the navel, revealing a lace bra with a crystal heart where the cups met.

"No," I said.

"Yes," Francine said. "My friend here has a date tonight with a rich, handsome, and smart man she has a ton in common with. She wants it to go well."

The girl smiled, eyes lighting up like the Vegas strip. "We specialize in that."

"I don't want him to think I do this for everyone," I said.

"He won't think that. We'll make sure. Do you have a budget in mind?"

"A hundred?"

The sales girl seemed undaunted, but Francine held up her hands. "More."

"Francine!"

She pulled me aside, next to a Swarovski crystal-covered bra. "You have credit cards?"

"Yeah, but—"

"Do you have a balance on any of them?"

"Well, no."

"When was the last time you spent anything on yourself?"

"I'm not a stylist. I'm a teacher. We're notoriously broke."

"Once, Vivian. Once, you can carry a balance on the card for one thing for one guy. I'm not saying to get in over your head. I'm not saying to go into bankruptcy. I'm saying maybe you should trust yourself. Trust you're spending too much just once and it's not some downhill ride. Treat yourself as well as you treat everyone else."

I looked around the store. If I was going to treat myself, it was going to be for more books and more things for the kids. But that little bra made the salesgirl's chest look so nice, and the mannequin next to me with the black stockings and garter, the way the stockings stopped at the upper thigh, highlighting the tiny string of a bikini and the place he wanted to put his tongue... I shuddered.

"I want stockings like this," I said. "And if I get this stuff, I'm pulling a dress out of my mom's closet, even if it's boring."

"Perfect. The more boring, the better. He'll die when he sees this underneath."

I filled my lungs with confidence. "He may or may not, but I'm pretty sure I will."

Francine put her fists in front of her mouth to hide her smile, but she couldn't stop herself from stamping a foot in glee. "Let's go!"

She pulled me back to the salesgirl, and I gulped down all my shame and followed her. I was giving myself a ton of mixed messages about what I expected from this evening. Poor guy. If he thought he was confused, he should have tried living in my brain for a few hours.

nineteen

Vivian

I didn't have long to get dressed. I ran past Dad, who was standing at the counter and cooking something that smelled wonderful, so he wouldn't see the La Perla bag.

"Hey, peanut!"

"Hi, Dad!" I said as I walked by.

"You staying for dinner?"

"Um, no. I have a date," I called from the den.

"What?"

Shit. I shouldn't have told him. "A date, Dad!"

I rushed into Mom's old room. I slipped into the closet and snapped the door shut.

A knock came soon after. "Vivian?"

"He's coming at eight. I'm nervous. I'm going to have a stroke. Please don't make it worse. Don't even mention it. Just don't even say anything."

A moment of silence.

"All right. I'll save you some dinner for later. Or tomorrow."

"Thank you."

He shuffled away. I heard the bedroom door click. Thank God. He was really leaving me alone.

I brought my stuff to Mom's bathroom because it was next to the closet where my dress was. I always cleaned between my legs, but that night, I was extra thorough. I bent over to see my flattened blond hairs. Was I supposed to shave?

Of course I was supposed to shave. I soaped up and took my razor off the shelf. How old was it? Should I get a fresh one?

I was being silly. Razors didn't have…

Expiration dates.

I had to stop myself to think about that. He'd agreed that we didn't have an artificial end date. That worked for me. But why was I going into this with my legs open? If we were going into spring training and beyond, then there was no rush.

Right?

Could I trust him? Could I trust that he wasn't going to use me and throw me away? Did it matter? I was a grown woman. Not terribly experienced, sure, but I was perfectly capable of enjoying sex when I wanted to. I didn't need artificial timelines any more than he did.

I put down the razor.

I believed all of that, and I wasn't ready. I wasn't even ready for what we'd already done on the kitchen bar stool. I needed to get to know him better. I lacked a very basic trust in our relationship, in him, even in myself.

Right. Okay.

I shut off the water as if the decision had nothing to do with my hair care choices and everything to do with the shower itself. But it was a punctuation at the end of the process.

Deep breath.

I toweled off and peeked in the bag. My new underwear was wrapped in gold tissue paper. I undid it carefully and folded it up. It was too nice to just throw away.

I laid out the black stockings and lace panties on the bed. The bra was the same as the salesgirl's but had a star in the center.

"You wear this when you want to get laid. Not when you don't." I said it to myself because I was the one who needed clarity.

I wanted to wear it because I'd just sold the farm to get it.

As long as the dress covered it, I was okay. That was what I told myself as I chose a bra-hiding burgundy dress with long sleeves and a flouncy knee-length skirt. It was so chaste I would have worn it to work if it wasn't so expensive and rare.

Done.

"Here goes," I exhaled.

I got the stockings, panties, and garter on, and I was hooking the bra when the bed buzzed. I rifled around for my phone.

I can't wait to see you

I smiled to the phone. Another text came before I could reply.

Wear something comfortable

Now was the time. This moment. If I was going to prepare him to be refused for tonight, then now was the time to warn him.

About that

I want to take it slow

Slow is my middle name

That's not true

My middle name is Beaumont, but that's a secret. If you tell another soul I'll deny it

Dashiell Beaumont Wallace

It had a terrible ring to it, and I laughed to myself.

LOL

Next week I'll cook you Mom's Scotts/Norman specialty. We'll see who laughs then

I bit my lip. He was planning something for next week. That was a good sign. I typed something polite into the phone then felt the skin of my hips goose-bump, and I looked down at my body. I was texting him in this getup, and I was going to see him in—

> Wait. Are you driving? You shouldn't text and drive

I'm out front. In the car. I got here early and didn't want to crowd you

I saw myself in the closet mirror. I looked like the mannequin. A little less waxen. A little more human. A little like a sex kitten.

Holy shit. Was that me?

It was, and I was pretty hot.

> Come in. I'm ready

I slipped on the black heels. Turned and looked at the seam down the backs of my legs. My ass cheeks stood firm and round in the warm lights, curving the back of the lace panties. I put my hand on my ass and felt the warmth of my own palm.

I'd just turned myself on.

Deep breath.

I put on the dress and a little mascara.

"Someone's here for you, peanut," Dad said from the other side of the door.

"Coming." I stuck the ball in my little beaded bag. It bulged. I felt like the bag. Bigger on the inside. Too full. Ready to burst out of my casing.

Dad was at the front of the house with Dash, who wore a suit and carried flowers. They were laughing about something. Me? I had no idea. I was stuck on the bright bouquet of daisies.

He'd brought me flowers. No one had ever brought me flowers.

"Hi," I said. Whispered. Breathed.

Dash's eyes ate me alive, and my skin folded outward to the dark, raw parts where I wanted him to touch me.

"Hey," he said. "Your dad was telling me you were a ball girl back in the day."

"Dad!"

"Five more minutes and I'd get the pictures out."

Mortifying. Me in my little ponytail and white pants, chasing after fouls.

"And what you guys did for game six last year," Dash added.

I didn't think I'd been gone that long, but Dad talked fast.

"It's a funny story." Dad shrugged, and I rolled my eyes.

It was only funny the way Dad told it. We'd bought tickets on eBay, which was completely against the rules unless you bought a four-hundred-dollar hat that happened to come with two nosebleed tickets. When eBay had taken the listing down, we'd done a reverse search on the ticketholder's email, hunting her back to Lancaster. Then we drove up there in my Nissan, up the mountains while my car choked and hitched, almost got eaten by her four angry pit bulls, paid her cash, and made it to Dodger Stadium with not a second to spare.

"It was crazy," I said. "We almost missed the national anthem because of traffic on the 5."

"I struck out that night, I think?" Dash said.

"Stand-up double, two Ks, and a walk, actually," I replied.

"I only remember the strikeouts." He looked at the flowers as if he'd forgotten he had them, and he handed them to me.

"Thank you, they're perfect." I didn't know what else to say. They were.

Dad took them from me. "I'll put them in water. Get out of here. The two of you. I want to go to bed already."

Dash shook his hand and led me outside, where a black Volvo sedan waited for us in the driveway. I paused, trying to remember if he'd had a Volvo the other night.

"Like it?" he asked as he opened the passenger door.

"You had something different yesterday."

"That one got in a little fender bender."

"Are you okay?"

"I went to the doc this morning. My arm's bruised, but that's it. It was nothing."

"Nothing? You got a new car."

"This one's safer. Get in before I put you in." His lips tightened as if holding back a smile.

He'd have loved to pick me up and put me in. I might not have minded it either, but Dad was watching. He'd have denied it, but he was watching.

"Where are we going?" I asked when he got behind the wheel.

"Someplace fun."

I felt the scratch of lace on my skin as he drove. It wasn't uncomfortable. It reminded me of what I was wearing under the simple dress. I crossed my legs and folded my hands in my lap.

"Did you eat?" he asked.

"A little."

"Can you wait a few hours? I have someplace I want to go first."

"Sure."

Traffic was nonexistent as he brought me into downtown.

"Dash, I don't want to bring this up..."

"But you kind of are."

"The pin."

"It's fine," he said.

"I can't tell you how bad I feel."

"Then don't."

"I feel like it's my fault."

He took my hand out of my lap and squeezed it. "If that glove hadn't been taken, we wouldn't have met."

"I know but—"

"You were worth it. If I'd been given the choice to trade that good luck charm for you, I would have done it in a second."

Was this the same guy who'd wanted to pre-dump me? I was confused, but I wasn't ready to replace... what? Important artifacts? His sister?

I shook it off. He was just talking.

"Well, when I wish, I wish big. You should have me and the pin."

"I went to that library ready to pound on your desk and demand you find it or I was going to call the cops. But I saw you coming down the hall, and it all went out the window."

"Thank you. I would have broken down crying."

He squeezed my hand. "Glad I didn't."

After the red light, his hand stayed in mine, even when he turned onto Pershing Square and stopped in a red zone. A man in a tuxedo rushed toward the car and opened his door.

"Hang on," Dash said before getting out. After chatting with the tuxedo guy and handing him the keys, Dash crossed in front of the car. Then he opened my door. "He's going to park it downstairs in the lot."

I took his hand and stepped onto the sidewalk. "You could have taken me down there. I've been to the Pershing Square lot before."

"Not looking like you do. It's filthy down there. You're too good for it."

"Silly," I said even though I loved every word.

We held hands and walked into the square. It was empty and mostly dark. The playgrounds were locked, and the temporary outdoor skating rink was bathed in white light. The booths were locked. The skate rental had been dismantled until next Christmas season.

"I hope you're a size seven," Dash said.

"In what?"

"Skates."

I gasped. "Are you taking me skating?"

"You're taking *me* skating."

"It's closed."

"Not tonight it's not. Not for us," he said, opening the gate to the skating area.

"Oh, Dash, I love this!"

His smile was so wide it could have just about broken his face.

Once we were on the turf-covered platform that surrounded the rink, another man in a tux handed us two pairs of skates.

"Thank you," I said.

I threw myself onto a bench and kicked off my heels. Inside the boots were a new pair of good, thick socks. Excellent, because the stockings were a hundred fifty dollars and would have gotten ruined in the skates, never mind my feet.

Dash held a pair of hockey skates as he said a few quiet words to Tux Man, who nodded and disappeared.

"This is so great!" I said. "How many guys in black suits are helping with this illegal trespass?"

"It's totally legal and paid for." He laced his boots up quickly. "They're just parking the car, keeping people with cameras away, that sort of thing. Here, let me help you." He kneeled in front of me and methodically tightened my laces.

"The cameras," I said. "That's why you don't do interviews. You don't like cameras."

He stopped lacing and put his hand on my calf, brushing his thumb on the smooth stocking. "I like these."

"Stay below the knee, sir."

He looked up at me, all mischief, and tied the laces without breaking our gaze. "Really?"

"Really."

He leaned down and put his lips on the inside of my calf. I gasped. Having him so close to home when we were outdoors made me wild. Even if no one was around, the presence of the sky above felt as if Los Angeles was looking.

"I can respect that," he whispered. "For now."

He worked his mouth up along the inside of my leg. Pressed my legs open. Kissed inside my knee. I gripped the edge of the bench.

"Are you wet, Apples?"

Wet? Wet was an understatement. I was soaking a pair of panties I couldn't afford. "I'm not telling."

He stood and held his hand out for me. "You don't need to. Come on. Show me what you got."

I took his hand, and we went onto the empty rink.

My muscles remembered what to do, pushing side to side,

balanced in movement. I couldn't have worn a more perfect dress to allow my legs proper movement, though keeping the underwear under wraps would be difficult. I pressed down the flared skirt.

He skated to me, pants fluttering against his legs, grace and power in male form.

"You skate?" I said.

"Everyone in Ithaca plays hockey." He circled me twice, and I spun to keep my eyes on him. "I was a traitor when I went to baseball."

"Why did you change?"

"Love. I just loved it." He grabbed my hand and pulled me along.

The wind blew my hair all over my face, and I sped up to catch then pass him. "What did you love?" I said as I passed him.

"The downtime. You can process every play, then there's this burst of activity, and all the processing just clicks. Like dominoes. All the calculations you made in the past two minutes, it fills in like an equation."

"And you catch the ball."

"Sometimes."

"Always."

He put his arm around me, and we circled the rink. I turned my face to the sky. The speed, the scratch of blades on ice, the crisp January air, this man's ridiculous body next to mine. My heart felt lighter than it had in a long time.

He twirled me under his arm then pulled me with his arm around my waist. We synchronized our steps, laughed when we missed, turned, and did it again.

I didn't know how long we were circling before he got ambitious and sent me spinning to the center of the rink. It could have been an hour, but when he did that, I forgot what I was wearing and went into a scratch spin. It was slower than I did when I was more practiced but fast enough to pick up my skirt.

When I slowed down, he was standing still on his skates,

mouth open, hands slow-clapping.

"What are you gaping at?" I asked, still thinking it was the spin that had impressed him. I skated over to him, and he pulled me into his embrace.

"We're going now," he growled.

"So soon?"

Before the words had left my mouth, his hand was up my skirt, tugging on the top of my stockings. He'd seen what I was wearing under the dress. In the exhilaration of skating, I'd forgotten I'd expose myself in the spin, and now I had his arms around my waist, his lips finding mine, the thrust of his body pushing me back against the wall.

"You wore those for me?"

"I'm wearing it for me." I didn't believe myself, but I said it anyway.

"I'm going to eat you alive." His mouth coursed the length of my throat, and his hands gripped my ass.

He'd been attracted to me before. I knew that. But I didn't know what a garter belt did. I'd hoped it would make me a little hotter. I hadn't known it would make him crazy.

The sudden increase in heat sent my alarm bells screaming. It was too soon. He wasn't committed to me or my feelings. My sexual arousal had always been tightly tethered to love, romance, the promise of something more. A future. We had none, and I was clear about that. It was the weight that spun me in his centrifuge. We were just bodies, and I couldn't drag him down. I couldn't weigh on him.

I was burning up from the inside out, melting flesh and bone against him. I couldn't put together a thought, only a series of images. All were affected by gravity. Falling. Sucked down. My consciousness, thought processes, ability to keep my body from molding itself to his got swept into the black hole of our shared need.

"Wait," I gasped.

"What?" he answered in my ear, breath hot, hands settling on my waist.

What did I want to say? Did it have words? I just needed to

stop breaking apart into a million hot shards, or I was going to lose my mind.

"I mean it. I didn't wear this for you. I just didn't expect to be doing scratch spins."

He nodded once. Slowly.

"And I don't even know you. It's too soon for you to take me home. I'm scared of getting attached to you. Really scared."

"The feeling's mutual."

Mentally, I stopped dead in my tracks. Whatever train my thoughts had been on screeched to a halt between stations. I looked in his eyes, searching for a bit of guardedness, a little double meaning, but there was none. He wasn't lying.

"I tell you what," he said, drawing his finger along the ridge of my jaw. "Come home with me, and let's get to know each other. But we can reserve sex for later."

"Define sex. Penetration? Coitus?"

He laughed. "You sure you don't teach sex ed?"

"I'm trying to make it less appealing."

"Didn't work. But I'll use your words. I'll get my mouth on you, my hands all over you. We can enjoy each other tonight, and I'll fuck you later."

"Those weren't my words."

"I meant the words you were thinking."

"You're a little crazy. Do you know that?"

He dropped his hands, smoothing down my skirt. His cheek against mine, I felt him smile. "Any man would get a little crazy around you."

I put my hands flat on his chest. He was so solid, so real, yet he'd mistaken me for a woman who drove men wild. He saw some mirror image and not the real Vivian. What would the anti-me do right there, with her hands on him and his body so close she could feel the heat coming off it?

"Take me home, Dash."

twenty

Vivian

He drove up to the hills, hand on the stick shift, mine on top of it, but he didn't say much. I'd never wanted anything as badly as I wanted his body and his time, but he wasn't talking.

Neither was I. I had nothing interesting to say besides *fuck me*, which I couldn't bring myself to utter, and as he clicked the box that opened his garage door, I wondered if I was doing a good job of being the anti-me.

"Vivian."

"It's all right. You don't have to."

The garage yawned before us, and I wondered if I had my Ryde app ready.

"I want to." He squeezed my hand and looked into my eyes in the darkness. "But I'm sticking by my word. I'm not fucking you. Not tonight."

I wanted to reassure him that I could easily be talked into all kinds of things, but cautious Vivian and reckless Vivian agreed it was time to shut up.

I shifted in my seat, and my skirt slipped over the tops of my stockings. I pulled it down. He laid his finger on my thigh and drew it over the stocking, pushing my skirt back up. He looked out the windshield as if he needed a moment, then he turned back to me, leaned forward, and spoke softly yet with force.

"Open your legs."

He put a hint of pressure inside my knee to part it from the other one. I went liquid and squeaked, so intense was the pleasure that gushed out from my center.

"Go on," he whispered.

I parted my knees, and he watched. My hands were at my sides, braced against the seat, the only clue to my heightened nerves.

"That's so good." He brushed his hand inside my thigh. "Sweetapple, I'm going to make this a night you never forget. Everything I ask you to do is for your pleasure and mine. Communicate with me if I ask. Tell me what you like."

"You're a bag of tricks, Dash Wallace." I barely got the words out around the dryness in my mouth and the chest-inflating heaves of my breath.

"You are too." He pulled the garter strap and sat up straight to pull the car in.

He got out of his side and opened my door. If I'd asked for it, I could have gotten out of it regardless. Right? But I didn't want out. I'd had sex for intimacy and love, but I'd never had sex strictly for pleasure.

All I had to do was ask him to stop if I wanted him to stop. Stop holding my hand up the stairs. Stop guiding me into his house. Stop turning on the soft lights.

Stop being nervous.

"You hungry?" he asked.

"I'm okay. A little. I'm not sure." I laughed nervously, and he smiled, plucking an orange from a bowl on the counter.

He dug a nail into the leathery skin and said, "Take the dress off, sweetapple."

I paused. He didn't say please. He didn't even look at me as he peeled a chunk off the fruit. Then he glanced up. I should have felt threatened by the way he looked at me. He was being bossy. He expected me to just do what he said. But his expression was kind and gentle, and I wanted all the things he'd promised.

I undid the side zipper, pulled my arms free until the sleeves were inside out, and let the dress fall down.

He ate me alive with his eyes. Toes to head, he made a meal of me, then he split the orange open. "Open your mouth."

I didn't. Not until he faced me, then I remembered I was

supposed to do what he said. I parted my lips, and he brought a wedge to them. I opened up more, and he slipped in the orange.

"You're nervous."

"A little." I chewed.

"Why?"

"It's been a long time."

Another wedge. I took it in my mouth. It was delicious.

"That's a crime." He fed me again. It was nice. I let myself feel cared for.

"Thank you." I was grateful for his sensitivity. I was willing to give up my power and take a few orders, but I wasn't ready to go full bore into whatever the essence of his kink was.

"More?" he said when the orange was gone.

"No, thank you."

He took my hands and looked at me in my expensive lingerie and high heels. I'd definitely gotten my money's worth at La Perla. He stepped back into the hall and led me by one hand into his bedroom.

All the lights were out but a nightstand lamp. King bed. Very few pillows. Geometric bedspread made to hospital corners. Dark wood. A patio with two chairs overlooking the city. What else? I couldn't even take it in.

He stopped me at the foot of the bed and took my chin in my hands, pointed it upward, and kissed me. His tongue filled my mouth, owning it, commanding it to respond. I gripped his lapel and tried to get his jacket off, but he took my wrists and pinned them behind my back with one hand.

He lost it a little just then. I felt it in the movements of his body and the way he breathed into me. Pinning my hands did something to him, and it did something to me as well.

"Take me," I whispered.

"Oh, I will."

Still holding my wrists together, he slid his finger inside the cup of the bra. It collapsed under the pressure, and my rock-hard nipple appeared. His mouth closed on it, licking and sucking, driving pleasure between my legs until I could barely stand. He let my wrists go and pulled the bra up, then he twisted one nipple and sucked the other.

I made a noise that was a word in some language, and he responded with a deep-throated groan. I wove my fingers into his hair and let my eyes flutter closed as he took my breast in his mouth. His hair was sticking up when he stood straight again and pulled my bra over my head.

"You ready?" he said. "I'm going to eat your pussy now, and you're going to love it."

My hands covered my crotch. It was a reflex. I wasn't even thinking about it, but I was suddenly seized with the fear that he wouldn't like it. That I was dirty and gross.

He pulled my hands away. "What?"

"I told myself that I didn't want to, so..." *Deep breath.* "I didn't shave or anything."

"You're supposed to have hair, sweetapple. You're past puberty."

How could I explain what Carl had said? Anyone would have thought I was crazy to even listen to it. But I didn't want this first time to be burdened by my ex-boyfriend's hang-up about unsanitary hair.

Dash didn't miss a beat. My expression was enough.

"Come on." He pulled me, but I resisted. "Trust me."

He yanked me again, and I followed him into the bathroom. He flicked on the light. The room was twice the size of mine and gleaming white. I caught myself in the mirror, bare-breasted and gartered in black below the waist.

"What are you doing?" I asked when he reached into the cabinet.

"Making you comfortable." He took a leather envelope from the shelf.

"Oh, no no no."

"Oh, yes yes yes."

"No. Really, we can just skip the oral satisfaction tonight."

"Take those panties off, or I'm going to spank you, Vivian. And you're not ready for that. Not if you want to get to work on time this week and sit still behind that cute little desk."

He wouldn't spank me if I didn't want him to, but the threat of it got to me. I unhooked the garter belt.

He undid the string on the envelope.

I got the straps off the tops of my stockings.

He took out a shiny silver straight razor.

"Don't you have a safety razor like a normal person?"

"If I can do my face, I can do you. Come on." He patted the counter. "Get up here."

I hesitated. He picked me up and plopped me on the vanity.

"Lean back."

I was frozen. Simply frozen. One that he'd be so close to my most sensitive parts. His face. His eyes. Observing it so intently. Two, that he'd have a blade.

But his expression didn't give an inch. Trust him or not. Surrender to doing things I'd never done before, just for a little while, or walk out.

Before I could do anything, he put his hands on either side of my face and brushed his lips with mine. "I want you to be comfortable, and I'll make you uncomfortable to do it. I still promise you I'm going to make this as good as it can be."

"I know." My voice barely worked. "We're just breaking through three comfort zones at a time. I feel off-balance."

He leaned back, stuck the knife in his teeth, and picked up a mug and brush. "We are. Don't make me go for the home run." He said it around the blade, and it was as sexy as anything I'd seen.

He put a little water in the mug and swirled the brush around, still biting the knife like a savage. I couldn't take my eyes off him, still in his button-down shirt and jacket, me nearly naked before him.

He put the knife to the side. "Come on. Open your legs."

I couldn't breathe. I relaxed my legs but didn't open them. He did it with the slightest pressure between my knees. He inspected the softest, most vulnerable part of me. The ugliest part. The part where all the shame lived. My lungs got very small, and the insides of my legs tingled as if I were in free fall.

"Do you remember in *Eternal Joke*?" He drew his hand across my belly, down to the tuft of blond hair. "That scene where Captain Gastronome is on the Aegean?"

I flicked the mental pages of the book. There were a hundred barely connected stories in it. "The one that made me seasick? Yeah."

He put the brush below my navel. It was soft and cool running down, down to where I couldn't feel the touch of the brush against my skin anymore.

"Do you think he knew his wife was below decks, fucking what's-his-name?"

He lathered me from clit to navel. My excitement came from inside, more at the idea of his attention than the touch of the soap.

"I think he only loved the sea."

"Until he caught them." Dash crouched down, razor in hand. "Then he loved her again. Because he'd lost control of her."

"He was such an ass. Honestly. I hated him."

The razor touched the line where the hair started, scratching the skin harmlessly.

"You're hard on the guy. He had a club foot, you know. I can barely stand upright on a boat deck with two good feet."

I couldn't look. Between Dash's inspection and the sight of the sharp edge, I was compelled to jump ten feet. If I did, the bloody gash and the ruined evening wouldn't be his fault. The flat white ceiling was about to become my entertainment.

"No one asked him to be a ship's captain."

"Ouch," he said, and inside I jumped a little because I thought he'd cut me.

I looked down, and all I saw was my near-hairless body and Dash Wallace an inch from my pussy, attention laser-focused.

"You don't give a disabled veteran an inch."

"He loved the sea more than his wife! And he told her to her face. What is that even? Who says something like that?"

His eyes flicked to mine. Was the blue warmer than it had been? Or was I seeing them differently? "She loved him for it."

I straightened and put my finger up to make a point. "She *fell* in love with his sea-captain-ness. But that's not sustainable. A girl can't sit on the bench while the sea's up to bat all the time."

When his body jerked with a laugh, I shifted a little out of fear he'd cut me. But he wasn't even close, and the laughter was so beautiful and real that my fear disappeared in a *poof* of my own delight.

"You're right." His attention went back between my legs. "I must have been caught up in the way he compared the color of the sea to wine."

"Storm is burgundy; calm is chianti."

"And us, the incompetent waiter's cork bobbing."

I laughed again because the passages were funny and the connection with Dash tickled my heart.

"Stay still now," he said. "Just a little more." He waved the knife.

I wanted to laugh, but I was trying not to move. Stillness was hard enough with blood screaming to the surface of my pussy as if getting three nanometers closer to him would get me off.

"Your pussy is gorgeous."

The lack of seduction in his voice sent blood to my face. He said it as if stating a fact. The same way I was reciting meaningless facts to stave off the fear. The capital of West Virginia (Charleston), or the quadratic equation (X-equals-negative-B-plus-or-minus-the-square-root-of-B-squared-minus-four-AC-all-over-2A), entire pages from the LAUSD protocol handbook.

"You blush easy." He stood and snapped a towel off the rack. "I like that."

I sat up straight while he ran warm water over the towel. I had been shaved clean without a nick or a cut.

"I like that you don't play a game at being experienced or naïve. You are who you are." He wrung out the towel. "Lean back again."

I leaned back but didn't use my arms to prop myself up. I

relaxed completely into the mirror. It was over. I felt as wrung out as the towel and as warm as the water. Tension flowed out of me. I could have gone to sleep if every nerve ending between my legs wasn't begging for release.

Dash put the warm towel on my belly and wiped the soap away, then down, he pressed it against me. I drew a hard breath in and arched my back. The warmth and the rough texture was enough to set me on fire. I pushed forward into it.

He put his hand on the mirror and kissed my forehead, my cheek, my chin while rubbing me with the warm towel. "You're right on the edge. I could see it. You're so ready to come for me. If I wait until I eat you, it's going to be half a second. I want it to last."

I could barely see him past the red film of my orgasm. I held it back but wouldn't be able to for long. "I don't want to yet. I want to wait for mine."

"Yours? Do you think you're only coming once?"

I nodded because I couldn't make a single word. Couldn't even think or control my body. The towel on my clit brought all my sense to it, rushing to the surface, blacking out everything. My back stiffened and arched. One hand curled on the edge of the vanity and the other gripped his shoulder. I howled to the ceiling then collapsed like a flag in a dying wind.

His lips landed on mine like an avalanche. We kissed in a flurry of hands, tongues, lips. He shrugged out of his jacket and tossed it. I reached for his buttons, but he moved my hands to his belt. We kissed while I yanked it open and he unbuttoned his shirt.

Pants open, I reached for my prize.

"Oh, Dash. I…" I looked down at it. I hadn't realized how big he was when he'd pushed me against the railing of my front steps.

I didn't finish the sentence. I didn't know if I could get it down my throat, but hell if I wasn't going to try. Before I could ask myself how I would do it, my feet and the floor parted company as he threw me over his shoulder and tossed me onto the bed. I landed with my legs open.

He stripped off the rest of his clothes. He was magnificent. An athlete. It was his job to be perfect, to tighten his abs, rip his biceps, work his thighs into powerful machines. I started to close my legs so I could turn, and he grabbed them and held them open.

"I did a pretty good job, if I do say so myself."

"I'm sure you did." I put my arms out for him.

He grabbed my wrists and pulled me forward. I was tongue-close to his beautiful dick. I looked up at him and opened my mouth.

"Not yet," he said.

"Please." I wanted him to come. I needed it. "I'll enjoy it so much more if I know you're satisfied."

"I think you're stalling, sweetapple."

"Stalling? I'm just moving this off my desk so I can enjoy myself."

"You're moving my dick off your desk? It's like *paperwork?*"

"Well, no. It's really nice paperwork. But a lot of paperwork. Like an eight-inch stack of cardboard."

"Cardboard?"

"I didn't want to imply floppy," I said. "Rigid like corrugated. Or…" We were both laughing so hard I couldn't even think of the word. "Something. Look, I'm really new at this."

He was laughing, and I smiled. I liked this. Liked him. Liked that he was in control but we could talk. And with that laugh, he stopped being a baseball god. He stopped being the athlete, the performer, the graceful shape between the bases. He stopped being perfect batting form, and he stopped being the mysterious guy who never interviewed. I thought I'd been seeing just him all along, but I hadn't. Not until he laughed, naked before me, did he become no more and no less than a man.

He got on his knees so he was just below my eye level, more or less, and we laughed together, kissing on the edge of the bed.

"Okay," he said when he slowed down. "You want to suck

my dick?"

"Get up to the plate."

"One 'bat' analogy and you're getting a spanking."

"Thanks for the warning."

He stood. I sat up straight and guided his cock to my lips. When I had it, he gently gripped the hair on the back of my head.

"Just your mouth," he growled.

Just my mouth. I'd never done it that way. Never been anchored by a man's grip on me. This must have been the control thing. I let myself fall into it, giving up power, surrendering to his grasp.

Yes. I could do this. I was free to do it, and I was free to like it.

I shifted, opened up, and let him guide himself along the flat of my tongue. I pressed down the back of my tongue as if I was at the doctor's office and pushed forward.

He breathed an *aah* then groaned an affirmation, pulling out. "I underestimated you."

Looking up, his face toward me, framed by his pecs, his forearm cutting my vision as he held my hair. I turned back to his cock. I'd taken all of it. I could do this. He guided it into my mouth again, and I took it again, holding my breath, nose catching the tickle of his hair. He pulled out quickly and pushed back in.

"So tight and sexy," he said through his teeth. "I'm not fucking you tonight. I'm coming in your hot little mouth. I'm going to fuck it. Are you ready?"

I nodded as much as I could.

"Breathe," he said.

I breathed, leveraging myself against his rock-hard thighs. I took his length again in long, fast strokes. He pushed. I opened my throat, let him in. I breathed when he let me. He thrust down my throat in increasingly urgent rhythms until his body went rigid, fingers hooking and tightening in my hair, groaning loudly as he came hot in my throat.

He smiled down at me. I swallowed.

"Lie back," he said, brushing the hair out of my face. "You were saving this for last."

Little white butterflies took flight in my tummy. He pulled my knees apart.

"I'm nervous," I said.

"I know." He ran his face along the inside of my thigh and up to the center, where he kissed gently. "But trust me. I love this, and you will too."

This was a first. I'd never had a man's mouth on me, and I bundled nerves and expectation in my chest, waiting for it. I felt his tongue on me as a slight flutter I could barely discern, but it was the thought of it that made me gasp. As the pressure increased, I could barely hold myself together. Nothing I'd imagined had prepared me for this direct line to an orgasm. He pulled it out of me. Licked and sucked away the layers between myself and my climax, changing his motions as soon as the payoff reduced. I threaded my fingers in his hair and pulled his head into me, and just when I thought I'd come for sure, he pulled back.

"You all right?" he asked, smiling.

"I'm good," I squeaked.

He readjusted himself and put two fingers in me then flicked my clit with his tongue. I bucked. He flicked again. I squirmed against his fingers.

"Do you want to come?"

"Yes."

"Is that how we ask for something, Miss Foster?"

"Yes, please."

He gave me a little suck. "Ask again."

"Please let me come. Please."

"That's my sweetapple."

He laid into me, sucking, licking, and biting until I tried to push his head away. He moved my hand and kept going until the pleasure subsided, regrouped, and flooded me again.

He collapsed on top of me. I kissed him, tasting myself on his mouth.

I was delicious.

twenty-one

Dash

She left in the morning, while it was still dark and pouring winter rain. I drove. She wasn't getting in a cab in the rain, in the dark. Those people didn't know how to drive when there was any kind of precipitation, never mind at night.

"Thank you," she said. I could barely hear her over the windshield wipers. "Last night was pretty amazing."

The previous night had been a warm-up. I hadn't even fucked her. Hadn't blindfolded her or tied her up. She only came three times. Her ex-boyfriend had apparently fucked as if he was driving in the rain.

"Never settle for anything less, Vivian. I mean it. You're a sex goddess."

"Oh, stop!"

She was beet red. I couldn't see her face in the dark or with my eyes on the road, but I knew it was true, and it made me want her all over again.

I rattled around the files in my brain, trying to find the right words to convey how beautiful and sexy she was because words like beautiful and sexy were overused and generic. She was unique. But I came up with nothing. I gave my attention to the road and holding her hand. No mean feat considering I hadn't taken my meds since the day before.

We got to her house. It was still pouring, and the clouds kept the street dark.

"I forgot an umbrella," I said.

"It's not that far."

I got out and went around, opened her door, and put my

139

jacket over her head. We ran to the door. She jangled her keys out of her purse. My jacket was a shitty covering, and drops of rain ran veins of hair over her face. She swung the door open and looked at me with those porcelain-blue eyes.

"Thank you, sweetapple." I kissed her quickly. "Go in. You're getting wet. And the heat's getting out. You don't have stock in LADWP."

She laughed harder than I deserved and went in.

I dashed to the car and sat behind the flooded windshield.

I knew what I wanted to say.

> Shall I compare thee to a summer's day?
> Thou art more lovely and more temperate:
> Rough winds do shake the darling buds of May
>
> Then more stuff about how summer isn't long enough and it's hot and shitty sometimes
>
> And then the thing I wanted to say in the car
>
> But thy eternal summer shall not fade
> Nor lose possession of that fair thou owest;
> Some other stuff I forget...So long as men can breathe or eyes can see: So long lives this and this gives life to thee

That's the nicest thing. You're going to spoil me

> A guy's gotta do what a guy's gotta do. I'm driving, so we'll talk later

I shut off the phone and pulled away. The rain let up on the way east. Los Angeles rain always shuts off like a faucet when the sun comes up. When I got home, I went out front. The air was usually clear after a rain, and I could see all the way to San Pedro.

Which was fine.

What wasn't fine was what the rain had done to the slope in my south-facing yard. It slid downward. The steps were covered in mud, and when I say covered, I didn't mean it was messy. I meant the steps would have to be excavated by a crack team of archaeologists to prove they ever existed.

Cancel Youder.

Where would we work out? What hill would we climb? I was too tired to deal with another change. I was going to bed for a few hours, then I'd cope with the general state of collapse.

And her.

The one thing that wasn't collapsing. She was unsustainable but necessary. I'd given her flowers and poetry. Another break in my routine. Another mistake. But I wanted her to feel good. Compulsively almost. I couldn't help but build her up even if I knew I'd fail her.

The sheets smelled like her. I got five hours.

twenty-two

Vivian

Back to the coffee shop on Olympic. I didn't even have to ask Francine where to meet anymore. When I'd called her at the crack of dawn and said I'd just gotten back from Dash's place, she said she'd meet me in ten minutes and hung up.

It had taken her thirty minutes to get there, but I never worried that she was bailing on me or that I hadn't identified the meeting place. The coffee shop with the black umbrellas out front and no name.

She came back with a latte for herself and an espresso for me and stacked our phones behind the napkin holder to let me know we weren't to be interrupted. Leaning forward in her chair as if she wanted to open my head and peer in, she said, "Tell me everything."

"Okay, so he came to the house—"

"Did you do it? Go all the way? Home run? Do the deed?"

"No, but... other things."

"Skip to those. Then work back."

Francine also ate dessert first whenever possible. She didn't believe in postponing joy. So I started at the end and worked backward as best as I could. It wasn't easy.

"He shaved you? Why? God, please say he's not another Carl with the hang-ups."

"No, it was me. I wanted him to."

"Really? And? I've never let a guy do that before."

I shifted in my seat. "It was fine but..." I dropped my voice and got as close to her as the table would allow. "The rubbing. It's like I can feel everything. I'm so aware of it."

"Aware of what? Your pussy?"

"*Shh.*" I looked around. The place was dead, but there were photographs of people with ears behind me. "Jesus, Francine!"

"Totally normal," she whispered. "You're going to be horny all the time now."

"You didn't tell me."

"You didn't ask."

A bleeping rendition of "Take Me Out to the Ballgame" came from behind the napkin holder.

"Are you serious?" Francine asked. "You gave him his own ringtone already?"

"He put it in this morning."

I wasn't supposed to take the call, but I reached behind the chrome box and grabbed the phones then passed Francine hers and tapped the green circle on mine. "Hello."

"Hey, sweetapple. Did I wake you?"

"No, I'm having coffee with a friend."

Francine smirked at me and bit her lower lip then fanned herself with her hand as if she knew how his voice made me feel.

"I can still taste you," he said.

Down below, where sensitive tissue had direct contact with fresh underwear, I went on high alert. I wanted him to taste me again. Now.

Francine watched me over the rim of her coffee cup, half smiling.

"I'm with a friend," I repeated because my not-aloneness was the second most relevant thing on my mind.

"When can I see you today?"

I didn't answer right away. Dad and I were going to clean the gutters then have dinner. I was free at some point, potentially, but though my body wanted to drop everything and see him, my head didn't want to be too available. "Today? I don't—"

"I want to get inside you," he said before I could finish.

I clammed up. My body started vibrating, and the shiver between my legs didn't allow me to speak.

That dick. That cock. That huge thing inside me, stretching me to get in. I gripped the phone as if it was the last ledge before I fell over a cliff.

"I want to see you come while I'm fucking you." His voice made pictures, and the pictures were absolutely filthy.

"Okay." Who wouldn't agree to that?

"This afternoon."

"This afternoon?"

He expected a yes or no answer. I shook my brain as if it were a vending machine and words were a bag of chips that wouldn't drop from the silver spiral.

"I have to do some things around the house with my dad this afternoon, and I should nap at some point, or I'm going to look like a ragmop and..." I now had seventeen bags of chips at the bottom of the machine when I only needed one. "The gutters, anyway, they look like hell, and the roof leaks if they get backed up and rain is coming next week, and I start work so we can't wait."

A sharp pain in my calf ended the sentence. Francine had kicked me.

I mouthed *ow*.

She held up three fingers.

"Three?" I asked her.

"I'll be at your place at three," Dash said and hung up.

twenty-three

Vivian

I'd been babbling to Dash, but I hadn't been lying. The gutters were a mess. One of the five deciduous trees in Los Angeles grew in our side yard, and every year it exploded in red and orange then shed like a hound dog. The neighbors hated us, and in the months between the shedding of the leaves and the rains, I hated us too.

I stood on the roof and surveyed the work. I was about two-thirds done. Dad stood in the driveway with a rake, wearing a puffy winter coat he'd bought to ski in when Mom was alive. Mrs. Klein stood in her bedroom window, undoubtedly wondering why we didn't do the normal thing and hire a guy to clean the gutters.

"I'm *schvitzing* in this jacket."

Schvitzing meant he was hot. "Take it off."

"I'm bundled. How's it going up there?"

"Okay?" I went girl-style and, as a lead-in to unpleasant news, asked the answer instead of stating it. "I don't have too much time. He's coming at three, and I haven't showered."

I wondered if my position on the roof meant the whole neighborhood knew that I smelled and a guy was coming.

"That was quite a nap you took." He leaned on his rake. "Musta been up late."

What happened with his eye? Did my father just wink at me, thinking I got laid? Who did that?

"Easy there, Dad. You're not marrying me off so quick."

"I know. If you left, who would do the gutters?"

I crouched by a gutter full of leaves, arms outstretched, and

147

caught a mess of them between my palms, then I threw them on my father, who let out a Yiddish cry and waved his rake at me.

"I can't believe you think I'd stop doing your damn gutters!" I got another armful and threw them on him.

"Elder abuse!" he cried, swatting the flying, wet leaves with his rake. "Help! Police!"

"I'm still coming here for dinner! You'll never get rid of me." I went to the other side of the house and got more leaves, walked across the roof, and threw them on him as he laughed and coughed between hysterical complaints of abuse.

I stopped looking. I rained wet brown leaves on him from all corners, listing all the ways he wasn't getting rid of me and stomping on the shingles in my cowboy boots. When I grabbed the last handful, I looked down.

Two faces looked up at me. Dad's, of course, and Dash's.

"It's three already?" I called down.

"I'm early. I couldn't wait."

"I like this guy," Dad said, jerking his thumb to the guy with the filthy mouth and huge dick. "He said he'd help you finish up."

"He's wearing a jacket and dress shoes, Dad."

"He said he won't throw leaves at me. What more do I need?"

I took a few steps away and threw the leaves in the orange bucket on the roof.

"Oh," Dad cried as Dash started up the ladder, "now she's putting them where they go instead of pelting me with them." He shook his fist at an unjust God—or me or the gutters or Mrs. Klein, who wouldn't understand that he was joking.

The ladder rattled, and Dash's head crested the roofline. I crossed my arms and leaned on one foot, letting the heel of my boot rock in an arc.

"You need to give a girl a chance to, you know, bathe. Put on a little mascara. All that."

He put his leather gloves on my cheeks and kissed me. The neighborhood saw it. Probably Dad too. I didn't care. I ran hot and cold when his lips tenderly touched mine, greeting me with gentle passion.

"You know it's rude to be early, right?"

"Yup." He kissed me again.

"It's unseemly."

Another kiss.

"Inappropriate," I whispered to get another kiss, then I dropped my voice to barely audible. "As bad as being late."

On the last kiss, his lips came off mine with a pop. "I'll help you with this, then we can go."

"Will I get to shower?"

"If you must." He stepped back and put out his arms. "Let's take a look at that downspout."

Dash knew what he was doing when it came to gutters. Apparently the job had to be done three times a year in Ithaca. Since his father was a wounded veteran from Michigan—where you mowed your own damn lawn and took care of your own damn house—and since Dashiell was the oldest son, three times a year, he cleaned the gutters. An hour after he'd started my house, he'd not only told me all about his dad, his two-story, gutter-clogged childhood home in a frozen wasteland, and the sloped roofs that had nearly killed him four times, he'd also finished up the job perfectly.

"You ready to go?" He slapped his hands together to get the grime off.

"Sure. Where are we going?"

He lowered his voice and pointed to the driveway where my dad slowly raked the leaves. "We're going to finish that guy's birthday present."

twenty-four

Vivian

Dash helped Dad with the leaves while I changed. I put on a wool maxi dress with a tiny black-and-white geometric pattern. It had a matching tote that fit a wallet, a notebook, a Kindle, a phone, and a secret birthday baseball.

Dash drove up the 101, hand in my lap, thumb stroking my hand absently.

"English lit," he said. "I figured if baseball failed, I'd have that BA. I didn't know it didn't work like that."

"Wait. Is that how you memorized so much Shakespeare? It's freaking me out."

"It's a long story."

"Okay? Were you in drama club ten years running or something?"

"English class. Seventh grade. I was just getting this weird fuzz on my face, and the thing with the voice? I sounded like two rocks smacking together. We were doing a semester of Shakespeare's comedy and a semester of tragedy with Mrs. Newman."

"You had a crush on your teacher?"

"A crush? Oh no. This was true love. Okay, let me start from the beginning. She was a black lady with a little Caribbean accent. A good Christian woman. Like, all turtlenecks and long pleated skirts. One day, she was marking up my paper, and it was so much red. I had no idea what to do with a comma. Still don't. But I was sitting at her desk, and I saw her from the side, and I could see her eye on the other side of her glasses, and she had these lashes that curled up.

151

They were short, but I'd never seen lashes with that much curl. I didn't expect it. I felt like I was seeing inside her, and I got really turned on."

"Oh, wow."

"Yeah, and I realized she had breasts and hips. And lips. I mean, she was gorgeous, and it wasn't flashy, but she was stunning. I fell deeply in love with her."

"And she taught you how to seduce her with Shakespeare?"

"Mrs. Newman? Fuck no. Are you kidding? She'd never. I decided I was going to win her when I turned eighteen. So I memorized all Shakespeare's romantic shit. All the sonnets. All the quotes about love and sex. I figured in six years, I'd be ready for her."

He turned off the freeway. He didn't continue the story. I punched his arm.

"Ow. What?"

"What happened?" I asked.

"What do you mean what happened?"

"When you turned eighteen?"

"I don't know. I had a girlfriend by then. I mean, come on, sweetapple. I wasn't really going to spend six years pining for my married English teacher. I just, you know, grew up."

"But in the meantime, you had a ton of love sonnets to seduce women with. Nice job."

He laughed and touched my face without looking away from the road. "Never occurred to use them before. I only pulled out the big guns for you."

He pulled down a private road. The gate was open into a short stretch with a dozen big houses.

"I wasn't that unattainable."

"Maybe not. But it seemed like you'd appreciate it." He turned off the car. "Got your ball?"

"Yup."

We kissed, and I thought I'd never been so happy in my life.

twenty-five

Vivian

Greg Duchovney was a closer. He kept his hair and beard long because it was lucky, earning him the name "The Samson of Elysian." He didn't have more than fifty pitches in him per game, but of those fifty, eighty percent were brilliantly placed tricks of air and physics. The rest were signs he was getting tired. That was why they called him "The Forty."

"Jesus, Wallace." Duchovney turned the ball over in his hand, a blue Sharpie wedged between two fingers. "You John Hancock or something?"

"There's room," Dash said, stretching up to turn on the third air heater in the yard. The gas flame whooshed to life. "Stop whining."

Duchovney had a brace on his left knee. It was quite a contraption of brushed metal wingnuts and rods, bridging the space between the outdoor couch and the coffee table. I had a hard time keeping my eyes off it. Though it didn't look as though Greg was uncomfortable, the titanium cage told a story of pain.

I tried not to giggle when he handed me back the ball, signed. I was at his house for dinner as his friend's girl, not in the stadium as a giddy fan. So I tried not to throw his stats back at him or tell him how he'd been robbed of a Cy Young Award two years earlier. Dash had already warned me against mentioning the accident. He didn't say why. He just said I shouldn't bring it up unless I was pressed.

And I wasn't. We got all the way through dinner with two professional baseball players without bringing up knees, trips

153

and falls, the good or ill health of anyone in the world, the pitching roster, or the Cactus League. Yet once we had established the life story of the dinner's newcomer (me), we talked about nothing but baseball. The deftness with which painful subjects were skirted was world-class but exhausting. When Dora Duchovney started clearing the table, I jumped up to help.

Dora had an accent straight out of Minnesota, which made sense. Duchovney had been a rookie with the Twins and failed as a starter.

"Thank you so much for not asking," she said, rinsing dishes as I stacked and scraped. "I mean, I'm sure you were raised to ask how someone's doing when they have a leg that looks like that."

"Dash told me he wouldn't want to talk about it. I get it. My dad has arthritis, and he says he feels like it defines him. He has lots of other things to talk about."

"Yes. Well, I'm sorry about your dad." She ran the sponge over the edge of the carving knife too fast, nearly cutting her thumb.

"He's all right. Will Steve get better though? What's the prognosis?"

She shook her head. "He's never playing again. And you know, unfortunately, baseball defines him, so he's pretty down." She rinsed her hands under scalding water. "It was such a stupid accident." She shut off the faucet and snapped the towel, rubbing her hands as if she wanted to break her fingers.

Duchovney had picked up a chopper and was taking a step to throw the ball to first when he tripped on the ridge between the pitcher's mound and the grass. But it wasn't just a little trip and catch. He'd been moving forward too fast, and the catch had unbalanced him. The edge of his foot caught and twisted.

It should have been nothing. Except that he'd been unlucky. A series of tiny angles and trajectories had broken his tibia.

"It didn't look like anything on TV," I said. I'd expected

him to get up and walk away.

Outside, Dash and Greg leaned on their chair arms, engaged in serious discussion.

"I know. Just bad luck. But he started taking apart everything he did before the game."

"It was the second game of a doubleheader. It was late."

"And he was tired. But I made him these meatloaf sandwiches for every game, and on that day, I made him one and not two." She reached for the stack of serving dishes, slipped, almost fell over the open dishwasher, caught herself, and laughed. "Golly. I'm not even drinking."

"He doesn't blame you, does he?"

All the buttoned-up subjects of dinner must have gotten to me because the question was wildly inappropriate, yet it slipped out as if through the fingers of a clutched fist.

"I'm sorry," I rushed to explain. "That's ridic—"

"He tries not to," she cut in, closing the dishwasher. "But how can he not? I'm not the best housekeeper already." She indicated the half-done counters. "And we had a cook. I made the sandwiches, but the cook let us run out of meatloaf. I should have kept on him. I feel like I let it all slip. The sandwich. Everything. So he doesn't have to say much." She snapped the towel off the sink. "Anyway, my goodness, you didn't come here to hear this nonsense. Are you traveling with our Mr. Wallace this summer?"

I was caught off guard. Did that happen? Did I want it to? Now I felt like the one putting the brakes on the relationship because the thought of leaving Dad and my life for months to chase around a pro ballplayer overwhelmed me.

The screen door scraped open before I could answer. Thank God, it was Dash in his polo and jeans, a demigod slipping half in, half out of the human-sized house.

"You need help making coffee?"

"Coming right up!" Dora's smile was meant to lighten up the room, but knowing what was behind it made it look sad.

twenty-six

Vivian

I'd never gotten the entire twenty-five-man roster from any winning year on a single baseball. It was a fan's wet dream, yet as the shape of the ball in my tote pressed against my thigh, it had an uncomfortable memory attached.

"She blames herself for what happened," I said in the car on the way home. It was dark, and the traffic was at that in-between place where it was open enough to go fast but too close to do it safely.

"Yeah, that's pretty normal."

"I think it's crazy."

"It's baseball. Normal is crazy."

"'He's mad that trusts in the tameness of a wolf, a horse's health, a man's love, or a whore's oath.' Or baseball."

He chuckled. "Yeah. If Shakespeare played ball." He got off the freeway. "And it's a boy's love. Not a man's love."

"No, it's man. I'm sure of it."

He shook his finger at me. "Boys don't know how to love. Men do. See *Romeo and Juliet*. The entire thing."

I turned in my seat. "Are you for real? Romeo didn't know how to love?"

"They both ended up dead. So no." He headed up into the hills. We were obviously going to his place, and I was all right with that.

"You really need to stick to the sonnets, buddy. This is *King Lear*. It's 'man.' And Romeo Montague is the greatest romantic hero ever in the world."

He didn't do more than *tsk*, shaking his head like a

disappointed parent. "First you get the quote completely wrong, then—"

"You are out of your league on that, mister."

He just nodded, but there was plenty going on in his head. I wanted to open it like a book and savor every line before using it to convince him of my personal Shakespearean truth.

His garage slid open, and he pulled in. The lights went on.

"You're not getting any tonight until you see it my way," I said, not meaning a word of it.

"I have all night, sweetapple."

He got out, crossed in front of the car, and opened my door. He closed it behind me with a *whup,* and he led me up the stairs and to the front patio that overlooked the city. Before I could breathe, his lips were on mine, his hands were on my hips, and his tongue could taste my next sentence.

In the basin below, traffic hummed and bushes rustled. In this space, his kiss was the dark night and the full moon, the spin of the earth, and the slow, purposeful drift of the clouds against the charcoal sky.

He pulled back long enough to breathe. "It was boy."

"Man."

He kissed me again, softly, with the entirety of his lips, and even as I leaned forward to extend the touch, he pulled away.

"Boy. And, Miss Foster, this is your last chance."

"Man. A man's love is not to be trusted. And Romeo's love was real. Are you going to kiss me again or not?"

"Turn around and look at the view."

I paused before doing it. The view seemed harmless enough. From behind me, he took my bag off my shoulder and dropped it on the glass-topped table. He ran his lips along the curve of my neck, found a space, and bit down just hard enough to make my eyes flutter closed and my knees bend.

He pushed me to bend at the waist until my elbows were on the table and I felt his erection on my ass.

"I think we can look it up," he said, drawing his hands down my back, "but first, you need to see it my way."

"I do not."

The first breath wasn't out of me before he'd pulled my skirt up, exposing my white cotton underwear to the night air. He kept one hand between my shoulders, and the other stroked my ass over my underpants.

"You do," was all he said before I felt his palm meet my bottom.

I gasped.

I groaned.

Something.

Both.

He did it again, and my groan mixed with a cry in a new kind of sound. He stroked and hit me again. The sting wasn't half as powerful as the feeling that my pussy had exploded just to get closer to him so his hand would reach me a split second sooner.

His finger slipped under my panties and slid along the wet skin.

A long groan escaped me.

"You're wet. So wet."

He hooked his finger in the crotch of my underwear and pulled the panties down to mid-thigh, then he spanked my bare ass. The sting was sharper, more concentrated, and the pleasure stirring between my legs was fuller.

"Boy," he said then smacked me again.

"Man," I gasped. "Trust not a…" I couldn't finish the sentence as he put two fingers in my soaking wet pussy.

"Romeo was a dopamine addict with no common sense," he said.

"Well, of course not! He was 'a boy' in love. A man's love."

"You're asking for it, sweetapple."

"'Trust not a man's love or—'"

He got each cheek, spanking quickly on one side then the other then the backs of my thighs, which weren't ready. I never thought I'd find such a thing pleasurable, but it was more than good, more than a turn-on. He was waking up every nerve ending between my legs as if they'd been sleeping.

He stopped long enough to stroke my pussy, my clit, to

159

enter me with two fingers and stroke a hard nub inside me.

"What were you saying, beautiful?"

"Nothing. I wasn't saying..." The words dropped into sucked breaths when another finger flicked across my clit over and over. "I'm going to come."

"Yes, you are."

I hadn't thought he'd say that. I'd thought he'd stop and wait until I was on my back or until we were inside. But he kept going. Flicking and rubbing, holding me down between my shoulder blades as the view of the city blinked in the darkness.

My body stiffened and clenched around him, and I exploded in a cry I was sure the neighbors heard, hips pumping against his hand.

"God, you are so sexy," he said, tenderly pulling me up when I was no more than a puddle of broken breaths and gelatinous bones.

"I don't think I can stand," I said, half joking.

"That's not what I had in mind." He picked me up and carried me to his bedroom.

twenty-seven

Vivian

Dash undressed me slowly, and I stood naked before him, then he pulled his shirt over his head, undid his belt. The buckle clacked, and then it whooshed out of the loops. We drew circles on each other's bodies with our fingers and tongues twisted together and teasing.

"I can't decide how to fuck you," he said. "I want to take you in every position. I want to fuck you like an animal and a saint. I want to keep you on the brink for an hour and take four orgasms from you. I can't do it all tonight. I'm kind of pissed about that."

"We don't have an expiration date. Remember?"

"We don't." He rolled on a condom. "But I'm impatient. I want it all right now."

I watched him kneeling above me, a perfect body in the sum of its perfect parts.

I held my arms out for him. "Take what you can."

He didn't lean down, just kneeled where I could see him. "Open your legs."

I loved it when he demanded my exposure. So I did it, letting him see me, all of me. He opened my knees wider, ran one hand up my inner thigh, and put three fingers inside, stretching me.

"You're so tight. So wet and tight."

He guided his dick to my opening and pushed forward, holding my legs open, fully in my view. I didn't think I'd have enough room for him, but I did, and his length glided against every surface I had. He angled himself to press against my clit, stroke it with his cock, until the pain of him subsided and only the throb of an awakening orgasm remained. He leaned down and pushed his dick into me, owning me with his eyes and his attention.

His breath caught. He liked it. He liked what he was doing to me and how close we were. I reached for him and pulled him close, closer, as close as I'd been to another person, and still it wasn't enough. I wanted his soul inside me, a melding of skin where we touched, an unbroken circle of pulsing attention and awareness.

"Vivian."

He only said the one word. A prayer. A supplication. A breath from his heart to mine.

I put my hand on his cheek and said, "Yes."

When he looked as if he was about to lose himself, I lost myself too. Physically, I came and came hard, arching and stretching under him, pinned to reality by the force of the way he fucked me. But emotionally, seeing him as lost in the moment as I was, unable to stop himself from closing his eyes and groaning... he gave me more than an orgasm. He gave me the sweetest release.

Afterward, when he was still on top of me and planting kisses all over my face and neck, he said, "You knew the Lear quote was 'boy.'"

"I realized it on the patio."

He pulled back a little until his nose was astride mine. "But you didn't say?"

"You gonna spank me for lying?"

"Not tonight, sweetapple."

"Are you getting hard again? I don't think I can go another inning."

He pinned my hands over my head and kissed me. "When you're still sore two days from now, I want you to remember who fucked you so hard you can't walk."

I couldn't. I really couldn't come again. I certainly couldn't let him inside me again.

Well, maybe one more time.

twenty-eight

Dash

Terror. Absolute, all-consuming, skin-searing fear. Like a frog in a pot of water that got hotter and hotter until it was too late, early January became mid-February, and I was still fucking her. Compulsively. I had her on my kitchen floor. My shower. My car. I fucked her face with my cock and my fingers. I ate her pussy and sucked her nipples. I came on her tits, on her back, down her throat, inside her. I put my hands under her clothes as soon as I saw her, held her hands behind her back, spanked her, blindfolded her, and still there was shit I hadn't done.

I hadn't tied her down. I hadn't gotten a finger in her ass.

There was *so much*.

And I was running out of time.

I hadn't made a plan because a sensible plan meant either we cut the cord at spring training, no negotiations, or I told her what I told the other ones. It's casual. It's friendly. It's non-exclusive.

But I couldn't because if I said shit like that to her, she would walk.

So there I was, watching her drive away at the crack of dawn so she could get to work and wondering what the fuck I was going to do, when my phone buzzed.

Hey, bat boy. I'm getting the hotel

A week.

She got the hotel a week before I landed in Arizona. She'd done it every year since my first winning season. Janice. Nice lady. Ass like a pear and God... what else? Nice hair, I

163

guessed. Divorcee. Her ex got the kids for that week, or she got a sitter. She made sure of it. She met me at the field. I signed her shirt. Met her at the same hotel. She was waiting. Same every year. Every winning year, it was boom boom boom. The year I hit .225 between opening day and the All-Star break? When I couldn't remove my glove from my ass before July 4th? That year we'd changed something critical, and there I was. Schmuck of the century.

So now what was I supposed to do?

Pace around. Not worry. Tonight was Joe Westlake's Spring Training Dinner, and she was going. I wanted her there at the same time as I didn't want to go.

I texted Vivian because I had to. The only thing that calmed me down was putting something sexy in her lap.

> I can't wait to get my mouth on your cunt tonight

Guilt for leading her on. Relief that I was being honest. One text could be both. I didn't know how to exist inside my own contradictions.

twenty-nine

Vivian

We didn't have an expiration date.

But we did.

I spent weeks in a state of perpetual soreness. I'd never been sore like that, and if someone had told me it was the most pleasurable feeling in the world, I wouldn't have believed them. But it was. I walked around school gingerly every day and went to his house every night to get sore all over again and started over the next morning.

I found myself in the hallways, carrying a stack of books and stopped dead, looking at some random corner, imagining the flick of his tongue on me, hearing his voice in my ear. Waiting for my phone to buzz.

I can't wait to get my mouth on your cunt tonight

Is that from Hamlet?

Shakespeare didn't have enough words to describe how delicious you are

He'd gotten filthier as the weeks wore on, until the words *cunt* and *cock* didn't make me flinch anywhere above the waist.

I got on birth control, and without the extra step, we wound our bodies together even more easily. He was considerately merciless, bringing me to orgasm repeatedly, pounding me insanely with a dick that never got tired or worn out, and keeping me up late talking about the silly nonsense people talk about between kisses.

Mondays, Wednesdays, and Fridays, a wrapped basket of fruit showed up at the office. Mostly apples. The kids went nuts when he sent a dozen pineapples once. Iris would never have a vitamin C deficiency her entire life with the amount of fruit she ate. Jim and I peeled them in the faculty lounge, and every kid in the school came by the library to have a piece. I thanked him by screaming his name at night, every night.

And the clock wore on.

The days on the calendar didn't slow down for us.

His workouts got longer, and he came to me sweaty and sore. The smell of him. Testosterone and musk and the leather of a worn-out ball. He was rougher after a workout. More passionate. Less talking. More bending, twisting, grabbing. He growled lower and fucked harder. I couldn't come enough to satisfy him.

But if I didn't see him right after a workout, if he dressed and we went out... if he was showered and shaved and ready... he was not just powerful and strong but commanding and purposeful. I trusted him, and even as I took pleasure in that, I called myself a fool. Because I knew what was coming. His workouts weren't getting harder because he had nowhere to go.

"They look good this year," Jim said, handing me my crappy black coffee.

I was wiped out, as usual. Sore pussy. Knees a little rubbed from being on them. Overtired. High as a kite. "Yeah."

"You might have caught yourself a winner."

"I don't think I caught anything," I said. "He's going to Arizona in a few days."

"You going to the Freeway Exhibition?"

"Yes." I rolled the coffee between my palms.

Every year, I looked forward to the game in the middle of the practice season. Every year, my hometown team played the team two hours south on the 5 freeway, and every year, one team creamed the other before they both went off to polish up for Opening Day.

This year, I didn't look forward to it as much because it

wasn't about me sitting with Dad all summer and screaming at the TV. It wasn't about sitting in the bleacher seats a few times during the summer. It was about Dash and me and what I could or couldn't expect from him.

It shouldn't have been a big deal all things considered. He'd come back.

"Right?" I said in a moment of insecurity before the season-opening dinner. "I mean, you live here. You're not disappearing into a black void and never coming back."

I'd been trying to talk about where we were going during the whole car ride and gotten my nerve up way too late.

"I don't want you to worry about that," he said, pulling up to the valet.

Guys in white shirts and black jackets opened our doors before I could press him.

He held his arm out for me, and I took it.

The dinner was at Joe Westlake's place in Pacific Palisades. More money than God. Normally I'd have taken a moment to absorb the riches of the mansion. The view. The gardens. The opulence. But I couldn't.

"You've been avoiding this," I whispered. "Dash, I can't. I can't not know what's happening."

"Shortie!" Westlake called. He wore his bow tie and seersucker jacket. Same as always, except now he was just another thing between Dash and me.

Dash shook his hand and introduced me as if I mattered. So I must have.

Right?

I hated feeling like that. Hated the way the gourmet food tasted like plastic. Hated being jealous of all the other girlfriends and wives for knowing what would happen next, what they'd be doing, who they'd be seeing.

I almost wished we'd agreed to part ways when the season started. This felt somehow worse. The not knowing. The insecurity. I hadn't thought this would feel like a bigger gamble, not because I didn't have the stomach for him leaving but because he'd already been clear, from the beginning, *he* didn't have the stomach for it.

"What's wrong, sweetapple?" he asked softly in my ear.

What was wrong was three glasses of wine. He drove when we were together, and after I'd told him how my mother died, he stopped taking even a sip when he was behind the wheel. So at Joe Westlake's house, I had one more than I should have. The nerves kept me from feeling tipsy until it was too late.

The property was a massive expanse of tight little gardens and concrete sections, all set with different chafing dishes from the best restaurants in Los Angeles. Nothing halfway. As usual. Third party like this in three weeks. It wasn't boring, but all I wanted was to be alone with Dash. I touched him more than I should have, tightening my fingers around whatever part of his body was close, feeling the hardness of his muscles under his jacket, knowing what the force of them could do to my body.

"So you're the schoolteacher?"

A woman. Raven-black hair and red lips. Black dress. Skin like porcelain and curves that needed a speed limit.

"Librarian." I let Dash hold me up. He was talking to Gerry Jonson. Lot of numbers. Stats. I'd have kept up if this woman hadn't assumed I didn't want to hear it.

"Oh, sorry," she said, sipping champagne from a flute. "How do you like being his good luck charm? Best thing ever, right?"

"Could be worse?"

I had no idea what she was talking about, but I must have looked more conversational than incredulous, thanks to the wine, because she smiled comfortably and rolled her eyes.

"I know, right? The life." She winked.

I smiled, but my chest cratered, opening from the center out, sand pouring in from the edges, wider and wider as the evening wore on until I thought I'd fall into it.

I was pretty sober by the time we got in the car. His hand rested on the gearshift, and I placed my hand over it.

"In a few days, you're going," I said.

He didn't say anything.

"I know this was a hard limit for you. Maintaining this over the season."

"Maintaining?" he snapped. "What's that mean?"

Maybe the alcohol drain had left me vulnerable, or maybe the weight of all my denials had dropped on my shoulders, but I felt as if I'd been slapped. I had a ball of gunk to swallow, and I had to take my hand off his before he noticed it was shaking.

And of course.

Of course, of course.

That was the moment I realized I was in love with him.

thirty

Dash

I didn't mean to snap at her, but I did, and I didn't take it back. I didn't soothe her. I didn't grab her hand back when she took it away. I wanted to, but a high-minded part of myself stopped me.

Terror took over my body. The walls squeezing in on me. The season and her and everything I had to do to prepare and hadn't. I was two years from free agency and could be traded at any time. Pulled out of the deck, paired with a third baseman and a relief pitcher for an inside straight or an outfielder for a winning hand. The disruption would kill me, especially if it happened in the middle of the season.

I had no control. None. Maybe she was shaking. Maybe she was upset when I snapped at her, but I'd been losing my shit for weeks. The moment she walked out, the moment I saw her again, and all the moments in between were a hell of anxiety.

"I can't tell you what's going to happen," I said.

"You can tell me how you feel."

"How I feel? I feel like the sky is eight feet over my head, a million tons and falling fast. I don't know what you want from me, but I'm pretty sure I can't give it to you. I tried. But I'm squeezed."

She didn't say anything for a long time. I wondered if I could take it all back between now and the next traffic light. She was so soft, so vulnerable. I'd never do better than Vivian Foster, but the conversation was like quicksand. I was in up to the knees and getting sucked down.

"I don't understand what this has to do with me," she said,

"or how I can help."

Of course she wanted to help. She was that wonderful. I wanted to touch her. Take her home. Reveal the body under her clothes and crawl into it until her hurt was mine.

"I have my routines. If I break them, shit goes crazy. And already I've broken a lot. I have to put it back together. I have ADD, and I know everyone says they have it. Everyone blames the fact that they can't pay attention on their ADD. Well, let me tell you this is different. Measurably different. I should be a failure at this sport. I shouldn't be able to play, but I am. And the only way is through medication and managing my input and my distractions. I get up at the same time. I do the same things. I make sure that when I do something outside the routine, I'm prepared for it. The season is coming. I walk a tightrope six months out of the year. And I do it by keeping control of my environment. You turn my life upside down."

"I get it."

"You do?"

She nodded, and I took it at face value. I believed her. She was good. She understood. And that made the next suggestion seem sane and hopeful instead of insulting and demeaning.

"So we could just keep it geographic."

"What does that mean?" She sounded hopeful, as if I'd thrown her to the wolves then told the wolves to take a cigarette break. I felt filthy.

"Well." I had a moment to stop myself and say something else, but when I glanced at her, she looked so optimistic and beautiful I forgot who I was, and mostly, I forgot who she was.

Stop it, Dashiell. You're going to lose her, and it's going to hurt like fuck.

"We could do it this way." Not being able to look at her while I drove made it easier to say. Stupidly easier. "I have mostly night games, and you're off in the summer. I could fuck you senseless every afternoon I'm in LA."

"And when you're not in LA?"

I didn't know what made me think she wouldn't ask that or that it could be answered easily. Maybe I'd hoped she'd just know and be okay with it. But no. She was too smart for that, and I was too stupid to understand why.

"Well, when I'm not in LA—"

You're really going to say it?

Dance around it.

Say but don't say.

"Then we're not together."

"Meaning?"

Meaning she was going to make me say it.

Stand firm.

Everything is riding on this.

It hurts already.

"Meaning, I just... I have routines. Things I do to make sure I perform. And I can't do them if we're together."

"Such as?"

Fuck it.

I came to a choice in the road, where I could go toward figuring us out or trying to go back to normal. I chose the hard-won routines that had made my career possible.

I continued south on Beverly Glen instead of turning east.

I knew that wasn't just a direction on a compass. It was a decision made too quickly, under pressure, when all choices were cruel.

She didn't look at me. When I glanced at the right side mirror to make a turn, I saw the back of her head. She lived close by, in her father's house. He'd be there for her. That seemed important. If she was upset, she'd have someone who loved her better than I did because before it was even out of my mouth, I knew that even if she agreed to be my LA fuck, I wouldn't do her the disrespect of allowing it.

"There are women I see," I said. "It doesn't mean anything. Not like you do. But it's a ritual, and I can't stop because of you."

"I see."

"Look, you can't come between me and what I've worked for my whole life. I love fucking you, but if I stop playing ball because of it—"

"I never told you to stop playing."

"If I slump, I stop."

"Everyone slumps."

"I do not." I roared it, pointing at her, leveling the truth. My truth.

If I stopped fucking pussy from the city I was playing, I stopped winning. I wasn't turning back. Shit was going to get really blunt and really ugly if she pressed me. I was going to tell her where exactly I needed to come and how. Then she was going to cry.

God. This was a mistake. All of it. I hated anyone hurting her, and that night, I hated myself. I was repulsed by my own heart because it was small and mean and only had room for my own desires. I was a disgusting man.

"If I didn't like you," I softened it because I cared what she thought of me, "if I didn't think about you every second of the day, I would have just left. But I can't do this."

"You intended this the whole time," she said, looking out the side window.

"No. No, I didn't." I pulled up in front of her house.

"Liar," she whispered so softly I barely heard it.

"I thought it would solve itself."

"Whatever."

She opened the door, and I cracked mine, making the dashboard *ding ding ding*. I was supposed to open her door. It was a habit. But she was out and gone, slamming the door and running up the stone path.

Getting out first and opening the door for her was a promise of something more. A promise that I'd be careful with her body and her heart. As she ran up the steps and pushed the door open without needing to unlock it, I knew I'd broken that promise.

If I couldn't keep my word with a woman like Vivian, I'd never be a worthwhile partner to any woman. I sat outside, coming to terms with the fact that she was it. She was my last chance at love, and I'd blown it. I'd had a choice between a woman I could love the rest of my life and baseball.

I'd made the only choice I could have, and I had to be okay with that.

By the time I got home, I'd resigned myself to a life alone but secure, steady, and predictable.

Packing was easy. Sleeping was hard. Impossible.

The sheets smelled like fucking.

I stripped the bed, made it again, and stared at the ceiling until morning.

I missed her already.

thirty-one

Vivian

I wasn't surprised. I'd known deep down that it wasn't going to work, so I was as good as someone who had cut the bungee cord and jumped anyway. So I fell and fell hard, but I wasn't shocked when I met the ground.

"Of course I'm bummed," I said to Francine as I pulled blue and white balloons off the shelf.

She was helping me get supplies for Dad's birthday party and had a baseball piñata under her arm. "Yeah, but you're doing everything Dodger blue. Got the baseball balloons and the piñata. He's too old for a piñata."

"We have nieces and nephews who will be there. Should I get this silver fringey stuff?"

She snapped it from me and put it in the cart. "All I'm saying is, when Carl did that thing, you wouldn't listen to Procol Harum for... how long? Ever?"

"I never really liked Procol Harum in the first place."

"And you wouldn't go to the Singapore Lounge forever."

"This is different."

"It was shorter?"

"Yes. Shorter. Also I came out of it sad, yeah. I wanted it to work. I still wished it had. And I'm nuts about him. I cry, Francine. I cry every night. But it's because I miss him, not because I think I'm worthless."

"You're not worthless."

"That's what I'm saying. It was him. Not me. I wasn't too boring. I was actually too much fun." I did a little dance with my shoulders and snapped up a stack of blue cups.

My shimmy belied the depth of my tears. After he drove away, I'd taken two sick days and just bawled. My father shook his fists at heaven and threatened to sue the league for something, anything. I couldn't calm him down because I was in such a state. I could barely breathe, much less argue him out of taking legal action.

On day two, my eyes ached. I put an ice pack over them and, through the cold blackness, explained to my father that it was all right. I'd stop crying soon. I was in love with Dash Wallace. He didn't love me, and not only did that have nothing to do with any of my shortcomings, there wasn't a damn thing I could do about it. Dad didn't say anything.

But late on day two, he exploded when I stood in front of the fridge, looking at the cold inside as if it were a fish tank.

"That son of a bitch. I'm going to kill him." He leaned on the counter. He was having a bad day but refused to admit it while I was upset.

"It's fine, Dad."

"What I don't have because of the arthritis I make up for in bludgeons. I can hit him with my walker. I don't care if I go to jail. And God help him. That's all I have to say. God help him."

I shut the fridge. I didn't even know how to be angry. I couldn't work up the energy for it. I remembered why I was there and opened the freezer.

"It's fine," I repeated, getting out the ice pack again. "I'll get over it."

"I don't understand it. When I was a young man—and it wasn't that long ago if you ask me—when I was a young man and a woman like you came along, there would have been a fight. Big fight for you. Now they fight to see who can treat the best women the worst. It's disgusting. Taking pictures of their schlongs."

"Dad, really?" I put the ice pack over my eyes to reduce the cry-swell.

"They're all intimidated. That's the problem. They don't know how to act, so they act like animals, and they push the best ones away because they're afraid you'll wake up and realize you can do better. Mark my words, he'll either be back or be in the paper with someone so far beneath you he feels like a bigger man. You wait. It's gonna happen, and either way, you're still better than any man deserves."

"I don't think it's about deserving." I took off the pack. "I don't think it's a contest."

He grumbled something I couldn't make out, and I tossed the ice pack back in the freezer.

"You're a beautiful girl, you know that, right? Just say you know."

"I know. I'm also funny and sexy, but you can ignore the sexy part. I'm just..." I sighed, and the breath caught in a sob I dismissed for later. "We had a great time."

"I hope so, peanut. You didn't sleep in your own bed for weeks."

"Yeah." My tone was rueful. I couldn't help myself. All the hours I'd spent wrapped in his sheets, laughing and crying his name, flashed in my mind like a high-speed slideshow. "Anyway. I have today to wallow in grief, then I have to get back to work. Should I make the jambalaya?"

"If you cut the carrots."

"Deal. What do you want for your birthday dinner?"

"It's six weeks away."

"It's something to look forward to."

Francine and I were going out later to get his decorations and order his cake. Though Dash had licked envelopes on invitations, my time with him had kept me from doing anything else to get ready for the most epic surprise party in generations.

"Can you get the potato pancakes from Merv's?" Dad asked.

"What's wrong with the ones I make from scratch?"

"Eh, they're a pain in the ass. Just get from Merv's, and then you get the sour cream right there. It's easy. And the soup. You can get the soup. You're done."

It was clear he really wanted the matzo soup, which I'd

never gotten right. The balls always fell into a goopy paste. Well, he was going to have it. After the party store, Francine and I stopped on Fairfax Ave and ordered the full-on Jewish deli New York spread.

Maybe I couldn't make Dash happy, but I sure as hell could make my dad happy.

thirty-two

Dash

Hey bat boy

Janice texted a few hours after I got in. I was barely at the hotel when she tapped me. She understood me. She followed all the rules. She knew what happened when the rules were broken.

But the next line. The one I had to text…

Hello ball girl

And that was it. There would be no more communication until the next day. First day of spring training. I went to the practice field with Youder and a couple of the guys. It was a full-size field with bleachers and dugouts that hadn't been dug. The locker room smelled of feet and asshole, and we snapped towels and joked around.

I didn't think about Vivian.

There's only one ball girl.

Not once.

That was over.

Vivian. She was the ball girl. A real one.

I was back to normal. So there was no reason to think of her or regret my decision.

At all.

This is going to be weird.

Right?

Day one was the usual clown show. Pitchers and catchers had been there a week and were a little better organized, but the rest of us were just a bunch of fat assholes who had forgotten how to think. We played like Little League for the morning, and in the afternoon, we signed balls for fans at the bottom of the bleachers. A few dozen diehards and locals, and at the end of the line, a pretty woman with dark hair and brown eyes.

I took her ball. "Hi, ball girl."

Yeah. That's not going to work anymore.

What was I supposed to replace it with? And could I replace it?

"Hey, number nineteen. I got us at the Westin."

I signed the ball. It was the right hotel. Was the hotel or the girl the thing that kept me out of the slumps? Maybe. I hoped so. "Our room?"

She winked. "Yep."

I handed her the ball, signed. She beamed every time. I liked that.

"See you at seven. Be ready."

Her eyes twinkled. *Ready* meant one thing. Naked. One time she'd been clothed, and that had been my worst opening. It had taken a month to fix it. Not until I fucked Rose in New York did I start playing like I should have.

"You coming to dinner tonight, Wallace?" asked Randy. He was already after-shaved and clean-pressed.

I was still in a towel. I felt slow. "Nah, got someplace to be."

"That girl?" He raised an eyebrow. "The one you brought to Westlake's place?"

The locker room was loud and boisterous. I barely heard him.

"Nope," I said.

"She was fuckhot."

"Shut up, Randy."

"She going to be your Los Angeles fuck or what?"

"Stop talking."

"Because if not, I love to tap fans. They're—"

I wasn't as slow as I'd thought. Not with my hand

completely bypassing my brain and grabbing his throat or my arm getting in on the action and slamming him against the lockers.

"Fuck—?" he choked out. He grabbed my arm, clutching, fingernails digging.

I didn't even feel it. "I said to stop talking."

A little *gack* escaped him, and he swung at me. The upbeat noise of the locker room was shut off as if it had a switch. I wanted to choke the fucking life out of him, and I squeezed.

I didn't squeeze. My hand had a life of its own. Dashiell Wallace didn't choke people.

I'd warned him.

Little fuck.

"Dash!"

A voice behind me. An older, wiser voice. Youder.

"Let go before I clock you."

I glanced at him. He had a bat over his shoulder. The entire team stood behind him.

What the hell was I doing?

I let the little fuck drop. He pushed me. Ran at me. Forty guys rushed in to keep us apart.

Part of me wanted to kill him. Part of me wondered what had just happened. I was still wrestling with wanting to wring out that little bitch, and I was watching myself act like a fucking animal.

I was pulled into the showers. Dropped on a wood bench.

"All right, all right!" Youder shouted, arms out, body between me and the guys who had dragged me off that asshole. "Everyone out!"

Grumbling. Hand-slapping.

Randy's a dick.

First day. Always fucked up.

See you out there.

When it was just him and me, Youder sat next to me.

"I lost control," I said. "I'll write him a fucking note."

"He's a moron."

"I'm going to get fined."

"Yup. And you'll pay it."

"Do my penance."

"You got a real control problem, Shortie."

I faced him. I was in a towel, and he looked spit-shined.

"Winnie was born in March," he continued, mentioning his daughter. "I had this adjustment period. A full fucking season with my head in my ass."

"That was three years ago."

"Yeah."

"Man, I practically had to play the bag for you."

"I know. And fuck you. Because we cover for each other. I had a new baby, shithead. I wasn't sleeping. Dana wasn't taking care of her usual because she had the baby. I wasn't eating what I usually did. Wasn't working out at the regular time. I wasn't doing any shit I was supposed to. Worst batting average in my career. And the errors? Well, you know about those."

Every word he said wound me up. My heart was inside a wire coil, and he was twisting it.

"I'm not changing anything, all right?" I said.

"That's not what I'm saying—"

"Everything is the same." I wasn't shouting, but my voice couldn't have been more definite. He had to believe me. Had to. "I'm not doing anything different than any good year I've had."

"How long can you keep that up?"

I stood. This was the shittiest day on record. "Forever, all right? Until I retire. Whichever comes first."

I went out to the dressing room, snapping off my towel.

Fuck him and his shitty story.

Fuck Randy and his mouth.

Fuck Vivian's sweet cunt and that laugh and her goddamned kindness.

I wrestled myself into my clothes. I had a date tonight. The same date I always had. And I had to replace the girls I'd lost in Oakland and New York because change was an error. It was a swing and a miss. It was a failure of effort.

I didn't have room to fail.

thirty-three

Dash

The Westin was nice. It was always nice. They'd changed a couple of the couches, but otherwise it was the same lobby I'd crossed at 6:58 p.m. on the first day of spring training every year since year two of my pro career. That was when everything had clicked into place. When being celibate stopped working and having pussy on me made me play better.

Pussy was the antidote to miscalculation.

Suite #19. My number. The door was ajar. That was part of Janice's turn-on. She was on the bed with her legs spread, wearing nothing but a smile. Someone could come in and see her naked.

I locked the door and turned the corner of the suite. I made sure she could hear me. I whistled as I dropped my stuff, took off my jacket. I made sure my buckle clacked when I undid it. Opened my fly and untucked my shirt on the way to the bedroom.

A single yellow nightstand light was on.

She was there, all smiles. Legs spread. Tits pointing up. Hands grasping the headboard. I slipped my belt out of the loops and threw it on the end of the bed. I'd use that later.

"Hi," she said. Her knees dropped another quarter inch as she relaxed.

I could see how wet she was, and I had a raging boner to match. "Hey."

"Wanna fuck?" she purred.

I approached the side of the bed.

The answer was yes. Yes, I wanted to fuck. Yes, I wanted

to have another .400. Yes, I wanted to lead the league in double plays, and yes, I wanted to come inside and all over her.

But not really.

She turned and made a pouty duckface, and the first thought that came to mind wasn't anything like, "I'm going to put my cock right between those lips," but, "Vivian doesn't make stupid fake faces like that."

And when she said, "Feed my pussy," and bit her lip, I didn't want to come back with more dirty talk. I wanted to laugh.

Janice and I didn't laugh.

If Vivian ever told me to feed her pussy, I'd laugh. She'd laugh. We'd fuck. I'd feed her pussy all night, laughing.

If I fucked Janice, there was no more laughing with Vivian. I couldn't go back to her with or without an apology.

If I fucked Janice or anyone else, the door back to Vivian was closed.

Everyone's going to laugh at you.

They're going to talk about you.

Feel sorry for you.

Are you ready to bat .200?

Are you ready to fuck up?

Are you ready for the slump?

I seized. I wasn't ready for that. I reached for Janice's knee to open her legs and stopped before I touched her, leaving my hand hovering.

"Thank you," I said.

"Not yet, baby."

"Thank you for all the good years. We had some great times."

She looked at me with big brown eyes and lips that didn't pout anymore. They were tight and defensive.

"I'll take care of the room, as always. But I can't this time." I zipped my fly.

She took her hands off the headboard and closed her legs. Sighed. I got ready for recriminations and a fight. But not too many. I had to get up in the morning. Even if I fucked her raw, I'd have left by eleven.

"You could have told me before I hired a sitter," she groused.

"I know. I'm sorry. I can cover it."

"I'm not a whore."

"I never treated you like one."

She looked at her watch but never made eye contact with me. "Whatever. Just get out."

I got out. I put on my jacket, paid the bill, got her room service, and sat in the rental car, shaking.

Jesus Christ. What had I done?

thirty-four

Vivian

The decorations were up. We were crouched behind sofas and chairs. My friends. Dad's friends. His brother and sister and their kids and grandkids. The house was alive, holding its collective breath as Dad's car pulled into the drive. He'd gone out for pre-latke-and-soup coffee with Sylvia, the lady from the deli counter at Ralph's. He'd changed his medication, and the rheumatoid arthritis pain had become less and less severe. He hadn't used a walker in weeks and only occasionally needed his cane. When he'd told me he'd had the confidence to ask Sylvia out instead of just asking her to peel the potatoes, my eyes stung with happy tears.

I hadn't wanted to meet Sylvia at a surprise party, but seeing as I couldn't change the party, I went to Ralph's to meet her on my own. Then I told Dad when I got home. Pretending she and I were just meeting at the party wasn't fair.

He looked stricken. "Peanut, I wanted to have a dinner."

"I needed pickles, and I know you don't like the ones in the jar," I lied. "She had a name tag. I said hi. She's very nice, Dad. And not just to me. To everyone. The lady in front of me was being a complete bitch, and she was still nice. Real nice. Not fake nice."

"Yeah," he said, flipping through channels. It was after midnight, and the pickin's were slim. "They send her to the worst customers. By the time they walk away, they're smiling."

He settled on one of the ESPNs, on some statistical yackety yack involving a players' strike that wasn't going to happen, and I didn't even think to ask him to change it. I didn't know what I was going to do over the course of the season, if seeing him on the field was going to hurt me too much or if even in the breadth of the stadium I'd feel the heat of his body.

But it wasn't the season yet. I had time. I had Dad's party the next day, and I had to get the library in shape for a funding drive, then I had summer vacation. I didn't expect to be over Dash Wallace by then, but I didn't have to figure out if I had to start rooting for Anaheim just yet.

That was why his face caught me off guard, landing in my throat like an olive I couldn't swallow. First in a rectangle in the corner of the screen, still and perfect, with a predatory look outward, with the header *Spring Training Report.*

Dad fussed for the remote while the announcer droned about something, but his hands were swollen and stiff. He couldn't find the button to change the channel.

"Sorry, sorry," he grumbled to my broken heart.

I hadn't said a word because it was crazy, but the sight of him brought it all back. When the picture flipped to clips of the Arizona practice field and Dash's body running across it, my sorrow hit a new low.

He couldn't catch a freaking ball to save his life. Tape of the pathetic drills looped over and over. Error. Error. Error. It was freakishly bad. I'd never seen him play like that. It was as if a Little Leaguer had stepped onto the field for a charity match.

"Stop," I said to Dad, leaning over so he couldn't change the station.

Scouts and sportswriters are calculating the odds that the current world champions will be in fourth place by the All-Star Game without Wallace's A-game. With Randy Tremaine's slugging percentage at a career high, there's speculation number 19's moving down to the bottom of the lineup.

They shot a second of him close. Profile. Walking off the practice field with his head down. He knew people were watching. He wanted to hide. He was ashamed.

How did I know?

I just did.

He'd hurt me. I knew he was sleeping with other women. I knew he'd forgotten me. I knew what we had together wouldn't be repeated, but I felt no joy in his failure. I was sick to my stomach for him.

The next morning, prepping Dad's twenty-five-man roster ball, I placed it in the little glass stand with Dash's big blue name facing up. I wanted to remember that confident player. That king of the Elysian. I wrapped the box in blue paper and immersed myself in decorating the house and entertaining the guests while Dad was out.

"They're here!" Aunt Bette said from her spot by the window.

I was in the center of the room because I lived there, so I didn't have to hide.

Sylvia and I had arranged it. She was going to let Dad walk in first. Tie a lace on her shoe or something. I'd left the door unlocked as usual.

"Wait," Aunt Bette whispered sharply. "Who is that guy?" She glared at me. "Didn't you say not to come after seven?"

Aunt Bette was always a little stern. I walked to the window amid the whispers behind the furniture and peeked through the seam between the curtains.

"Shit," I said.

"Mouth!" Aunt Bette shot to me.

Fuck her. My life had just exploded.

Dash.

Dash Wallace.

Three-time Golden Glove shortstop with a .380 career average and the gentlest filthy mouth was in my driveway with a huge bouquet of pink roses, opening the car door for Sylvia. I put my hand over my mouth. My lips remembered his, and my fingers told them about the sweet silk of his cock. It was my heart that shouted the loudest. Screamed for him to make me laugh, soothe me, goad me into those moments when I didn't worry about anything but how to please him. My nose and eyes tingled with the threat of tears, and my throat closed around a big lump.

Dash and Dad exchanged words. I couldn't hear them, but they were pointing at Sylvia. She laughed and waved. Dad sniffed the roses and shrugged. Dash pulled one out and gave it to Dad. He passed it to Sylvia.

"Who is that?" Aunt Bette hissed.

"Dash Wallace," I said, "He's a—"

"The shortstop?!" My eleven year-old cousin stood ramrod straight from behind the couch.

"Get down!" three people said simultaneously.

His father pulled him down.

"Friend," I finished.

The three of them came up the front walk, Dash and Dad talking seriously and Sylvia trying to stay behind. Dad wouldn't let her. Goddamned gentleman.

Well, the original plan had changed, and I was bursting out of my skin anyway, so I opened the front door. I was supposed to have eyes only for my father. It was his birthday. I was supposed to get him in the house. Shout surprise. Make sure he didn't have a heart attack. Give him a fraction of the love he'd given me over the years.

But I only had eyes for the guy with the flowers.

Don't cry.

"Hey," I said.

He was ten feet away and three feet below, all dressed up in a suit like the day he had waited outside my library. My heart sighed. I hadn't dared to hope he'd ever be in my driveway again, so seeing him flooded me. Joy first, then pain. Acceptance then rage. Forgiveness then bitterness. What had he been doing for the past few weeks? Who had he been sleeping with? Was he in for the weekend? Was he trying to make me his LA girl? I guarded my heart with tinfoil armor. It was the strongest thing I had against him.

"Your dad said you made potato pancakes," he said. "And I like potatoes."

"There's plenty," I replied. I wasn't going to ruin Dad's party with drama, so I stepped aside and made room.

"Birthday boy first."

"Ladies first," Dad said.

"Oh, I left something in the car," Sylvia said with her lilting Honduran accent.

Dad, of course, started back to get it for her. The slapstick comedy of chivalry in the front of the house was maddening.

"Dad, can you let Dash help her? I have an emergency with the matzo soup. I know you told me not to make it, but I had to try."

Sylvia was already at the car, waving for Dad to just get on with it.

He did. His knees still ached, so he was slow up the steps, but he finally got in the door.

"*Surprise!*"

The shout went up without a hitch, and Dad laughed and whooped right after. I heard it all, but I didn't see it. Dash had stepped into the doorway, and he filled my vision with his piercing blue eyes and talented lips. I couldn't tear my eyes from his face. His body. The heat coming from it. The smell of grass and summer. The tinfoil was crumpling.

"Can you forgive me?" he said softly.

"Not if you ruin my father's birthday."

He leaned in to kiss me.

And... no.

I pushed him away gently. "It's not that easy."

He stepped back. Nodded. Handed me the roses. "First step: I'm an asshole."

I took the roses. "Good start because you're leaving Sylvia standing on the steps."

He looked at her as she stood, waiting, then he smiled in that way that turned me into jelly. We got out of the doorway and joined the party.

When he came in, Francine's eyes went birthday-cake big. I shrugged, letting her know that if she was stunned, emotional, elated, curious, I was all that and more.

thirty-five

Dash

In a way, I'd spent the last six weeks planning to see her again. In another way, I was playing it completely by ear.

I'd tried implementing new routines in Arizona. This thing, that thing, then the other. The shame of going back to her with my tail between my legs was too much to bear. If I did that, I'd have to tell her everything. I'd have to have the guts to change my life around.

Every grounder I missed, every time I was caught looking, the walls closed in.

I flew back a month into spring training for an exhibition game.

The game didn't matter. I was a complete cockup. I was letting everyone down. I couldn't even pass a ball to Youder for the double play. He was ten feet from me. If I fucked up the season before his free agency, he was going to be offered a bag of shit. That was on me. I didn't want him to go, but I didn't want to fuck him over either.

I had to do this better. I had to get control.

I dug out the stairs on the slope. Turned out the roots of the avocado tree had been holding the mountain up, and now the ground was going where water and gravity told it to go. So I could shore up the hill, which I did, but I had to unearth the steps. Otherwise, the only way to get down was to slide and slide.

I stayed back half a day and drove to her school. I watched the library windows for a sign of her. Stayed in my car and waited for her to walk to her crack-pipe car. The rear passenger tire needed air. I took the pump out of my trunk and filled it. I noticed it was as bald as a turnip and hustled back into my car like a criminal. I wondered if I could change it completely before she got out.

I missed my opportunity. She left with that guy. The one from the Petersen. He touched her shoulder when he said good-bye, and I wanted to rip out his arm. I opened the door to do just that, getting a foot on the pavement. She got in the car and was far away from him before I even stood straight.

This was me.

This was the core of me. Slow. Misdirected. Impulsive. Unaligned with the rhythms everyone else walked to.

I hadn't fucked Janice at the Mesa Westin, and without that, the rest of the preseason rituals were forgotten or rendered meaningless. The last time I'd felt right was when I was with Vivian.

I had to go back. All the way back, before I'd built anything. I was running out of time. I had to accept that I was obsessed with her, ask for forgiveness, and rebuild around her. Without her, I'd not only be worthless all season, I'd be plain worthless.

When I saw her in the doorway, I knew I'd done the right thing. Anxiety molted off me. I left it on the sidewalk like an old skin.

I couldn't keep my eyes off her. I didn't touch her. Barely spoke to her. The room was populated with Dodger fans, and they were all very nice. I talked about the previous season and the upcoming one. Showed one of the kids how to throw. Caught her glance whenever I could.

Her father opened his signed ball after dinner.

I signed hundreds of balls a year, and I had no idea what they meant to anyone. I didn't know if they went in the trash or on solid gold pedestals. But I did know what happened to that ball.

He turned it over in his hands a few times, looking at all the signatures. I couldn't see his face.

"All twenty-five from last season," Vivian said, wringing

her hands.

"You give me such *naches*," he said. "I'm *kvelling*."

I didn't know what he was talking about, but a collective *aww* went up in the room when he put the heel of his hand to his eye, rubbing away a tear. Vivian hugged him, and he clasped her as if she was about to run away.

I sat with my drink in my fingers and knew why she didn't want an expiration date. She couldn't just take her pleasure and go on with her life. She had a bare minimum expression of love, and it was the love her father had for her. She wouldn't take anything less.

And why should she? She deserved the best a man had to offer.

An hour later, I got a taste of it. I went to the kitchen to drop my plate in the sink, and her dad was there, pouring himself a glass of water.

"I didn't get a chance to wish you a happy birthday," I said. "My timing was terrible."

"Thank you." He popped open a clear plastic pill box and emptied it into his palm. I started back into the living room, where I had been having a great conversation with his brother on pitch counts and foul balls, when he stopped me. "She's not a plaything."

"I realize that."

He looked as though he didn't believe me, and I didn't blame him.

"I don't want to be that dad who gets in his daughter's business where he's not wanted…" He tossed the pills back and took a big gulp of water. "But don't be a fucking *putz* anymore."

"I won't. I don't know what a *putz* is, but I'm sure I can stop being it."

"It's a man who takes women for granted is what."

"I won't. Not Vivian ever again."

"Good. Now stop making eyes at her and ask her if she needs anything." He winked.

That was a relief because I knew I wouldn't get anywhere with Vivian if her father wasn't on board.

thirty-six

Vivian

I'd used paper plates, but on the buffet, I put out the good serving trays. None fit in the dishwasher, so I stood over the sink, washing them by hand. The water was near scalding, and my hands were wrinkly. I could see the yard from the window in front of the sink. The remainder of the guests were around a table outside.

Dash drank from a water bottle and laughed at something my uncle said. He'd talked baseball with anyone who asked, took some pictures, signed some stuff, but had become part of the furniture in the first hour.

That was, if whenever I looked at the furniture, I had to check to make sure my buttons were fastened. He managed to catch my eye from across the room, over cake, while telling the story of his game-winning hit in game four of the World Series, and every single time, he didn't break the flow of whatever conversation he was having. Not a millisecond. Yet I could feel his thoughts tracing lust all over the surface of my body. He was an exceptional multitasker.

I hadn't mentioned the *Spring Training Report,* and I wouldn't. I didn't yearn for his stats. I craved his touch and his laugh, his Shakespeare quotes and his attention. Even his awkwardness. Everything.

I turned away from the window to dry the oval serving tray and stack it. When I turned back to the sink and looked out the window, Dash wasn't at the table.

I saw him in the glass's reflection and felt his lips on the back of my neck. With a reaction that was no less instinctive than breathing, I tilted my head to expose my skin to his kiss. He let it linger, moving to my shoulder, warming me with his breath. Every cell in my body vibrated for him, and every sinew of my heart cried foul.

"My body says yes," I said, "but I want you to listen to my voice."

He drew his lips along the edge of my ear, and I leaned into him.

"Stop," I whispered, hoping he'd ignore me.

"Stop what?" He slipped his hand under my dress.

"Messing with me."

"I'm not." His finger curled under the edge of my underwear.

I was wet, soaked, and he was a quarter second to feeling it.

"I want you. I want to watch you come." His face was so close to me I heard him swallow. "I miss you."

Just those three words said softly, with his fingers between my legs, opening my heart and body to him, and the lump that had been wedged in my throat all night nearly choked me.

I turned to face him. He removed his hand from my underwear. I put my hands on his chest, keeping a barrier between us. "Dash—"

"No." He pressed two fingers to my lips. "Let's do this fast before I take your clothes off. I made a mistake. A big mistake. When you drove away, you took my destiny with you. I felt like my future was pulled out of me."

I leaned back on the sink and crossed my arms.

He took his fingers from my lips. "I know what you're thinking, and there are no other women. None. There's only you and the ways I've failed you. You don't have to give me a second chance. I know that. But I want you to. I'm going to beg you if I have to."

I'd thought the tinfoil over my heart would crumble, but it didn't. In the flame of his words, it was blown open, charred black, and turned to flakes of ash.

"You can't do this again," I said. "I'm fine without you. I want you, but I won't be hurt repeatedly while you figure yourself out."

"I've figured it out. It's you. You're the end of all the figuring."

"That all you got?"

"'The very instant that I saw you, did my heart fly to your service.'"

Shakespeare. He was full of shit. He had to be. But my mouth and my tongue found his, colliding in a crush of need. My arms uncrossed and went around him, embracing the fresh-cut grass scent, the attention of his lips, the fire that dropped down the base of my spine and settled between my legs in an explosion of desire that was close to painful.

Dash hitched my knee over his hip and pushed his erection against me, and my pussy remembered what my brain had tried to forget. I gasped and groaned, eyelids fluttering, body shifting into him, his breath on my face a reminder of how close he was.

I was going to say something about the people outside. How they could come in any minute. It was getting late, and someone could walk in and see me putting my legs around him so I could feel the length of that gorgeous cock against me.

But I didn't have time. Not a second. He got a hand under my ass and picked me up. I wrapped my legs tighter around him.

"Which way?" he asked.

Which way?

Down, of course. Inside. Hard.

I heard a chair scrape outside and the rhythm of voices.

"Down the hall." I pointed. "Through the den. Door to the right."

By the time I said "den," he was already carrying me through it. He threw me on the bed. Tape and wads of wrapping paper and ribbons bounced with me as he shut the door.

Was I breathing? Yes, I was. So hard and fast I couldn't even feel it.

He stood over me, pants tight in the front where his dick

was hard, and yanked his belt open.

I asked myself if I trusted him. If I let him in and he hurt me again, the wounds would be in a different place. He'd open me where the hope lived—the hope that he'd come back, that we'd have a second chance, that what we had was meaningful and real. I couldn't imagine the pain of it.

I sat up. He pushed me down. Kept his hand just above my sternum, leaning against it as he got his hand under my skirt. He hooked his finger around the crotch of my underwear and yanked them down and off. He was so dominant. So in charge. Every worry dropped off me and my defenses went with them, replaced by a vibrating desire. He folded his lips inside his teeth when I groaned.

"I don't have anything." I pointed at my dresser as if that meant anything. "No condoms."

He pulled me up, turned me onto my stomach, and pulled my hips toward him.

"I'm taking care of it." With that, he put two fingers in my soaking pussy and pressed against the place where pleasure lived.

I swallowed a scream.

"No, no, sweetapple," he whispered. "There's a full house."

"Sorry, I'm just… it's so good."

His fingers left me, and I was disappointed for half a second, exhaling, getting myself together to have the quietest orgasm in history. Closing my eyes. Steeling myself.

Fabric against my lips. Pushing. Lace. The smell of my pussy.

I opened my mouth to complain, and what the heck?

He was shoving my underwear into my mouth. *Holy what?* I turned around to tell him this was my good underwear. The La Perla's. Hundred fifty dollars. I didn't want to eat a hundred fifty dollars' worth of lace. French panties didn't come halfway around the world to get ruined by my teeth.

Too late. Looked as if that was exactly why they'd made the trip.

He had the birthday ribbon around my head in the split

second, and he was knotting it, securing the underwear in my mouth.

Didn't he say something about being an Eagle Scout? Because the knot went in quick, and his fingers were back in my pussy, which found ten new reasons to be wet.

He leaned against me, the skin of his dick and the fluttering touch of his shirt on my ass. "Today. Now. You're mine, you beautiful thing. No one else is going to have you."

I made some vowel sound against the lace that was thirty percent complaint and seventy percent give-it-to-me.

He only heard the seventy percent, sliding his dick in as though he owned the joint and setting my pussy on fire. I was close before he entered me. Once he was buried inside, I went someplace else. A place with no words, only colors.

Heaviness on my back, between my shoulder blades, and I fell under it. He pushed me against the bed. I lost myself in his thrusts. Unable to speak or move, I was only made of vibrations. I didn't think the promise of pleasure could expand further until I felt pressure against a place that had never been touched, and I squeaked.

"Hush," he said, pressing a wet finger against my ass.

I had to obey. I wanted to. His thrusts shifted to a painfully slow pace. Every inch of his finger in my ass, every inch of his dick inside my pussy.

Gradually and deliberately, he filled me. I hadn't known it would be good. I'd had no idea. It was too much. I couldn't hold it. I was on the left side of an orgasm, pushing against the membrane to the other side, but he wouldn't let it break.

Outside. Dishes. Laughter. The other side of the door. People.

"Where's Vivian?" someone called from the hallway.

I was pushed closer to the edge, almost caught with my underpants in my mouth and a finger in my ass. Fear buzzed and amplified the pleasure.

"I'm going to fuck you hard," he whispered, pressing me down. "Don't make a sound."

Pain shot through my ass and transformed into something

else when he stuck two fingers in. Not pleasure necessarily. A presence. Another anchor.

I came with a sob. I felt my ass pulse against his fingers. My body tightened like a guitar string and broke. I cried. Just cried into my hundred fifty dollar panties. My ass was released, and he was above me, lips at my ear, breathing staccato as I felt a warm liquid on my lower back.

We breathed together.

Well, he breathed. I was still sobbing.

"Vivian? Are you in there?"

It was Aunt Bette. Dash fumbled with the ribbon, biting back a laugh. It wasn't funny, but it was, and I couldn't help but laugh myself.

"Vivian, are you all right?"

My underwear expanded, and Dash plucked it out, his lips on my cheek.

"I'm fine," I said from under him then whispered, "You owe me a hundred fifty dollars, mister."

"I owe you a cleanup back here too. Jesus, did someone jizz on you or something?"

I wished I had the underwear back because I had to cover my mouth I was laughing so hard.

"Are you coming?" Aunt Bette said from the other side of the door.

"No, I—"

Already came. I stopped myself mid-sentence before I blurted it out. As if he could read my mind, Dash bit back his own laughter.

I swallowed mine long enough to answer. "I'll be out in a minute."

I pushed up, but he wouldn't let me go. "I want to make you come again. And again. And again. You're magic, you know that?"

"I'm about to be a family spectacle."

"Please tell me I can get to a sink without going through the hall."

I pointed at the bathroom door.

"Don't move," he said.

He kissed a butt cheek and went to the bathroom. The water ran, and I let my body sink into the mattress. I didn't know how stressed I'd been until the tension went out of me.

The sink ran, and he came back buttoned up, carrying a white washcloth. He straddled me, and I felt the warm roughness of the cloth on my back.

"I have to be back by Monday, early," he said.

"I have to clean up tomorrow."

"I can get a staff of people in here to make this place sterile while I fuck you dirty."

He got off me and patted my back, indicating he's gotten me clean.

"That's a great offer, but…"

But what?

But I had plans.

But it's weird.

But a part of me is just flat uncomfortable with it.

Which part? I searched the hallways and doorways of myself, looking for the words to describe my unease. Feminism, adulthood, personal responsibility—all were perfectly fine with him getting people to clean up the party.

"And then," he said, putting his nose to mine, eye to eye, filling my vision in a way I had been convinced would never happen again until he'd shown up in my driveway with roses. "And then we have to talk about when you're going to start traveling with me."

There. The unease was there, and it exploded like a land mine.

There was a knock at the door again.

"Peanut?" It was dad.

I pushed Dash off me.

"Give me a minute." I opened my drawer and rummaged around for new underwear. I hopped into a plain cotton pair.

Dash was standing in his suit, watching me, looking at me in a way that only hinted at his delicious depravity. I checked the mirror, straightening myself until I didn't look as if a man had just had his fingers where the sun didn't shine. He was visible in the mirror, hands in his pockets.

He wanted me to travel with him. What did that even mean?

Another knock.

"Dad! I said one minute!" I snapped.

"Is Mr. Wallace in there?" It was Jacob.

He and I looked at each other. I guessed there was no denying it. Jacob continued without pause while our gazes were locked.

"I want to say good-bye, and my mom said not to bother you, but I am anyway."

Dash didn't look away. "I'm here."

I opened the door. The room probably stank of sex. I could only hope Jacob wouldn't recognize it or notice the crumpled panties on the bed.

Dash went to the door and patted Jacob on the back, said something encouraging, and headed out. I caught myself in the mirror one last time before I went to be a good hostess.

Travel with him.

I didn't look just-fucked as much as I looked terrified.

thirty-seven

Dash

"Think about it," I said in her driveway.

She wasn't coming home with me. She wanted to be with her father on his birthday. I understood it, but I hadn't expected it, and I felt as if she was unspooling my rope from the mooring.

"I will." She looked at her shoes.

I didn't believe her. At least, she wasn't going to think about it the way I needed her to think about it. She was going to talk herself out of it. I could tell. She wasn't giving me the openings to convince her.

"I'll put you in great hotels. There's one in Chicago with an indoor pool under a retractable glass roof."

"Sounds nice."

"You'll have great seats. Skybox for every game."

"Okay."

I couldn't see what she was thinking. She was hiding. I took her chin in my hand and pointed her face toward me. If I could make her understand how important it was, she would stop looking away. She would say yes, and we could make plans right now instead of doing this weird dance of denial.

"I need you," I said, crouching to get at eye level.

She was a shitty actress. I could see the confusion all over her, and I understood it. I'd just dumped her a few weeks earlier. Broken her heart. And there I was, inviting her to travel with me and be mine in front of everyone. Of course she doubted my commitment.

I kissed her. She tasted of rosewater.

"I'll call you in the morning," I said.

"I'm glad you came," she said, hugging me.

We kissed a few more times, and I let her go back into the house, but I knew what I had to do. I had to make sure she believed I wouldn't drop her again. That my commitment was real.

She wouldn't be impressed by the luxuries that came with travel. I should have known better than that. It wasn't too late. I could sell her on fun, on sex. I only needed to earn her trust again.

I couldn't sleep. I juggled three balls, then four and I fell into the comfortable pattern of my disorganized nature.

I'd tried to teach her to juggle but everything fell she gave up and sucked me while I tried to keep them all in the air squealed when the balls fell on her concerns were real even though I didn't know what they were going to have to go back with or without her, but I'd fuck her all week so I'd be on base four times out of ten this season if I was right, she was the thing that was going to have to drop the others only Diane would be hard she was sensitive no fear like it was going too fast I had to make Vivian comfortable maybe she was afraid of planes or didn't want to leave her father all right for Youder to go free agent if I had her by my side I could play and forget this slump and go into the season strong.

It all made sense to me.

I was deep in the rhythm when I was distracted by the double ding of my phone. I dropped everything.

thirty-eight

Vivian

Dad had taken painkillers and retired to bed with Sylvia. There were two bedrooms between his and mine, but I sequestered myself in my room and took a long shower. I made sure Sylvia didn't see me when she tiptoed out. But once all was quiet, I sat in front of the television with my wet hair and let the blue light of the TV flicker in the dark room. I didn't even know what I was watching. A little sports. A little news. *I Love Lucy* came on, and it was as funny as ever, but I just smiled at their twin beds.

As if a hot potato like Ricky Ricardo was keeping a separate bed with that firecracker of a wife. She was always trying to interpose herself into her husband's business. Half the comedy was about how enamored she was of show business and how she didn't understand the work or preparation the job took.

I didn't have that problem.

Working for the LAUSD wasn't a sane person's dream. But it was my job. Sure, I could leave, and there would be twenty librarians to take my place. That wasn't the point.

Was it?

I liked my workmates. I loved the children. Hell, I had the whole next week off for spring break.

And I loved Dash Wallace. His return had been as much relief as I'd ever felt over anything in my life. I didn't see why I'd have to choose between them, but if I traveled with a baseball player over the course of an eight- or nine-month season, my job would be *kaput*.

I took my phone off the coffee table and flipped through a

211

bunch of stuff I didn't care about, then I did the one thing I couldn't get off my mind.

> Are you up?

It took too long for him to answer. I assumed he was asleep when the phone buzzed in my hands.

I was just thinking about you

> I can't travel with you

I was thinking how you looked gagged and held down

> It's not that it's my job or anything, but it is

There's something so fucking explosive about containing you and then making sure you can't contain yourself. It's like a nuclear bomb going off on my cock

> I need to have a life of my own

(...)

(...)

Was he thinking about an answer? Was he considering what I was saying? Or was he gone? Was my seriousness so unwelcome? How could I not be serious? There were 162 games. About half would be away games. Of the fifteen National League teams, eight crossed two time zones and required travel days.

I wasn't a calculus teacher, but the math for me being home and having any kind of consistent life was out the window.

He didn't answer. I paced a little, considered texting him again, but I had to assume he needed space. I had to trust he wouldn't just disappear. All those things were true, but I was still human and, yes, insecure. I was getting more and more anxious as the minutes passed, and when a text came in, I jumped.

I suggest you fall asleep in your ice skating dress

Why?

Good night, sweetapple. Opening day tomorrow. I need to sleep

I stared at the phone. Nothing. No sexy talk. No Shakespeare. No last good night. No running dots indicating he was typing.

Good night

The message was marked delivered, but I had no idea if he'd read it. Maybe he really had gone to sleep. Well, good for him. He knew what he needed for his life to work, but I didn't know if I was as clear about my own. I'd never had to think about it before. I just did what I had to do to make a living, maintain my relationships, finish school, coast from one day, week, year to the next.

Wasn't that sad? It would be so easy for me to just pick up and travel the country with him. Fourteen to sixteen regular season cities—with just one in driving distance. And what would I be leaving behind? My dad, who was fine without me. Friends like Francine who would probably pack my bags for me in the name of living my own life. Jim. Iris. All the kids. My city.

For a guy.

Really, it was all about me leaving everything behind for a man. Even if everything constituted a dozen intangibles, it was *my* everything.

thirty-nine

Vivian

I only knew I fell asleep because I woke up, and I woke up hard. *Morning Stretch* was on TV. Seven women in leotards, kicking and bending.

And up and down and kick and up and down and kick and knock knock knock and up and down and kick and bang bang bang and kick and tap tap tap and up and down and—

Tap tap tap.

I bolted up. Someone was knocking on the window behind me. It looked out onto the driveway. I peeked out past the curtains.

"Dash, you asshole."

He stood just below the sill, smiling in the blue morning light. The sun was barely up. I had gunk in my eyes and sleep saturating my system. I opened the window.

"I read lips, you know," he said.

"What are you doing here?"

He had on a hoodie and sneakers. He'd never come to see me looking like that. Even in my half-sleep, I noticed the difference in the way he dressed had nothing to do with how beautiful he was.

"Did you wear what I told you to wear?" he asked.

"What?"

I'd been dreaming. I remembered it as he was finishing his sentence. Something about shoveling dirt over a hole filled with books. All my romance books. I shook the sand out of my brain.

"I'm wearing sweatpants, same as you," I said. "Why are

you here?"

"I forgot how sexy you are in the morning."

"Who's that?" came Dad's voice from behind me.

I turned. He was in boxers and a T-shirt, hoisting a baseball bat over his shoulder.

"Dash."

"Did you tell him it's five thirty in the morning?" He lowered the bat.

"He's wearing a watch. I think he knows."

"There something wrong with the front door?"

I turned back to the man in the drive. "Dad wants you to come in like a normal person."

"Coming around," he said, projecting his voice. He stepped forward and whispered, "But you're coming with me now."

"After I shower."

"Nope."

He jogged down the driveway before I could respond. We met at the front door. He looked crisp and clean and ready for anything. Ten percent of my brain was still on the couch.

"Dash. What are—"

He craned his neck to address my father, who was leaning on his bat. Dad's hips hurt. He never knew what kind of day he was going to have until he woke up in the morning.

"I need your daughter for a few hours."

"Take her. Just don't break her."

"Funny, Dad." I put my hand up to Dash, ready to explain the desperate need for a shower and a change of clothes, but I didn't have a chance.

He grabbed my wrist and tugged. "Come."

"Seriously, I need to wash up."

He yanked me out the door. "No time."

I grabbed my bag and let him pull me to his black Volvo. "We're not seeing people, are we?"

"It's five thirty in the morning. Only priests and bakers are up."

He opened the door and tried to kiss me. I gave him my cheek.

"This is all you get when I don't brush my teeth," I said.

"Very considerate of you. Get in."

I got in, and he got behind the wheel and handed me a bottle of water from the center console.

"Drink. You'll feel as good about your mouth as I do."

I took a long swig. I did feel a little better, but I was still going to withhold kisses out of playful spite just to see how long I could resist.

He sped down San Vicente, which was empty, and onto La Brea.

"Where are we going?" I turned on his radio. He had a hip hop station loaded, and I left it but turned down the volume. Hip hop was all right sometimes.

"Echo Park."

"The King of Elysian Park going to show me his empire at sunrise?"

"I have to if I want to get you to work on time."

"Lucky you, I'm off all week for spring break."

He smirked as if he wanted to say something he couldn't. I was just glad I'd showered before bed.

"You asked me a big thing yesterday," I said as he stopped for a red light. We'd be on the freeway in a minute, and this was his last chance to take a long hard look at me.

"I did. And I still want you to travel with me. It's not that big a deal."

"I'm sorry?"

The light changed.

"Lots of players do it. When someone's important to them, they just make arrangements."

He meant it wasn't a big deal *to him*. I had a few dozen responses, but I held my tongue. I didn't want to tell him I had third graders who were less self-centered or that I was glad it wasn't a big deal for him since that made what it meant to me as irrelevant as he thought it was.

I tried not to get mad at him for being a jerk or at myself for not having a big, important life.

"You nervous about this afternoon?" I asked.

"Why would I be nervous?"

His tone was just a little sharp. I didn't know if he was aware that I'd seen *Spring Training Report* or if he cared.

"Opening day. Duh."

The hills of Elysian Park grew in the distance.

"Yeah, well, I'm kind of glad spring training's over. I'm ready to get out there."

"How did it go in Arizona?"

"You saw the exhibition games."

What did I have the right to say? What was my role here? We'd been broken up during that time, and we hadn't even mentioned his poor performance. We'd been too busy ruining my good underwear.

But he was kind of asking, wasn't he?

"Were you feeling all right?" I didn't know how else to put it.

He surprised me by smiling. "No, not at all."

"Bellyache?"

"Yeah, a two-month bellyache called Vivian-itis." He exited at Elysian Park and wound through the back ways.

"Shut up." He was making my face and neck tingle again.

"Symptoms include desperate longing and an inability to do anything but feel like a douchebag. Patient can't do shit on the field but stand there like an ass, wondering what the fuck he's doing with his life. It's chronic. No known cure."

"We'll try to manage the symptoms."

He pulled up to a back gate where a security guard sat by a portable wood stand. The guard was older than dirt, with a big smile and a bounce to his step as he approached the driver side.

"Number nineteen!" he exclaimed. "You're early. Grounds crew isn't even here yet."

"I know." He handed the security guard his license. "I'm just making sure it's all there."

"I think you'll be pleasantly unsurprised." He crouched to look through to me. "Hello, miss. Do you have a license you can show me?"

"Oh, sure." I fished it out, and he went to his little stand and wrote down our license numbers. "I still don't know why I'm here."

Dash rested his head against the back of the seat, eyes running up and down my body and landing on the bare ankle over my Keds. He stroked the bone and the skin along the edge of the sneaker. "If I tell you, it's going to be weird."

"I like weird."

"Good."

The guard handed back our IDs and hit a button on a little grey box he'd taken out of his pocket. The chain-link fence swung out.

Dash pulled forward.

Dodger Stadium was not a suburban, outer-city stadium. It had landed like a spaceship in the middle of the densest part of the city, with a huge forest of a park on the west side and the concrete crease of the Los Angeles River on the east.

The south crescent of the stadium was three hundred acres of sixteen thousand parking spots. I'd seen the lot full, clothed in darkness and spotted with floodlights. I'd been stuck in it for an hour, trying to get out after the eighth inning of a late-season blowout and during meaningless mid-season games. If there was a better way to plan for the exodus of sixteen thousand cars, no one had come up with it in time for Dodgers Stadium.

But that morning, the lot was empty as a winter's day, its grey as uninterrupted as a Christmas sky. The stadium below looked shoved into a corner like an afterthought. I took a deep breath. I'd never come in this way. Never seen the structure from that angle on such a clear morning. It was both diminutive and majestic.

"It's overwhelming," I said.

"You should see it from the field."

He twisted down into the lot, and everything fell back into proportion. After a few more checkpoints, we pulled into the back of the stadium, where an empty spot waited among many. The sign at the head said "Dash Wallace #19."

"It must all be worth it for your own spot at Dodger Stadium."

"Money's pretty good too." He shut off the car but didn't move.

I waited. He tapped the wheel.

"Why am I here?" I asked gently. "It's hours before game time, and you have plenty to do, I'm sure."

"Trust me."

Did I trust him?

He hadn't earned it.

But I did. I needed to. The alternative was unspeakably dreary.

"We're already at the stadium, slugger, and the sun's barely up. I must trust you."

He pulled back and took a look at me, eating me for breakfast, before getting out and opening my door. I took his hand and stepped out. When my little rubber sole hit the asphalt, I'd accepted a challenge I didn't think any living woman could meet.

forty

Dash

In hindsight, I was crazy. At the time though, I was getting control of my life. Being proactive. Solving problems. Fixing what was broken. All of those phrases seemed sensible when put next to what I was doing.

When she was finally in arm's reach, I knew everything would be all right. She would forgive me. I could have her again. Shit started clicking. It wasn't anything I could point at. I wasn't playing, so I didn't have any stats, but my guts stopped twisting. I felt hopeful. Not skipping-on-daisies hopeful, but I didn't dread getting on the field for opening day.

The bowels of the stadium were empty and scrubbed clean. The floors and walls would get progressively filthier over the season, but now they smelled like pine and bleach. New things.

"Wow," she said when I turned on the lights in the locker room. "I never thought I'd see this."

"How unimpressive is it?"

"Not special at all." Her eyes were as big as donuts, fingers drifting over everything. She stopped at my jersey. WALLACE and a big #19.

"I wanted you to see it before it got too busy."

She plucked my glove off the shelf and put it on her left hand. "No pin. You sure you're okay with that?"

"No choice, really."

"Here." She whipped off the glove and slapped it against my chest. I took it and she touched her right earlobe with both hands. "I still feel bad about the pin. I'm not a superstitious person, but let's pretend it matters." She got the gold hoop with the pearl at the end off her ear.

"You don't have to," I said.

"I know. Where should we put it?"

We huddled over the glove and found a strap the little earring fit around. I kissed her when it clicked. I kissed her long and hard, pushing her against the lockers because I wanted to thank her as much as I wanted to own her completely.

forty-one

Vivian

When he kissed me, it was as if he forgot himself for a minute, and I was no better. We were both rudderless in each other. He put his hands between my legs, four fingers flat on my crotch. The fabric of the sweatpants didn't stand a chance against him, yet it was too much of a barrier.

I reached for his dick, groaning when I found the shape of it.

He pulled back, panting. "Fuck, woman."

I heard a click or a tap from somewhere in the building. Not the locker room itself but close enough to remind me that we weren't alone. But he didn't pull away. He kept his hand still and on the warm, damp spot between my legs, his body so close I could see the brown flecks in his blue eyes.

They narrowed a bit before he spoke. "Come on."

He took his hand off my crotch and wove it in mine, leading me away.

"Where are we going?"

He didn't answer but pulled me alongside him, out of the locker room, past a long stretch of cinderblock hallway with buzzing fluorescents overhead, into a bigger area with benches and shelves full of equipment. He smacked the push bar of a nondescript door.

I assumed there would be another hall, another minimal room, a private place for us behind it. Instead the doorway opened into pure open space.

I stopped.

He pulled. "Don't be scared. No one's here yet. Almost no

one. The grounds crew is on the way. We don't have long. They'll start wiping seats and heating up the hot dogs. I wanted you to see this. I wanted you to imagine me out there, thinking of you."

I wasn't scared, and I wasn't worried about who was there. The stadium was empty. Just fifty thousand or so unoccupied seats. But I needed a moment to appreciate where I was going. Because the open space wasn't directly across the outfield or across the parking lot. It was the view from the dugout. I hadn't seen it since I was a ball girl.

I hadn't even been allowed in the dugout as a ball girl. It was sacrosanct, and superstition dictated only players, coaches, and managers in uniform could enter.

"It gets disgusting by July," Dash said when I stepped onto the concrete.

It was scrubbed clean. Every corner. Every surface. Every object I'd seen on television for years jumped out at me. The beige phone. The wood bench and bat rack. The bins of blue helmets.

He closed the door behind me.

The field was enormous. The seats went on forever. In the rows, people walked like ants on vertical pavement. Security guys checking for people and packages that didn't belong. I remembered them from my ball girl days.

"It seems bigger on the inside than the outside," I said, leaning over to touch the gravel.

I felt his hands on my shoulders then down my back, pushing me forward. I put my other hand down to steady myself, and he curved his body over me.

"You're a fucking knockout," he whispered in my ear, hooking his fingers in my waistband.

"What are you doing?"

"I told you to wear a dress." He yanked down my sweatpants.

I stopped breathing. The morning air hit my bottom. He'd gotten the underwear too.

"You are not—"

"I am. I'm christening this field with your orgasm."

"Jesus, Dash, I can't."

I had a reasonable explanation for why I wasn't going to let him fuck me in the dugout, but his arm snaked around me, and his finger found my clit before I could get a word out. All the air left my lungs. My clit was hard and wet and ready for him to turn circles all over it.

"What if someone…"

I couldn't finish. He unzipped, and the sound of it made my pussy clench and pucker for him.

He pushed my legs open with his foot. "No one's coming but us."

His dick at my opening, dry on wet, a four-alarm fire where we touched. I glanced all over the field. No one was looking. But it wouldn't take more than a glance for us to be a spectacle. No one did. They were far away and doing their jobs.

Slow and steady, he pushed forward inch by inch, almost methodically. I was so soaked for him he didn't have to thrust.

He pulled me up and spoke in my ear. "Act natural."

"You're joking."

He slid out slowly, his finger circling my clit. "Kind of. But try anyway." In again. Slow again. My eyes fluttered closed when he buried himself completely inside. "I want to fuck you on every base and eat you out in centerfield. I want to play every game with your pussy on me."

"Yes." I would have agreed to anything, logistics be damned.

"I need to come inside you."

His fingers gathered sensation like cotton candy in a sugar mill.

"Do it. Come in me."

"Show me first. Show me how you come."

His finger twitched a little differently, flicking instead of circling, while he got the length of him inside, filling me with him. My hips pushed back, begging for more, and he pushed his finger down. My muscles stiffened, and my mouth opened with soundless satisfaction. I let everything go and came in the Dodgers' home dugout.

"Thank you," I gasped when his finger slowed and stopped.

He pulled me back, letting his dick slip out. He grabbed a waist-high bin of bats and helmets and wheeled it closer.

"Come back here. Put your hands on the edge." Looking up, he changed the angle so I couldn't see the stands anymore. "I'm not going to be able to be discreet about pounding you right now."

I didn't ask how discreet we could be if someone came through to the dugout because from behind me, he pulled back the skin of my thighs and licked my sensitive pussy. My groan echoed in the empty space.

"Shush."

I felt his dick again, and again he didn't pause. Just used my wetness to slide inside. Not slowly. No, this time, he slammed into me. I had to brace myself against the bin as he did exactly what he'd promised. He took me from behind, pounding my pussy deep and fast, hands gripping my hips for leverage.

"Harder," I said. I wanted him to break me with it.

"All of it." I knew from his voice that he was close. "Take all of it."

"Yes."

He went as deep as I thought possible, balls slapping my clit, the base of his cock pulsing against me, grunting like the sexiest animal on the planet.

When he slowed, I turned to see his face above me. He pumped me one last time and pulled out.

"I declare this stadium christened," I said.

He pulled my waistband back over my ass. "Not yet."

"Not yet?"

He bit his lower lip and shook his head. I didn't know what a girl had to do to christen a stadium around here, but I was about to find out.

forty-two

Vivian

We stepped onto the field. The grass was pristine, and the decomposed granite that made up the dirt parts was smooth and even. The lines hadn't been drawn between the bases, but the square sacks that marked the bases were pristine white in the rising sun.

"It's been a long time," I said.

"Since you were on the field?"

"Yeah. Ten years. I was fifteen, and everything seemed as big then as it does now." I spun to look at the stands.

"I was playing college ball ten years ago." He pulled me to home plate. "Here, touch this."

"Touch what?"

"Home plate."

I leaned down and stroked it, thinking there was a texture he wanted to share, but once I did it, he took my hand and led me down the first base line.

"My first day on the job," I said, "I wore makeup because I thought I'd be on TV. By the second week, I barely brushed my hair."

"I bet you were still beautiful."

"Hey, I was too young for you, mister."

"Right. Forgot."

I jabbed him with my elbow. "How is it no one ever gets an interview with you?"

"I did *Rolling Stone* last May."

"On camera."

"I don't come off well on camera. Tag first."

"What do you mean? You're on camera all the time. You're gorgeous."

He pulled me back and pointed down. "Tag first."

He tapped first base with his toe. I stuck out my foot and tagged. Satisfied, he took my hand and walked me toward second base.

"When I was a kid. Second grade. Fourth grade. Up to sixth. I was a mess."

He stopped talking. I waited. I dealt with kids all day, every day. I knew what a kid with problems looked like, but I didn't know what young Dashiell with problems looked like. So I waited while he paced slowly to the next base.

"I didn't know how to regulate myself is what the therapist said. And I was both overstimulated in areas and under-stimulated in others. My brain wasn't wired right. Still isn't. But it's subtle, so it looked like I was just disrespectful and inconsiderate." He put his finger up and looked at me finally.

Once I could see him, I knew that what he was saying might have seemed inconsequential, but it was critical for him, and the words came hard.

"I was talking to my friend in the hall. Second grade, I think, and we were in line for the fountain. We were talking about, Jesus, who even remembers... something about drinking from the fountain and spitting it out. How far it would go if the drain wasn't there. And I wanted to show him how far, so I spit in his face."

I laughed.

He smiled. "It's funny now. At the time? I got suspended. It was always something like that. I had zero impulse control. When I had a tantrum, I had a fucking tantrum. Right? This is going somewhere, I promise."

I squeezed his hand. "You're not boring."

"Whatever you say. Tag second."

I leapt forward and landed both feet on second base and cried victory. "Stand up double."

He high-fived me. "Nice play."

He tapped second with his toe and took my hand so we

could continue to third.

"Okay, so my parents loved me," he said. "They gave me everything, and they were at the end of their rope. My mom... one day she took video of me flipping out so she could show me what I looked like. Maybe if I could see it, I would catch myself before I lost it again, right? And knowing she was doing that, seeing her with that little camera? I went... crazy."

He shook his head, his expression changing from mild amusement to shame to horror to courage to dismissal to guardedness in flashes so quick I had no idea how he was feeling. He stopped at the midpoint between second and third. Though he turned to face me, he looked up at nothing in the stands.

"So I hit my mother."

I felt how difficult it was for him to say it. If he had told a million people before me, you'd never have known it because it seemed so hard I could have been the only person in the world he'd told.

"I was in sixth grade, but I was big. It was the low point of my life."

I squeezed his hand. He'd been in sixth grade. Eleven or twelve years old, yet he carried it like a dead weight on his soul.

"And the cameras," I said, leading him to third. "You remember that when they're on you."

He pointed at two spots in the stands. "There and there." He pointed up at the announcer's booth. "There." He turned to the scoreboard and walked backward a few steps. "There and there. A couple more. When I'm playing, I'm fine. But as soon as I talk, I hear the way I screamed, and I feel like I'm that out-of-control kid again." He barely paused, glancing at me then away. "You think I'm crazy."

I tagged third. "No. Crazy is thinking you had to hit your mother. Sane is making sure you don't do it again."

He tapped the base and put his arm around me, walking me home and holding me tight.

"I did," he said. "I got it together."

"What did you do?"

"My dad wrestled me down, but it had all gone out of me. My mother had a bruise on her cheek and that little bit of video. It did the trick. I saw myself, and I hated it. I got my shit together. I took my meds. Kept a journal of how I felt until we hit the right ones. I let my parents set routines, and I stuck to them. I played baseball because I needed something to fill my time when hockey was off, and it was..." He put his hand on his chest and directed it outward as if the world expanded from it.

"Less chaotic," I said.

"Exactly."

We made our way to home plate. The sky was fully blue now, and the birds of Elysian Park had quieted a little.

"I was good. I was at home with baseball. But I set my routines, and I need them. I can't... I can't play without them."

He didn't say anything else until we got to home plate and stepped on it at the same time. He put his hands on my face and looked at me directly, as if putting a tunnel of attention between us. His thumbs rested on my cheeks.

Why hadn't I seen it the night before? Or an hour ago? Why hadn't I put it all together from the exhibition games and the spring training video? He was coming apart at the seams.

"You," he said. "You threw it all in the fire. Things started collapsing right before you, and when you came, everything went to hell. It's you. I denied it because if I let you in, I had to start over. I tried to bend it around to not want you. But I can't deny it anymore. There's no center without you."

I was breathless. I wanted this, heart and soul. I could fall into him in a blink and lose myself in him in a breath. I wanted him, but it was too much. He was asking me to be the conduit between him and his talent. To be responsible for his center, his routine, his very sanity. I didn't know how to be a man's center. He brushed his thumb along my lower lip.

"I'm just a regular woman. I'm not special."

"I disagree."

He kissed me, flooding me with his needs, commanding my

body's response while my mind was drowning in its own questions. I had no resistance in me.

"Will I see you tonight?" he asked.

"Dad and I always watch opening day together."

"I figured. I got him a seat too."

"Wait! What? Where?"

He motioned thataway. "Behind the dugout."

Oh.

My.

Fucking.

God.

I was about to gush, but he cut me off. "If you want a skybox—"

"No! God, no. It's too far. You read my exact wish."

"I want to see you in the stands for every game. Can you?"

"I'll try, Dash. I'll try."

I wanted to discuss the finer points of traveling while holding down a job, but he kissed me, and I figured I'd let the details take care of themselves.

forty-three

Vivian

To say Dash Wallace played brilliantly on opening day would have been a gross understatement. To say he owned the field and commanded the game would have been closer but not quite descriptive of the way his confidence turned into action.

After they'd won with the starting shortstop coming up to bat four times and getting a BB, two line drives no one could touch, a stolen base, and a two-run homer over the left field fence, the announcers Dad played on his phone asked each other if he'd been joking around during spring training. They wondered how the guy who'd swung at everything but what he was supposed to managed to keep up the act for two months.

I knew it

VIP parking was worthless. I couldn't leave in the eighth inning of the blowout. I had to stay until the end since, you know, I was sleeping with the shortstop. Dad and I were stuck in the traffic out of Elysian Park, which was always ten times better than the traffic onto the freeway.

Dad let me drive his car. His knees were aching after the long day of getting the house back in shape.

My phone buzzed in the center console again.

"What's happening with this thing?" Dad grabbed it.

"Dad, really?" I didn't want him to see the texts between Dash and me. Awkward.

"He says he knew it."

The traffic opened up, and I went right on Sunset. "Please don't scroll."

233

"Knew what?"

"I have no idea, and I'm driving. So forget it for now."

"I'll ask him."

Knew what?

"Dad, really?" I snapped the phone away.

Ding ding.

I couldn't look. I was going thirty on Sunset, and the lights were synchronized for a westward trip, so there would be no stopping at a red.

"Let me see," Dad said, hand out.

All I needed was for my father to see something about Dash's tongue on my pussy or the way I sounded when I came. So I pulled over.

"I'm looking," I said. "But back off."

"I'm a curious man, and that was some game he played back there."

"It was." I put my back to the driver's side door and tilted the phone just a little so I could see his response.

You're my lucky charm

I didn't answer it. I pulled away from the curb and thought about it.

His lucky charm. That was a nice thing to say. Everything about it was right and good, and I should have been happy. It was nice to be needed. It was nice to be the good thing in a man's life. Baseball was very important to him, and if I was the charm that made him play better, no matter how ridiculous that was, it should have made me happy.

But it didn't.

I must have looked pensive or something, and I was so in my own head about the responsibility he'd laid on me that I didn't think about my father's reaction.

"That guy's a *putz*. That's it with him. You're done."

"What?"

"I'm not letting him in the house. Do you hear me?"

"Why?" I asked.

234

"What do you mean why? You got that look on your face. The one you had when he was a *putz* last time. I don't have the stomach for it. I'll kill him first."

"Dad—"

"I know I'm getting old—"

"It's not—"

"I've had it."

I tossed the phone in his lap. "Don't scroll up. Just look at the last two, or you're going to give yourself a heart attack."

He looked at the screen. "I'm strong as a horse," he mumbled, putting on his reading glasses. He looked at the screen again.

"Don't scroll," I said.

"He's lucky." He replaced the phone in the console and folded his hands in his lap. "I'll let him live."

I worked really hard not to laugh at the idea of my semi-mobile father murdering Dash Wallace—trained athlete—with anything less than a firearm. He loved me.

I dropped my hand over his and squeezed it. "It's going to be all right."

"Why do you have that look then?"

The most obvious answer was "what look?" but I didn't want to lie. I knew what he meant. I changed the subject instead. "Do you want to eat at Café Sid?"

"No. I have a stomachache from that thing they called a frankfurter. It tasted like salted Styrofoam. Why are you the lucky charm? And why did you get a long face when he called you that?"

I made a left off Sunset so we could go home. "It's a lot of responsibility. And I'm afraid if he has a losing streak or something, it's going to be my fault."

"Your fault?"

"Well… that he's going to blame me."

"*Oy.* I've never seen two people make up so many problems."

We shot west on Beverly, but I couldn't take it. I wasn't making up a problem. If I was going to be in his life, I was going to be more than a rabbit's foot on his keychain. I pulled over in a red zone and snapped up my phone.

> I don't want our relationship to be
> contingent on your batting average

I was a hundred percent sure he was still at the stadium, talking to the off-camera press. I tossed the phone in the back. I didn't even want to be tempted by it.

"Oh, no," I said, pulling around the corner of our block right around three in the afternoon.

A Volvo was parked in our driveway. Parking in someone else's driveway was a big no-no in our neighborhood and usually the result of a sense of entitlement or an honest mistake. I could see someone leaning against the driver's door, and once I got around the car, I could see who it was.

"Crimeney."

"He's fast, that guy," Dad said.

I pulled up behind the Volvo. The car's color was a deep, molten gold, and Dash Wallace was tapping on his phone. He put it in his pocket when we got out of the car. He ran to help Dad but was brushed off.

"I'm fine, Mr. Four RBIs."

"I had a good game." He looked at me with half a smirk.

"That's a flashy car." Dad swung his cane at it.

"It's a Volvo."

"It's gold," I interjected.

"It's insoluble." He fell into step next to me. "And it's yours."

He put his hand over mine, clasping it. I felt the hard box of the key in his palm. When I pulled my hand up, the key was in it.

I stopped. "Dash."

"Let's take it for a spin."

I stopped, looked at it then Dad, who was at the door, jingling his keys. My mouth was open. I didn't know what to say. I wanted to accept it. My car was worth four hundred dollars, and it needed a three-hundred-dollar tune-up.

"Go!" Dad dismissed me with a wave. "Go with your *khaver*. Buys you a car." He shook his head, mumbling, "Couple of *mensches* here."

"What does that mean?"

"A minute ago you were a *putz*. *Mensch* is a big improvement," I said.

Dad opened the door, waved, and shut it without even asking if I wanted to come in. I faced Dash, my *khaver*—boyfriend. Out of my league yet somehow in my life.

"I want to talk about my batting average," he said.

"Me too. And I'm driving."

forty-four

Vivian

I'd never thought much of Volvos. It wasn't a Mercedes or a Porsche or anything. But I got it. As soon as the engine hummed to life and the RPMs cooled a split second later, I knew why it was a gold Volvo. It was safe. The sweetness of his gesture melted my corners into curves.

The driveway went around the back alley and onto a side street.

"You know I can't accept this, right?"

"Head north to Sunset. Take it east."

"Hello? Did you hear me?"

I headed north. The turn signal had a low, deep clicking sound that felt more expensive than the high-pitched clack of my Nissan's signal. The dash lights were crisp yet easy on the eyes, and the leather smell was ambrosia. All of the finest details—there to piss me off.

"Yes," he said. "I heard you."

"Well?"

"Well what? You're just uncomfortable with the size of it. The expense. And I'm uncomfortable with you driving that piece of shit you have in the driveway. So one of us is going to have to get over it, and since it's a matter of life and death over fifty-five miles an hour, I win. Left on LaBrea to Hollywood."

"Where am I driving? Can you tell me? I was raised here. I might know the place." My voice was saturated with irritation. When I looked at him, he was smiling. "What? Why are you grinning? Is there some kind of problem? Do you not take me seriously?"

"I do. I'm sorry. Barnsdall Art Park."

He turned away and looked out the window. I knew it was because he was smiling. Even when he reached for my knee, then my thigh, he looked away.

"Stop smiling," I grumbled.

"Can't."

"Were you this irritating when we met?"

"I was charming. Very charming."

"Where did Mr. Charming go?"

"That guy didn't have staying power."

"But Mr. Irritating? He'll stick around?"

"Unfortunately. Go up to the top please."

I went past the gate at Barnsdall and up the hill. His hand crawled up my thigh, and my body had the usual response, which was something between highly aroused and melting into lava.

I parked.

Barnsdall Art Park sat atop a low hill in East Hollywood. Frank Lloyd Wright had designed and built a residence with a theater and art gallery overlooking two sides of the city. Because the parking lot was the only piece of the puzzle at ground level, the park was historically underused, making it a great place for a pro baseball player to walk around without being recognized.

He put his arm around me and led me over the grass. A few couples and trios sat in the stone alcoves, chatting and laughing in the late afternoon shadows. He led me to a ledge overlooking the north side of the park, in view of the Hollywood sign and the high contrast lighting of the setting sun over the hills. He brushed dirt off the top of the stone wall and offered me his hand.

I took it and sat on the ledge overlooking the city. He hopped over, onto the side of the hill.

"This is nice," I said.

He stood and wedged himself between my legs. "Vivian?" He linked his fingers together at my lower back.

"Dash."

"Seeing you behind the dugout meant a lot to me. I want you to be at every game."

I put my forearms on his shoulders and locked my fingers together. "I want to be there, technically."

"Technically?"

"I have work until the middle of June."

His expression was hard to read it changed so fast. But with the narrowing of the eyes and the tightening of one side of his mouth, I knew he hadn't considered my job an issue. Maybe he didn't consider it a job worth staying at in money or satisfaction. Both. Neither. Something else entirely.

Then I felt his fingers tap on my back, and his gaze went deep into the middle distance.

"You're counting," I said.

"I have seven weekday away games between now and June 10th."

"And? You think I can just take those seven days off?"

"Yes."

"As what? Sick days?"

"And after that, you just travel with me."

"That's nuts."

It was. How many red-eyes was that? How many mornings would I show up at school on no sleep? And how was I supposed to get away with that? Teachers only worked nine months a year, so unless we were actually sick, we were expected to show up.

"Listen." He pecked my lips before continuing. "You give notice now, and they have all summer to find another librarian. They'll be fine."

I pulled back. "What? No. Dash, really, I'm not quitting."

"Why not?"

What the hell? Had he lost his mind? How could he even pretend to not understand the issue here? It was so obvious to me that he was asking me to give him everything that mattered to me in exchange for... what? I didn't even know what was on the table.

"I'm not ready to change my life all around," I said.

"We change each other's lives. That's what we *do*."

"A couple of months ago, you couldn't even commit past March. Now you want me to quit my job and leave my father so I can travel with you?"

He couldn't step back much because of the slope of the hill, but he backed up as much as he could and put his hands on my thighs. Mine were folded in my lap.

"I know," he said. "I don't blame you for being cautious. But I want to reassure you that I'm serious."

I took his face in my hands and put my nose on his. He was a good man. A sincere and worthy man. I had a million reasons to drop everything and run away with him and only a few very important reasons to refuse. "I know you're serious."

"I don't think you do. I think I've made mistakes with you, and that's what's making you balk. So I want to undo those mistakes. I want you to know how much you mean to me."

"I get it but—"

"Marry me." He reached into his pocket.

No. Oh no. I grabbed his hand before he could dig in there and pick out what I knew was a ring. A ring bought too soon and for the wrong reasons. Maybe the only ring I'd be offered in my life, but nevertheless, one I couldn't accept.

"Don't," I whispered urgently. "Don't do this."

He'd obviously expected a different reaction. "Why not? I need you."

I shook my head to get the thoughts out. The ones where he was using me to fulfill his superstitions, the ones that demanded I tell it to him straight and lose him forever. They pushed against the filter, bulging and pounding against it.

"You need me for the wrong reasons," I said, pushing the rest of it back.

"What do you mean?"

That was all that thin membrane holding the truth back needed. The words burst out too fast, and they were hard and unkind.

"I'm not—"

Your good luck charm
Responsible for your failures
A toy

I bit it all back so hard I nearly coughed. I couldn't do it that way. I couldn't cut him down. The crux of what he was going through was lack of confidence, and I'd almost played into it.

"You're a gifted person," I said. "You don't need superstitions to be successful. Me, I'm just a trinket right now. But the talent is with you. All you."

"You're not a trinket. How could you say that?"

Of course he picked the one thing that would deflect the conversation from the real problem. I wanted to talk about his confidence and his ability. I didn't want to talk about what I thought of myself.

"You have to work on this idea that you're not good enough," he said. "You have to know that we're that good together. That you're different. Special. Better for me than any woman I've ever met."

"And you love me?"

"Of course I do."

Yeah. That was bullshit. I was honored and flattered. I was even tempted. His pseudo-declaration of love was the best he could do, under the circumstances, which were just awful.

"My father," I said, then I corrected myself. "My *biological* father. He and my mother got married in a whirlwind. He was an actor on the verge. Clint Eastwood was casting this western. He'd directed stuff before, but everyone was talking about how this was going to be a big deal for him. My father thought he was getting cast in it. It's hard to do forensics on a guy I never met, but he was vulnerable when he met my mother. His success was about to crush him, and from what my mom said, success was scarier to him than failure. She was that successful. She was in magazines and fashion shows. She'd survived it. She was a symbol of what he wanted to become and what he feared. He felt safe with her. They met and married in the space of two months."

243

Dash shook his head as if to clear it. "Wait. Who's your dad?"

"Nobody. Really nobody. Richard Harris got cast to be English Bob when my mom was pregnant with me, and my father flipped. Nothing she did brought him back to reality, and he blamed her. He said if she hadn't been pregnant, he would have gone out more, made more contacts. And when *Unforgiven* did well, everything crashed. They weren't strong enough to get through it, and he left her with nothing but a baby and a house she couldn't sell."

"That's not me."

I was torn. I felt the depth of his disappointment and disorientation, yet I couldn't change my mind to soothe it. "No, it's not you. Because you have real talent."

He looked away from me, and only in that redirection did I see how confusing this was for him and how I couldn't make it better. He'd exposed his deepest vulnerabilities, and I'd thrown them into the pit of his fears.

Well done, Vivian. Way to go.

"I love you," I said.

Those words should have come before he asked me to marry him, and he looked back at me as if he was shocked to hear them.

"We should go," he said.

That wasn't the answer I'd been looking for, but what could I expect?

He helped me down from the wall, but his touch was cold, and his eyes avoided mine.

forty-five

Dash

Before Ithaca winter set in, we got a cord of wood for the fireplace. My father bought rough brown twine to tie it together in manageable bundles. The sisal came in a tubeless cylinder, and we pulled the end from the center. There's a lot of wood in a cord, and we used yards and yards to bundle it, pulling from the center of the cylinder to take a length. We could use ninety percent of the spool, and the size of the thing never changed. It just got emptier and emptier, but it looked the same on the outside.

Until the last few yards. Then the shape would start to collapse, and the entire thing disappeared as if the invisible man had gotten undressed, and boom, I'd see how empty it had been all that time.

I walked her to the car and drove it back to her house, but my shape was crumpling. I was about to be stripped down to invisibility. I'd looked pretty fine and felt okay until she refused me, then I'd realized how little I had left at the core.

"I'm sorry," she said when we were halfway to her house.

It was the point in the drive where I could have gone in either direction: to my place, and a night of fucking, or her place.

"I understand." I didn't understand a thing, but I couldn't talk. I was about to fall apart, and talking would only use up the few yards I had.

I held her hand because it would reassure her and she'd stop talking. With that touch came a new unraveling. Had I lost her? Did my desperation drive her away? With that

245

thought, I was one layer of twine from complete collapse.

I parked and got out before we could talk this through more. I opened her door and helped her out. At the top of the steps, I stopped.

"The game tomorrow…" I said.

"Yes."

"Will you come? I have the seats for you."

"Yes."

"Will you still walk the bases with me?" I asked. I needed her to. For luck, yes. Because I needed the routine. But also because it meant she was beside me.

She barely hesitated, and that told me the truth of her response. "Yes."

"We're playing San Diego next."

"I want to go. Can I just go to your games when I can?"

"Yes, I"—*take a breath*—"I need you there. Whenever you can."

"Dash, you're fine with or without me. You have to believe that."

I put my fingers to her lips. I couldn't hear another word. She turned her head until my palm cupped her face, and she pressed it to her cheek, letting her eyes flutter closed.

I'd hurt her. I hadn't thought it was possible to hurt someone with an unopened ring box, but I had, and with that, the last of the string got pulled away.

forty-six

Vivian

"Why do you look like that?" Dad asked when I got inside. He was in his robe and slippers, boiling water for tea. His amber med bottles were out. If it was midnight and he was up with painkillers, the arthritis was flaring.

I got a cup from the cabinet, deciding to stay up with him.

"He asked me to marry him."

"*Mazel tov!* Where's the funeral?"

"I said no." I pushed my mug toward him, and he swung a teabag into it. "It's too soon."

"It is, it is."

"Why do I feel like crying?"

"I want to tell you something you don't know. Do you remember that boyfriend you used to have?"

"Carl?"

"That one. He used to call here all the time. After you broke up, I mean."

"What?" The teapot whistled just as I said it. "Why?"

Dad turned off the heat. "He wanted to know if you were all right. And I didn't like the guy. I didn't like what he did. I was mad at him. But he was very upset."

"Why didn't you tell me?"

"Why should I? He was wrong for you. If I told you how much that stupid ass cried for you—you with your good heart?—you'd just try to comfort him."

He poured hot water into my cup, and the water went from clear to pale yellow, releasing the waxy florals of chamomile.

"I don't have the energy to be mad at you," I said.

"Have the energy to realize it's hard to say no to someone you care about. Even for Carl the *schlemiel*."

I dunked my teabag, pinched it, and put it to the side. Carl had put a stake in my heart. I'd thought I'd never get over it.

And Dash? What had he done by moving too fast? Whipped the rug out from under me, from all my view of how things were and should be, and I was going to make contact with the floor. Hard.

"I'm afraid he's going to leave me."

When I said the words, my face tingled and crunched. That was my hard place, and by refusing him, I'd angled my body to hit harder and faster. My mouth filled with gunk, and my eyes burned with tears. In a second, I couldn't breathe unless I gulped.

Dad was there. He held me right there in the kitchen for a good ten minutes while I sobbed as if I hadn't been proposed to. I sobbed as if I'd been dumped.

forty-seven

Vivian

are you up?

It's 2am. Of course

(...)

(...)

You have a game tomorrow. You need to sleep

I can't

(...)

(...)

I'm sorry

No. I'm sorry

forty-eight

Vivian

My phone lit up. He was calling. The thing to do was to answer it. Talk to him. Tell him I loved him and accept his love even if he felt half-heartedly trapped into expressing it.

Or not.

Who was I to doubt him?

I was the sensible one, that's who. I started saying things to myself as the phone vibrated in my hand. Bad things.

I was an object.

When he got to know me, he'd dump me.

He couldn't hear me crying, and I didn't want him to. I rejected the call.

I'm not functioning well. I can't talk

He didn't answer for a long time. And why should he? He was the one who had put his heart on the line, and I was the one who was protected and fortified. Not only had I rejected his proposal, I'd rejected his call.

I'll walk the bases with you tomorrow

You don't have to

The next text came right after.

Your tickets are at the will call if you still want to come to the game. Otherwise, I'll see you another time

Another time.

Simple and polite. Nonspecific. Not demanding. Move along. Nothing to see here. Nothing but nothing. I couldn't call him and reassure him. I'd already said I couldn't talk.

Good night

I hit Send and started on the next text before the first even went through.

I love you

Both messages were delivered. The screen said so, but nothing came back. I had no way of knowing if he even saw them.

I tried to sleep and failed. My brain was too busy winding guilt around justification, knotting me into a braid of righteous self-reproach.

I should have just said yes.

But I couldn't have.

I fell asleep, sure I'd lost him, and woke up an hour later when the birds started whistling. Dash was the first thought on my mind. I didn't look at my phone. I was afraid of what I'd see.

I was tired. Tired of all the limits I'd put on myself. Tired of the box I'd built around my heart. I wanted to change but didn't know how.

Padding into the kitchen, gunk in my eyes and sleep in my veins, I found Dad already up. I loved him. I loved him more than my heart could even fit. The way he bent in front of the fridge so slowly, careful not to twist his joints, made me doubt what I'd decided during the walk across the house.

"Dad," I said.

"Good morning."

"Would you be mad if I moved out?"

He stood cautiously, closed the refrigerator, and leaned on it. "Mad?"

"Disappointed. Or whatever. Maybe the question is, 'How would you feel if I moved out?' But not far. As close as I could afford."

He laughed quietly. "I've been meaning to ask you the same thing."

I hadn't even considered the idea. This was Mom and Dad's house. This was my home base. My life was in this single-story O-shaped modernist masterpiece, and even if I was gone, it had to be here.

"You can't—" I stopped myself at the apostrophe. "Where will you go?"

"Somewhere smaller. I'm feeling all right with the new pills, but the steps aren't good in the long run. And this is really your house."

"What? No! It's yours."

He waved me off, which he'd done a million times before without annoying me. That morning, however, I was in no mood.

"You made sure Mom got this house, and when she was gone, you're the one who paid the mortgage and made it a home," I said.

"I only stayed so you had some consistency when your mother died. And now it's just a habit. Honestly, I don't even like it."

I had to swallow that hard. It was a complete turnaround. I had to sit down. "You don't like it?"

"I like the older style. And the neighborhood? Too many nosy old ladies. And I can't walk to the grocery store. I'm not going to be able to drive much longer, peanut."

I hadn't even wondered if I liked the house. It was the house I had grown up in, and when I left to live with Carl, the fact that it was there, and Dad was in it, was a comfort I took for granted.

"You should go if you're not happy here." I said it as if I was talking to myself, and in a way, I was.

Dad put his hand on my shoulder. "I am happy here. I *kvell* thinking of you doing your homework in the courtyard. Reading on that couch. I watched you for hours. You were the reason I was here, and lately I've been thinking I made you my reason too long."

"I thought you stayed because of Mom."

"For a few years, sure. I was a lonely grouch when I met your mother. After you came, I was a man with a family. My empty heart was full. You gave me everything. I stayed in this house to thank you."

I gulped back denials because I was the one who should have been thanking him. He'd built his life around me because it was what I needed. He'd taught me the purest form of love, but had I learned it? I choked back a sob.

"Believe me," I said, looking up at him, "I'm trying not to say I owe you the thanks. But being your daughter was the best thing that ever happened to me."

He patted my shoulder again then squeezed it. I put my arms around him and laid my cheek against his chest.

Dash hadn't answered the text, and I was glad. He needed to rest. He'd been tired and upset about his performance over spring training. One great game wasn't going to change that. He needed constant injections of confidence.

I was his serum.

I sat on the edge of the bed. My room looked over the vegetable garden that volunteered to grow on its own every year. I'd crawled out of that window every night when I was fourteen until Dad put a bell on the outside and I was busted. The walls had been painted twice. Dark blue over pink when I went to high school, and two coats of primer and white over that when I started college. I'd studied here, eaten here, fucked here.

I could move from this house to Dash's place in the hills. I could demand he and I get a new place. I could stay in this house. I could get an apartment. I could stand on my head and spit nickels. It didn't matter.

What mattered?

Someone needed me. A human being I cared about. The

way Dad needed Mom and he needed me. The house didn't matter. The ring didn't matter. What mattered was the evolution of a relationship.

My bio dad hadn't evolved. He'd needed my mother at a certain stage in his life, and when that changed, he didn't go with it, because in the end, he didn't know how to love her.

If Dash needed me to give him confidence now, that didn't mean he'd need the same thing next year or in ten years or after his retirement. I needed to be willing to give him what he needed and evolve later.

I feared he wouldn't be able to evolve, but wasn't that always the fear? No matter who I was with, we'd need to evolve. Wouldn't children, middle age, old age change us and change our needs?

I was going to be a zombie today, but a zombie with a completely changed attitude. No dream had come to change my outlook. No little spirit whispered in my ear.

No. Just a little rest for the brain.

Dash Wallace was the only man in the world I wanted.

I was going to be there for him one hundred percent. I was going to let him know that every day, every minute, until he put his heart back into us. If he needed me to walk the bases around every major league field in the United States, I'd do it. He'd own my summer and a chunk of my autumn. His rushed proposal wasn't going to stop me from loving him with everything I had. I could refuse it and still love him. I could put a ring around my heart.

I took a deep breath and committed myself to him.

Long haul. He was my responsibility.

forty-nine

Dash

I couldn't sleep. I put my phone on Do Not Disturb for the night and juggled three balls ten different ways. I was a fuckup. Everything was fucked up. Wrong. And those phrases just replayed as I tried to distract myself with the rhythm of the balls. You're a fuckup. You're a fuckup. She hates you now she thinks you only want her for luck do you love her do you even love her such a fuckup a fucking her is the best thing that ever happened to me with her body around mine she's mine no one else can fuck up you fucked up you fucked up...

When my arms hurt, I ran up and down my newly dug-out stairs in the dark, and I stopped when I tripped and thought I'd sprained my ankle.

My greatest fear wasn't a strikeout or even a string of them. I worried about making errors, but they were small potatoes when I thought about the other thing.

An injury. A career-ending injury.

I needed her. I didn't feel safe on the field. I didn't know how I knew it, but there was no question. She was all my luck in one little body. She was kind and beautiful and, yes, sexy as hell, but that was gravy.

I shook off the twisted ankle and stretched out on my bed for two hours, drifting in and out of anxiety-laced sleep.

She was right. That was the thing that kept me up. I'd been trying to slap a glass jar over a butterfly. That was bullshit. It was hurtful and stupid and bullshit. She saw right through it. Of course she did. And I'd just fucked it all up by panicking.

At six o'clock, the DND shut itself off, and I heard the

chorus of texts coming in from the kitchen. I went out to see what was so important.

Good night

I love you

Then a line where time had passed, and the last few came in real time.

Listen. I've thought about it

I don't think we should get married. I'm sorry. There's no reason

Not now. Not so soon

Maybe some day

You're right

She *was* right. I'd been stupid and impulsive.

The messages continued as if she wasn't even waiting for a reply.

But the now. Let's have the now. Let's do this together

If you need me, I'm there for you

I want to be clear. I WANT to be there for every game I can. I will do everything. I'll take red-eye flights and lose sleep if you need me to

I'll walk the bases with you, Dash. I don't need a ring to do it

Was she done? I had so much to say, but I didn't want to interrupt her.

I'll walk the bases with you

Nothing more came. The little rolling dots that told me when she was typing had stopped. It was my turn. I had to tell her what she meant to me. I had to use big words and gestures.

Infinitely big words. I constructed the speech in my mind before I tapped the glass, and I went for it. I said it big, and I said it loud. The relief, the love, the joy. I thought I was going to explode into a two-word sonnet.

Thank you

I didn't have any more words. Everything I felt was right there. But what did she need? I had to think of that, and I brushed away the gratitude to find clarity.

For forgiving me. Thank you. I own the
world with you by my side

fifty

Vivian

Nothing changed, but everything changed. Dash came to get me that afternoon, and though the stadium was too populated for him to fuck me in the dugout, he made do in the best way possible. He parked in a far off corner and fingered me in the car like a teenager, then he walked me around the bases, tagging each one. He introduced me to the grounds crew and kissed me at home plate.

"Two games down," I said.

"Hundred sixty to go." He put his lips on my forehead. So soft. So warm. He turned my insides to paste and exposed them to the comfort of his attention.

"I'm doing this because I want you to be happy," I said. "But you don't need me. You're a brilliant player. Period."

"Thank you," he whispered, and I didn't know if he was thanking me for speaking that truth or for playing along with his ritual. I didn't ask.

He played that night as if it was the defining moment in his career, and talk of his passion and talent was reignited in the post-game show. The third game was on Wednesday, and he had a car pick me up.

I got there ninety minutes before game time, and we walked the bases quickly, kissed, and I took my spot behind the dugout, where Francine waited in a puffy black coat and red beret.

"Larry and all of them are going to be at the bar on Friday." She handed me a large black coffee. "Including Carl. I know you avoid him, but I thought you might not have to

261

anymore?"

"I don't, but Friday isn't good."

She pouted. "Doesn't he have a game? Like... away? Not here?"

"Yeah. I have to be there."

She blew into the little hole in the coffee lid, making a low whistle. "I'm not even going to ask why," she said between blows. "I'm going to ask how."

"I have to leave work early and get on the freeway to San Diego. And when he's across the country, I'll get on a plane Friday afternoons and take an overnight back on Sundays until school ends."

"You know that's crazy, right? I mean, I'm assuming he's great in bed, but I'm sorry, I don't know if any man is worth all that confusion."

We stood for the "Star Spangled Banner."

"He is." I leaned in and whispered, "He's completely worth it."

She smiled, bumping me with her hip. "Good."

He was worth it. Every hour of lost sleep. Every inconvenience. Every moment I wanted to shake him and say, "It's your talent! Can you please own it so I can get to bed early?"

He needed the routine I gave. When he was away midweek and I had to work, I watched from a stool at the bar. His failures seemed bigger and his successes more modest. For a moment, I thought there might be something to the superstition. Maybe he did need me. Even if it was all in his head, maybe he needed me.

By June, I was wrecked.

"I think I miscalculated," he said in the airport after a night game in St. Louis.

I would be getting off the plane to be shuttled right to

Hobart Elementary, where Jim was covering the first half hour of the library schedule in case there was traffic.

"Miscalculated what?"

We sat on a leather couch in the first-class lounge. He draped his arm around the back and tenderly stroked pieces of my hair off my neck. I was flipping through a magazine, but the pages couldn't hold my attention.

"You have dark circles under your eyes."

"I can't think. I feel like I live in peanut butter." I tossed the magazine aside. "Two more weeks. Then I can go around with you all the time. I'll find an apartment when you have that double home stand in July."

"I don't like seeing you like this," he said. "I want you to move in with me."

"That's not going to help."

"You won't have to look for an apartment. And it'll just cut a step out of the travel."

"I don't know," I said, resting my head on his chest. "Maybe I'll get used to the peanut butter."

"I love peanut butter."

I bent my neck, resting my head on the back of the couch. "I love you too."

He kissed me, and I could have dropped off with the softness of his lips on mine and the smell of summer grass around me, but they announced my flight.

"Think about it," he said when he picked up my bag.

"I will. I'll see you Friday." I kissed him, grateful that he'd be home for the weekend series and I could sleep.

fifty-one

Dash

The slumps usually started at my second at bat if she wasn't there. Sometimes I walked or the other guys were at the top of their game so no one could tell. But I could. I felt it because things got harder. I felt as though I was hanging on by my fingernails.

"You're psyching yourself out," Youder said for the hundredth time.

We were on a plane back from St. Louis, and he thought now was the perfect opportunity to lay down more mentoring. I wanted to punch him sometimes.

I put my seat back. "I'm fine. It's up and down for everyone."

The truth of that, even as it came out of my mouth, had no effect on me. I was just saying words. I knew I was down when she wasn't there and up when she was. Any statistician could see my weekdays away sucked.

I had a hundred things to say about Vivian. But the most important was that with her, I felt loved. Really loved. All of me. The non-medicated, not-charming, awkward son of a bitch who read too much and had learned to juggle balls to calm down.

I sent her library fruit and candy, boxes of pens and sticky notes. Anything she mentioned the kids needed. It wasn't enough. She drove herself to the edge of exhaustion to be at my games. She had to quit that job because as nice as it was to be loved without limits, she was hitting a physical barrier.

265

She waited for me at the gate with a sign that said KING OF ELYSIAN. She wore a skirt, and if I looked under it, I knew I'd find something that would keep us up half the night.

I kissed her right there and took her home.

fifty-two

Vivian

He started kissing me when we were barely in the door, dropping his bags on the hardwood with a *clap*. He was more intense after a series away, less controlled. His hands went up my skirt and grabbed my ass hard. Yes, it hurt. Yes, it turned me on.

I kissed him back, reaching under his shirt for the hard muscle that waited for me. I felt suddenly empty, wanting, awake and ready.

He pushed me onto a barstool and yanked my legs open, exposing the new stockings and garter belt I'd bought for him.

"Yes," was all he said as he spread my arms over the counter. "Stay still. I'm going to taste that delicious pussy."

"Okay, I—"

I forgot the next word, and all that came out was a groan. His tongue flicked the inside of my thigh, a point of pleasure surrounded by the scratch of his stubble. He moved the crotch of my panties aside and ran his tongue along my cleft like a hungry man, sucking on me while holding my legs wide open.

I was wet, hot, pulsing in response to every flick of his tongue. He ate me as if he'd never done it before, as if he had to do it now or die trying. My arms stretched on the counter where he'd put them, and my back arched.

"I'm close, Dash."

He lightened the pressure of his tongue but didn't stop. My raspy breaths only uttered *please please please,* though I didn't know what I was begging for. When I thought I couldn't be on the edge any longer, he laid his lips on my clit and gently sucked the orgasm out of me.

When I could breathe again, he stood. His cock was monumental, pushing against the fabric of his pants. He wiped his mouth with the back of his hand.

"Welcome home," I said.

"Home?"

"To Los Angeles."

He glanced around. "You didn't move your stuff in."

I slid off the barstool. "I think I found an apartment."

He looked surprised but unshaken. "Where?"

"Bottom of the hill. Your hill. It'll be ready next month."

"Do you need help packing?"

Yes? No? There was a quarter century of crap in that house. Dad hadn't decided where or when he was moving, but I felt as if I needed to give him room and reason to go. So I'd found a cute one-bedroom behind a Craftsman.

"Can I let you know about the packing?"

"Stand up," Dash said.

I didn't have time to comply. He took me by the shoulders and got me to my feet, pulling my shirt up to reveal my lacy bra. He slid that over my tits, exposing the hard nipples to the air.

Pressing his erection against me, thumbs and forefingers circling the bases of my breasts, he spoke into my ear, "You're here all the time."

"But you aren't."

He closed his fingers around the apex of my tits and squeezed the nipples, twisting until my knees melted under me.

"You're so hot. I can't even think. Take your skirt up and the underwear down."

I hitched my skirt around my waist while he played with my nipples, and I got my underpants just below my ass.

"Take my dick out."

I reached for him, wiggling to get at his enormous cock. He was wearing sweatpants, so it wasn't long before I felt the skin of it against my palm and the drop of pre-cum waiting. I was ready for him again. With a final tug, he took his hands off my breasts and hooked a finger on my underpants, yanking them wide.

"Leg. Come on, sweetapple. Before I fuck these off you."

I pulled my leg through the opening, and my panties dropped over my left foot.

He pressed four fingers onto the wet ache between my legs. His eyes were on fire, and his lips were tight with intention as he rubbed my clit and slid three fingers inside me.

"Deeper, God, Dash, deeper."

He got his fingers in me and found the bundle of nerves inside, circling it, pressing it awake. I hitched a leg over his waist, and he took his hand away. I groaned.

"I want you here," he said, stroking my wet cleft with the head of his cock. "In this house."

"I'm here. But I want to—"

He shoved himself in me, and I gasped.

"Want to what?"

"Fuck. Dash. God. Just take it. We can talk later."

He got all the way inside, down to the root, grinding up against me. He pushed me against the counter, pinning me with his cock, pushing his body against my clit. I held onto his shoulders for dear life as he fucked me hard and slow, angling himself against me. I felt full, every surface stimulated, the pressure of his hips bringing my other foot off the floor.

His eyes locked on mine. His jaw set. He looked as if he wanted to tear me open and crawl inside me. And I wanted him to. Fuck me. Fuck my identity. Fuck my own skin and soul.

I wanted to tell him I was coming, but it was too late. I was shredded. Ripped open, and he came in the fissure, marking me with his name as it left my lips in a scream.

Our bodies moved together even after we were done. He wrapped his arms around me and carried me to the bedroom.

"Did you really get an apartment?"

His voice sounded deeper because my head leaned on his bare chest. He'd taken me from behind minutes after we got to the bedroom, and I was sore already. I didn't have another fuck in me. Not for at least an hour.

I picked my head up so I could make eye contact with him as he sat against the headboard.

"I want to explain."

"Okay."

"I love you. But I've only ever lived with my father and Carl. I'd like some time in a space of my own."

He took forever to answer, drawing circles on my cheeks and lines along my jaw. At least three seconds of staring at me as if memorizing me for his next trip.

I swallowed. I didn't think he'd be angry, but I was afraid of hurting him or shutting him down.

"I understand," he said. "I don't have to like it, but I understand."

I believed he wanted to understand, but I didn't think he actually understood at all.

fifty-three

Vivian

I ran as fast as I could. Coffee in one hand, sack of apples in the other. Purse over my shoulder, paper bag of used books on my wrist. The bag crinkled, the purse jingled, and the coffee splashed out of the little hole on the top.

I was as sore as I'd ever been. After I'd told Dash I was moving and described the little one-bedroom at the base of the hill, he spanked me and fucked me so hard I thought I would break like a china doll.

It was amazing.

But I'd overslept, and since I had to leave early to make the Friday home game, I had to get to work early. I was almost late. Sixty seconds to get to the library before the bell rang.

I nearly stepped right out of my shoe while getting up the steps, and my lungs burned as much as my pussy. When I crested the top of the stairs, I saw Jim coming from the opposite side of the hall. He stopped at the library door, keys swinging.

"Hey, you made it," he said.

I didn't have a full breath to answer. He opened the door just as the bell rang.

I dropped all my stuff behind my desk. Jim didn't have first period PE class, so he could stand there with his hands in his pockets while I unloaded all my bags and oxygen.

"Thank you," I said.

"No problem. Leaving early?"

"Yeah. But there's no class in here, and I can do my paperwork at lunch."

I dumped my apples in the bowl. The kids were on their way in.

He was still there, bouncing on his heels.

"Yes?" I said.

"I hate to ask, but I was wondering... could you score me some tickets for next week? Michelle's birthday?"

"Probably. How is everything with her?"

He shrugged. "Same."

"Breaking up?"

"And making up." He winked just as a hoard of kids lined up in the hall for first period. He backed up a few steps toward the door. "Let me know about those tickets."

"Will do."

I spent the day in a sticky fog. I needed sleep. I needed to stay home. I needed a week without an airplane. I couldn't focus on the paperwork I'd promised myself I'd do because I kept writing Dash a letter in my head.

It went something like, "Dear Dash. I love you. I'm tired. You did fine before you met me. You'll do fine again."

But I couldn't. When a man told you he needed you, you showed up. I'd learned that from my dad. He'd shown up for my mother even after she was dead.

"Miss Foster?" Iris stood a few steps inside the library, rubbing her eye with the heel of her hand.

I didn't have a class visiting, so the room was quiet. "Hey, Iris, how are you?"

"I'm tired."

I waved her in. "Did your mom take you to work last night?"

"No. *Mi abuela* took care of us."

I looked at her closely. Her eyelids drooped. She was falling asleep standing up.

I felt her forehead. No fever. We didn't have a nurse on

staff, so there wasn't much I could do. There was only an hour left until dismissal. I called the office and let them know Iris would take science class time to nap on the library couch. She was out before I even got a blanket on her.

Should I send a car for you?

I looked at my watch. If Iris slept for an hour, I could make it to Echo Park in thirty minutes, which was still an hour and a half before anyone sang the national anthem.

I have my gold Volvo. It's superfast

Are there any kids around? I want to tell you all the dirty things I'm going to do to your body.

He wouldn't talk dirty when I had kids in the library. I was usually watched by no more than dancing bears and clown cutouts at two, but little Iris, breathing in shallow sleep, counted as a kid.

It'll have to wait until tonight

Too bad

I'm shutting the phone at 2:40. Let me know if you need anything before then

He shut off the phone in the stadium to keep his mind on what he was doing, and devices weren't allowed in the locker room or dugout anyway.

See you later, Slugger

I shall say good night till it be morrow

I left it there and got back to my requisitions. I didn't notice the time again until three, and I sat straight with a start. I should have been locking up. That extra five minutes on a Friday, with traffic to Echo Park on a game night, was going to count for an extra ten minutes of travel time.

"Iris?"

She'd slept the entire hour.

I put my hand on her shoulder. "*Iris, despiertate chiquita.* Wake up."

I shook her a little and patted her. She didn't move, and her breath was so slight I couldn't detect it right away. I panicked, getting hot and cold at the same time. She looked too relaxed. Nothing was moving. Not her eyelids or her fingers. Nothing. I put my fingers on her cheek. She was alive.

Jesus. My head went crazy sometimes. Of course she was alive.

"Iris? Come on. Time to go."

She didn't look good.

That instinct that had freaked me out? The one where I'd thought she was dead? The instinct was right, but the conclusion was wrong.

She was not all right.

I picked her up. She was a complete dead weight.

I left everything at my desk and ran her downstairs.

fifty-four

Dash

She didn't come for the walk. I sneaked away after batting practice to call her, but she didn't answer, and the text I sent right after got no response.

Traffic.

Getting into and out of the north side of downtown sucked on game nights. And Fridays were generally bad.

Next time, she had to leave earlier. I couldn't deal with this.

I tapped each base, pretending she was there, but as we took batting practice, I had an empty mental place I tried to fill. Something I didn't do. As if I'd forgotten to brush my teeth. I had to go back and do it, but she wasn't there. Not in her seat above the dugout even during the national anthem.

Forty thousand people in the stands couldn't distract me the way the absence of one could.

At first, I thought it was traffic. But by the top of the ninth, her absence was assumed, and it turned from an irritation to outright worry. She wouldn't just no-show unless something had happened.

Yes, bases were loaded with no outs.

Yes, Rodriguez was coming up to bat. I had all that handled, but when I glanced at her seat behind the dugout, she wasn't there. I got annoyed with myself. I'd been so worried about my performance and the effect my rituals had on my play that I hadn't worried about her and where she was. I hadn't trusted her. Hadn't assumed she had a life that needed me as much as I needed her. She could slump, strike out, make errors.

And where was she? Was she all right?

Rodriguez was three and oh. One out. He was going to swing. He only needed to get it far enough for the sacrifice. Anything in his wheelhouse would be in play.

I hopped right when I saw the catcher's signal. Moved forward when I saw the batter move his front foot to left field. Back half a step when I caught a glimpse of how the pitcher held the seams of the ball. The crack of the bat reached my ears long after I knew where the ball was going.

And even then, I was off by about eight inches. The difference between catching it and missing. An out or an error. So I pushed off my toes a little harder. Leapt a little higher. Stretched farther. Still, as the millisecond unwound and the ball spun a little higher and I knew the batter was running, I twisted to get another inch out of my arm.

My wrist bent back predictably as the ball landed full force in the web of my glove, and I closed the fold around it. Then, having reached the apex of my leap, I started falling.

I was in an unexpected position, and my reflex was to protect the ball, not my throwing arm which, because of the last twist, had gotten into the space between my body and the ground.

When I fell, my body weight landed on my hand, and my wrist was at an angle I could not have predicted would result in the entire arm bending in a way it wasn't supposed to.

I didn't hear a crack or anything else. The entire stadium went silent with the held breath of forty thousand souls, and the vibration and volume of the silence funneled into pain.

But I couldn't just lie there.

Whitten was running home from third.

I held up my glove and opened my hand. Youder had probably read my mind before I even hit the ground. He skidded to my side, getting dirt on my face, and plucked the ball out of my glove.

The silence erupted into a joyful roar.

The last thing I thought before the stadium lights were blocked out by the shadowed heads of trainers and coaches was that this had happened because Vivian wasn't there, and I cared more about what had happened to her than I cared about my broken arm.

fifty-five

Vivian

The TV in Sequoia Hospital's ER waiting room had been set to the news, which was always depressing. I pitched the idea of the ball game hard, and I got a few sickly backers. They changed the station deep in the third inning. Dash struck out, and I crossed my fingers and prayed he did all right on the field.

Iris's head was on my lap. Everything had gone quickly and slowly. Having finally gotten a day shift, her mother was at work until six. Iris's brother was old enough to walk home with her, but he couldn't take her to the hospital. Her *abuela* wasn't answering the phone from the dialysis clinic. The rest of her emergency contacts, by some freak occurrence, were seriously indisposed. I couldn't wait for the office to make another phone call or get the nurse in, so I made an off-book executive decision that was probably going to get me fired.

I brought her to the hospital.

I'd expected them to tell me she was tired. I thought they'd roll their eyes at me, but thankfully, after only two solid hours of red tape and waiting, they took a blood sample.

They roused her enough to give her a piece of candy. She perked up as if it was Saturday morning.

Iris had suffered a sugar crash. She had undiagnosed diabetes, which explained the incontinence and constant exhaustion. It explained her rabid addiction to my bowl of apples.

Iris cried when they put in the IV catheter, squeezing my hand weakly. But it took exactly three seconds for her to wake up completely. She smiled and devoured the applesauce the nurse put in front of her.

Suddenly, I didn't care if I lost my precious job.

"*No han llegado*, I'll watch. Don't worry," I told Iris's mother when I finally got her on the phone. Her employment situation was so precarious that leaving to see her daughter in the hospital would lose her hours of pay at best and get her fired at worst. All she needed was a time buffer.

I stayed and tried to contact Iris's aunt and grandmother. All it would take was a few hours of my time, and I had a few hours. I was already slated to leave school early, so it didn't matter.

Not really.

Except it did.

Her aunt showed up at the hospital at seven o'clock, all apologies and tears, rattling off complex explanations and thank yous. My Spanish was good but not that good. I kissed Iris and her aunt and ran out.

I crossed the waiting room early in the ninth inning. The TV had earned a few new viewers. One out. Bases loaded. Dodgers up by one.

Rodriguez at bat.

"That guy's a clutch homer waiting to happen," said a middle-aged man with his arm under an ice pack.

Jesus! And three balls. No strikes. He'd be crazy not to swing at anything near the strike zone. If he touched the ball with the bat and it stayed fair, one man was coming home. If he got behind it, two men home. If he got it to the outfield, sac fly brought one man home. Which would put the home team in a terrible position in the bottom of the ninth.

Dash was a speck between second and third, hopping right then taking half a step forward.

I didn't know what kind of game he'd had. I'd only seen one strikeout. If it was bad, I would feel as if it was my fault, and he might act as if it was too. I felt as though our whole relationship pivoted on this play.

I hated that. As much as I loved him, I hated that.

Rodriguez swung. Everyone in the waiting room held their breath.

Line drive to left. Hard and high. Gorgeous Dash Wallace leapt for it, stretching the length of his body, turning in the air, catching the drive, and landing hard on his right arm.

Everyone in the room gasped.

Dash rolled and held up his left arm, serving the caught ball like an apple in a bowl. Youder, the second baseman, was already there. He grabbed the ball from Dash's glove and drove it home.

The runner was out.

Side retired.

Game over.

The sick fans in the emergency room at Sequoia Hospital cheered, but my eyes were glued to the TV.

Men were running onto the field.

Dash wasn't getting up.

He needed me.

fifty-six

Dash

The pain was broken apart by region. My fingers were numb, and my shoulder felt as if a blade had been wedged in the joint. Everything between those two points felt as if it had been twisted loose and rearranged.

"I need my phone," I said through my teeth.

I'd walked off the field after I was offered a stretcher. My arm was fucked, but my legs were fine. And Vivian hadn't shown up. It wasn't like her to be late, much less a no-show.

"Gonna call your mama?" Youder's voice came from the doorway of the training room, where I was getting a workover from three guys in white shirts.

"Vivian," I growled. "I don't know what happened to her."

"Does this hurt?" a voice asked right before a shooting pain went up my arm.

"Yes!"

"Where's the phone?" Youder asked.

"Locker."

"We're sending you to Sequoia," Marv said. He was the veteran trainer. A medic in Vietnam.

I looked down at my arm, but it was covered with cold compresses. "Fine."

"We're going to pull the stretcher into a gurney. It might jog a little."

"No fucking way. My feet are fine." I tried to get up using my good arm, and I had to ignore the pain in my other shoulder.

Marv pushed me down. "But your shoulder needs support.

283

The ambulance is waiting."

"Overkill, Marv! Total fucking overkill."

"The team's paying for it. Might as well use it."

They wheeled me out the door. I didn't forget Youder was supposed to get my phone, but it wasn't until we were outside and the flashing red lights of an ambulance lit the side of the stadium that I realized he still hadn't come back with it.

"Wait."

"What now?" Marv asked, not waiting at all.

I grabbed the edge of the ambulance with my left arm. For the first time since I was wheeled out, I heard the sounds of the parking lot. Horns, shouts, and cheers that got louder when I stopped the progression of the gurney. Fans waited for me behind sawhorses, and men with big network cameras stood in a special closer area.

"Youder has my phone," I said quietly to Marv. I didn't want the mics to pick up what I was saying.

"Probably."

"We have to wait."

"If you have nerve damage and we don't take care of it, you're doing a lot of waiting from the sidelines."

He was surprisingly strong, peeling my fingers off the edge of the ambulance entrance. He hopped in the back, and the other trainers got in too. The door was about to slam when I heard Youder's voice from outside.

"Wait up!" He appeared in the narrow slit between the nearly closed doors. "Nice game, Wallace." He put the phone in my outstretched hand.

"Couldn't have done it without you," I replied.

"You won't have to."

Before what he was saying sank in, the doors snapped shut and the siren started pulsing.

I called her anyway, hoping against hope that she was all right. I cared about my arm and my career, but not half as much as I cared about Vivian Foster.

fifty-seven

Vivian

My phone was in my bag, and I was on the 10 freeway. I couldn't pull over and get it, and I couldn't answer at fifty mph, which on the 10 was as close to the speed limit as I'd ever gotten near downtown.

The radio announcers celebrated the Dodgers' win, giving only the most perfunctory non-news of Dash's injury. They were waiting to hear, but he'd had the game of his career. I'd seen his single misstep from the waiting room. The strikeout in the third inning had been boxed by two doubles, a home run, and seamless fielding.

Once I took the exit and got near the stadium, traffic slowed down. Since most everyone was exiting, the lanes coming in had been blocked off to make more lanes coming out, and still the lot was locked up. I spun right and went back into Elysian Park, looking for the entrance Dash had taken me through on opening day.

My phone rattled "Take Me out to the Ballgame."

To hell with this. I pulled over and answered. The sound of sirens and voices came through the speaker.

"Dash?"

"Hey, are you all right?" he asked.

"I'm fine. I'm sorry. I'm so sorry."

"It's fine. I—" The signal broke up.

I got out of the car, trying to hear past the cacophony of crickets and the parking lot below. A backup of cars leaving the stadium passed. I'd never known about this exit, and it was still jammed.

"I tried to get there," I said. "But I'm sorry. I can't live with myself if you were right. Maybe there's something to it. Maybe you needed me and I failed you."

"I—you—listen—nonsense—"

Between the bad signal and the siren, I couldn't hear—

Siren?

The trees went red then nighttime green again.

The whoop of the ambulance siren came from the phone and from below. The situation explained itself quickly. The exit had been opened for the ambulance, and a few hundred opportunists had tried to use the exit before security had a chance to usher fan cars to the side.

I locked my car, left it on the side of the road, and ran down the hill, between crammed cars, waving at the driver of a Chevy who wasn't paying attention that, yes, I wasn't where I was supposed to be, holding my hands up in front of a news van, getting caught in the lens of an ESPN camera hanging out of the back of another van, until I was at the front of ambulance.

I ran around to the side and knocked on the driver's door. "I need to get in!"

The driver ignored me. I looked like a crazy fan, but there were hundreds of cars in the way. He couldn't speed away from me.

Right.

I texted Dash.

I'm here!

Where?

Banging on the door in a sex

sec

I ran around and banged on the back of the ambulance. I was sure I was going to get arrested. Not a doubt in my mind I would get hauled away, and the cameras from the two news vans were going to capture it all.

The doors clacked, and I stepped back so they could swing

out.

He was shirtless, sitting on the edge of a gurney like a god in a sling.

"Hey, slugger," I said.

I didn't know if he could hear me over the sirens and horns and yelling. But he smiled and was suddenly so well-lit he looked flooded with white. I turned to see the source of the light.

The cameras. He hated off-field cameras. Yet there they were, and he was right in front of them in a shirtless, vulnerable position. I wanted to protect him.

I turned around toward the cameras, but the reporters just came at me, barreling past my pathetic attempt to block their lenses. I fell, and from the ground, I turned back to Dash. He was half standing, right arm wrapped to the shoulder, left arm out to put his hand between his face and the lenses.

Or so I thought.

"Back off her," he shouted, his deep voice working a different sound spectrum than the sirens. "Just step back."

He was looking right at the cameras. I knew how much that bothered him. I knew he was seeing the parts of himself that shamed him the most. The parts he tried to keep under control.

The trainers tried to get him to lie down, and he shoved the older one away, taking the man's shirt in his good fist.

Don't don't don't.

Don't hurt him.

A replay of his episode with his mother, on camera, in front of the world, was about to happen.

"Dash!" I shouted.

I didn't know if he heard me over the din. Didn't know if it was my intervention that brought him back to earth, but he stopped.

The conversation between Dash and the trainer was wordless and brief. The trainer nodded. Dash let go, patting the guy's shoulder. I scrambled to my feet. Grimacing, Dash slid down to the ground and toward me.

"Are you all right?" he asked, left hand out.

"I'm fine." I took his hand but didn't use it to steady myself. I was pretty sure he shouldn't have even been standing.

I turned toward the cameras, shielding my eyes, and when I turned back, his lips were on mine. I took a breath of surprise then put my hands on his cheeks and kissed him back. The skin of the world sloughed off, and he and I were connected at the core, where everything was quiet but for the beating of our hearts.

"I didn't know what happened," he said. "I hated that I couldn't go find you. I saw a life in front of me where I couldn't love you, and I knew I'd never be happy again."

I must have squeaked, but I couldn't hear it. I only felt the sides of my throat stick together and release. In ten words, he'd wiped away all my worry, all my fear, and embraced me for who I was. Even if his career was over that night, he was still with me.

"You need a goddamned doctor," the old trainer interjected, yanking me out of my reverie. "Get in."

But Dash wouldn't listen. He looked at me as if seeing me for the first time, exploring me with his eyes. There was noise everywhere, questions being shouted at him, unnatural lights blasting his face white on one side.

"This arm's not going to keep me from fucking you so hard—"

"Stop. Before I blush in front of all these cameras."

He brought his gaze back to me. "I love you. I've never loved another woman. I was waiting for you, and I didn't even know."

Angry car horns from far away. The night birds of Elysian park. The whoop of the siren. None were as loud as his words. None came close to shaking my heart the way he just had. I felt grounded and ready to take off for the moon at the same time.

"Can you kiss me before I cry?"

He did, right in front of the news cameras as if he didn't care anymore. As if I'd taken away a measure of his fear. He held me with one arm, and I pulled away.

"We have to get that arm looked at." I stepped back.

The space in front of the ambulance had cleared, and fans were leaning out of their windows, hooting and hollering encouragement. I was mentally ready to go back to my car and meet him at the hospital, but Dash pushed me toward the ambulance, and one of the younger trainers grabbed my bicep and pulled me in. The doors slammed shut behind us, and in an instant, I was caught up in the bright lights and sounds.

The trainers pushed him to sit on the gurney, but he was smiling. Even when the trainer pressed his arm and his face contorted in pain, he polished it off with a smile.

"What are you so happy about?" I said, sitting as far out of the way as possible in the crowded ambulance.

"Nothing. Except that you're all right."

"I'm fine. I saw the way you fell."

"Just a flesh wound." His head twitched, and his brows furrowed as if he'd thought of something. "You saw it? Were you there?"

"I was in Sequoia with a student. She went into diabetic shock in my library."

"Can't have that."

I wanted to hug him but couldn't. He had three men around him, whispering things I couldn't understand. His body was so lucrative to so many people and so precious to me. I needed to be there, yet I felt as though I was in the way.

When it got silent and we were only waiting for the space between the stadium and the hospital to fold and disappear, I took my Kindle from my bag.

"What are you reading?" he asked.

"I started *Reaper's Weekend.* It's not bad. Guy's kind of a jerk."

"Can I see?"

I scooted close to him and handed him the device. A second passed as he glanced at the screen. The room clattered and rocked.

"Read with me," he said.

I remembered. He read when he was overwhelmed. It calmed him.

In the minutes I'd spent back there in front of the cameras and feeling like an interloper, I hadn't seen in his eyes what I saw then. He was broken and in pain, yet those things were nothing compared to the panic he held low in his gut. He was worried about his arm, his career, the one thing he'd ever loved.

"Excuse me," I said to the trainer next to me before I got up.

Crouching under swinging instruments and wires, I crossed to Dash's left side. I sat next to him as close as I could.

He put the device on his lap, and we read together.

fifty-eight

Dash

I assumed I was destroyed. A hundred ninety pounds landing on oddly bent bone and soft tissue meant I was finished as a ballplayer. The possibility of being on the field dropped into a void.

I could do other things. The possibilities spun around the edge of the sinking vortex. I could be a commentator. I could coach. I could write books on strategy. I could live off my savings for the rest of my life.

Each option sucked. I'd seen all of them as second-rate alternatives to the power of actually playing. But through the X-ray and poking and prodding (*Does this hurt? What if I do this?*) I had to stop rejecting them outright, and I could because Vivian was there with me.

Getting the X-ray took an hour. We read together, sitting side by side with my arm raised and iced on a rolling table. I could breathe with her next to me.

"What do you think they'll say?" she asked, looking at the screen.

"I'll never play again. Turn the page."

She clicked the button. "Come on. Really? It's not like there's bone sticking out of the skin or anything."

"My fingers are numb." I didn't want to go into it further. I didn't want to have to say or hear the phrase "nerve damage" until it came from a doctor.

In my peripheral vision, I saw her slight nod. I had no idea if she knew what numb fingers could mean or if she had intuited that I didn't want to talk about it.

I looked away from the screen at her face. Her hair had seen a long day, and the ponytail was coming out. Her forehead was topped with an inverted V and her face was framed with blond escapees.

"Jim wants to get laid," she said.

"He'd better look elsewhere."

"He thinks good seats at Dodger Stadium will do it. Personally, I think he'd get laid anyway, and I don't want to start a pattern of me getting tickets for friends."

If she thought my career was over, she wouldn't ask. She was a shrewd woman, but transparent. The request was her way of telling me she thought I'd be fine without empty platitudes.

I couldn't dismiss her optimism.

"I'll set you up with the PR department. They set tickets aside each game. Page."

She didn't have a chance to flip it.

"Wallace." The doctor came in, white coat flapping, a tablet in the crook of his arm. He was young and confident. Earring. Tattoo peeking out under his shirt.

"Doctor."

"Quite a catch."

Vivian held my hand. She was more nervous than I was. I liked that. It took some of the pressure off. She made me safe. Safe to fail. Safe to be nothing more or less than a roofer's son from upstate New York.

"You're a lucky guy," the doctor said.

The tension fell out of her. I heard it in a little nervous laugh that had a life of its own.

"I am," I said, squeezing her hand. "But how's the arm?"

"Nice clean break." He flipped the tablet to show me the X-ray. "With the proper care from yours truly and whomever else Major League Baseball can hire, you'll be back in by the All-Star game."

"His fingers are numb," Vivian said, throwing a ball before making sure the catcher was ready. She sat back deep in her seat, turning red in the cheeks.

God, I loved her. As a man well-acquainted with his comfort zone, I admired how easily she stepped out of hers on my behalf.

"We have some compression at the shoulder. Once the swelling goes down, I think you're going to be just fine. No guarantees, insert disclaimer, et cetera, et cetera." He flipped the tablet back into the fold of his arm. "I'll be back to set you in five minutes. Your manager and half the team are in the hall."

"Tell them to fuck off."

"All righty then." The young doctor spun on his heel and was behind a closed door a second later.

"Ready to turn the page?" I asked.

Amazingly, because she was Vivian and she was the woman I loved, she turned the page. She gave me space while still being present.

"We're going to need a code for that," she said. "Like 'turn' or 'go' or something."

"I wasn't joking," I said, changing the subject abruptly. "I might not play again."

"I know." Her eyes flickered across the page.

"Does that worry you?"

She looked up at me. "Does it worry *you*?"

"I asked first." I wasn't ready to put my true worries into words.

She wasn't either, because she swallowed so hard I saw the lump in her throat. She looked away then shut off the Kindle. "I'm afraid if you don't need me to walk the bases, you won't need me."

Her chin quivered. She cleared her throat. That had been a hard admission for her, and I wanted to say every word of love in every language in her honor. I wanted to rip those hidden sobs away. My arm hurt like fuck, but I could have killed a bear with it.

"Look, I—" She took a deep breath. "I'm fine. I think, with the game you had tonight, you know your talent isn't about me walking the bases or you wearing something on your glove.

You know you have everything you need. And I have everything I need. But man, I really love you."

"I can't believe I played at all. All I could think about was you. You. Not how you affected me, but you. How I treated you. I didn't know where you were. And it was you, but I was greedy. If you weren't with me, I'd miss you in the morning. I'd miss you drinking coffee on the couch. I'd miss a life with you. I may never play ball again, and I care about that. I care a lot, but I'll get over it. You? I'll never get over you." I took her hand in my good one, lacing the fingers.

"I can't believe you're reassuring me right now. I should be reassuring you."

Everything did seem flipped around. I was more concerned with her than with my arm. I worried about her career more than my own. Her unsurety made me unsure. Was this what it meant to love someone?

"I am reassuring me," I said. "I'm telling myself it's okay to doubt the purpose of my life. It's okay that I'm going to lose everything I depended on. I thought I'd built something stable, but I didn't. It was shit because what we have is forever. It can't be shut down. I can doubt everything, but I don't doubt that I love you."

She leaned her head back against the wall. "'Love is an ever-fixed mark.'"

"Be my ever-fixed mark. Be my north star."

I didn't wait for her to answer. I just kissed her long and hard. I kissed her with everything I had because I'd run out of words. Even Shakespeare had nothing to say I couldn't say better with that kiss.

I'd said I knew I couldn't control my luck and I was okay with that.

That I might not play again and it was all right.

I was a small man in a big world I didn't understand. A fool and a fraud. A gambler whose luck had run out. I was a meaningless ball of thoughts and fears with no control over the way my life unfurled.

But with her, I wasn't afraid.

Vivian

I missed games sometimes. I still had my job, and it wasn't glamorous or lucrative, but it was important. I had a father who needed me, and sometimes I had something else I had to do.

So I walked the bases when I could and made the first pitch whenever possible, but sometimes I missed games. I watched from the TV in my little apartment or at the bar with my friends. I heard them on the radio in my car on the way to Echo Park to catch the fourth inning.

But I'd never miss a second of the World Series. Especially not the seventh game of a nail-biter. And of course, my man's talent was all his, and walking the bases with him while he had our sex somewhere on his body was no help to him at all.

But for the World Series? We figured it couldn't hurt.

It was close from the first game to the seventh inning of the seventh game. The Boston Red Sox bullpen had never been better, and Los Angeles had to bring their best for every game.

I hadn't spoken a word to my father, Francine, Larry, or Dash's parents in two innings even though they surrounded me in the seats behind the dugout. There was nothing to say. We were all too wound up.

They'd been tied at one since the third inning, and both teams had come close to scoring. Right now, the Sox had three men on base with two outs. No one was breathing. Rodriguez had been traded to the Sox in September to get them through the playoffs, and now he was up. The same guy Dash had caught when he landed on his wrist. The hairline fracture had healed by the All-Star break, but I'd never forget how worried he'd been, how lucky he was, and how close he had come to ending his career.

I couldn't take my eyes off Dash, legs spread between second and third as though he could go either way. I watched him every second of every game, the way he moved and when. He chose a direction before the ball even left the pitcher's hand, and he was right about where the ball was headed every single time.

In the seventh inning of the seventh game of the series, Dash stepped right then took half a step back before the bat connected with the ball and went flying three feet to his right. He took another step and caught it, making it look easy, and retired the side.

We breathed.

I'd seen a hundred games that year. Nine hundred innings. When the fielder caught the final out of the side, he tossed the ball on the ground or to the ball boy and trotted over to the dugout. Dash looked at me and tipped his hat every single time. Every single time, I waved.

He didn't this time. He just stayed on the field. His teammates started back, but he stood there, tossing the ball, catching it, tossing, catching.

The PA system shuddered with the announcement of the seventh-inning stretch. Usually they played "Take Me Out to the Ballgame" and did some scoreboard games.

"What's he doing?" Dad asked. "Is he losing it?"

"I don't know."

The scoreboard went black, and the announcer's voice blasted out of the PA system.

"Number nineteen, Dash Wallace, has a request."

"Uh-oh," Francine muttered.

I knew she wasn't talking about the game. She'd come because the World Series was fun, not because she cared.

"Uh-oh what? Do you know something I don't?" I asked.

Steve Youder ran out to the field and tossed Dash another

ball and something black I couldn't see. Dash caught them both and juggled. He'd tried to teach me how to keep those balls in the air, but I just dropped all of them and we laughed.

"All I know is I was supposed to make sure you stuck around for the seventh-inning stretch." She put her arm around me and squeezed as if keeping me in place, and I looked up.

My face was huge. On the stadium monitor, my hands flew to my mouth to cover my blushing cheeks but not my eyes because Dash was looking at me.

He came toward the section I sat in, and words scrolled over my face in billion-point type.

Let me not to the marriage of true minds
Admit impediments. Love is not love
Which alters when it alteration finds,

He got to the rail, and Francine pushed me forward while holding me up.

"He's crazy," I said, clutching her forearm.

"Hell, yeah."

The field was five steps down, and she made sure I got there.

Or bends with the remover to remove:
O no; it is an ever-fixed mark,
That looks on tempests, and is never shaken;

Then, flashing under my big, blushing moon pie face:

Say yes.

He waited for me at the railing, and when I got there, he caught the two balls and a little black box. He was sweating and dirty, holding out the open box with scrapes on the heel of his hand from sliding into second in the fifth.

The ring was stunning. Three diamonds across, as clear and perfect as his eyes.

"Marry me, sweetapple."

I was too stunned to utter a word.

Francine elbowed me.

"It's gorgeous," I said.

"You'd better answer. I have to get on deck."

I paused, not because I didn't know what to say but because I wanted to run this moment over my tongue and teeth, have my senses give it form. But though baseball fans were terribly patient with balls and fouls, in matters of marriage, they apparently had no time for delay.

The chants of "Say yes! Say yes! Say yes!" started in the centerfield bleachers and rolled to the first base line until I couldn't put it off another second.

"Yes, Dash. Yes. Without a doubt, yes."

He plucked the ring out and tossed the box over his shoulder. The crowd went wild in a deafening roar, and after he'd slipped it on my finger, he kissed me over the railing. We held each other, one of us on the field, one off, locked at the lip and heart as Los Angeles cheered us on.

THE END

5-16

CPSIA information can be obtained
at www.ICGtesting.com
Printed in the USA
LVOW12s2052120416
483242LV00007B/856/P